HALWENDE'S REINCARNATION

HALWENDE'S LEGACY
BOOK 3

JOHN WEGENER

Halwende's Rencarnation

Written by John Wegener.
Published by John Wegener.
Copyright © 2022 John Wegener.
Copyright © 2022Cover designed by Fiona Jayde Media.

1

HALWENDE'S WAR

Everyone's eyes are on me after I make my announcement. Even Lilith, who has had eyes only for Sentinel since we arrived, is staring at me.

Adala looks dumbfounded, and Sentinel doesn't appear to comprehend my words at all. The others — Ishtar, Zabada, and Mamagal — stand rigid and stern-faced, shooting fleeting, uncertain glances at each other. The air is thick with tension as they attempt to absorb my message.

"This is a shock," Adala says at last. "You must explain this. But first, we must prepare rooms for our guests so they can freshen up. Then we can discuss this matter. And *you*," Adala glares at me, "come with me!"

I gulp and dare not disobey her. At her command, servants enter and usher the others to their rooms. I follow Queen Adala through to her private chambers in the royal palace's residential suites. As soon as the doors close behind us, Adala starts to weep, unable to contain her distress a moment longer. I rush to embrace her, but she pushes me away.

"Adala, please, I'm sorry."

"I don't know whether to throw you in prison or ravish you."

"I'd prefer the latter."

My words produce a wan smile to the angel for whom my soul aches. I try again to console her, and this time she relents. Moistening my jacket with her tears, she rests her head on me, her sobs slowly diminishing. I lift her chin and gaze into her emerald-green eyes. My heart races as I move to kiss her; her resistance melts as she responds.

We part, and Adala peers into my eyes, sadness on her face and teardrops dripping from her cheeks. "I thought you were dead. Or left, never to return."

"I promised to come back."

"Then, what happened?"

"My past life caught up with me. Please sit."

We retire to a sofa and rest facing each other.

"They captured me–," I begin.

Adala, distressed, grips my arm. "Were you hurt ... tortured?"

"I was. But I'm OK now. And then I had to help my friends. We'll discuss that later. But not a heartbeat elapsed when I didn't ache to return to you."

Adala's eyes fill again with tears as she stares at me with concern. Not knowing what to do, I hug her, and her warmth and scent charge me with emotions I can barely control.

"I'm still furious with you," she says in a calm voice as she pulls away from me.

"I bought you a space yacht."

"You did?" Adala's eyes sparkle with delight. "When do we leave?"

"In good time." I reach for her hands and hold them. "There are more urgent matters to discuss."

"Let's return to the others, and we will judge your news together. You may yet redeem yourself today."

"I promise you I will." I give Adala a warm smile.

"To the conference room, then."

"Can we pass by the kitchen for a bite to eat along the way? I'm starving."

Adala laughs. "Yes, we can."

We rise and leave. I grab a meat pie and an apple from the dining hall as we head to our meeting and consume them in almost one gulp. We are the first to arrive, but Sentinel and the others enter soon afterward, closely followed by Adala's young siblings Sigmund and Freida, and two of her generals, Tancred and Ernst. Reluctantly, I part from Adala and rejoin my motley delegation comprising Ishtar, Lilith, Zabada, and Mamagal. I have a stake in both camps, but I must stand with them as their leader and the cause of our current predicament. I sense nervousness within both parties as our reunion comes to order.

With a cough to gain our attention, Adala begins proceedings. "Helheim welcomes our guests from the outer galaxy." The visitors nod in acknowledgment. "Although it's still overwhelming to comprehend that another civilization beyond our planet exists, your presence today verifies Halwende's claims." She smiles at me before her expression becomes earnest. "But Halwende's return also brings us unwanted and disturbing news of our need to prepare for war — a war not of our making. Can you explain why?"

Our rebel delegation looks at one another, wondering who should speak. I suspect whose responsibility it will be, but I let the brief exchange of glances continue until their eyes gravitate to me. "I believe we've sorted out our speaker," I say, a faint smile hiding the turmoil inside of me. Our Helheim hosts smile in return.

My gaze falls to my hands planted on the table's surface as I build a framework around my recitation. Determined to give Adala as much of the truth as she — and Helheim — can take, I fasten my eyes on her and start. "As you know, I left Helheim for Santori with my rescuers intent on establishing trade agreements with other realms in the galaxy. What you don't know is that my rescuers, although true traders, knew about the bounty on my head in Eridu."

A buzz of surprise and confusion circulates amongst the Helheim people present, frowns disfiguring their faces as they digest my words.

"A bounty?" General Tancred asks, alarmed. "What for?"

"Please bear with me while I explain," I say, and the room falls silent. "Beyond these skies lies the Rigel Empire, of which I am a member. I was a leading general in the movement to overthrow the corrupt Emperor Shulgi and restore justice to the empire. It was my misfortune to place my trust in a peer who later defected to Shulgi's side because he lost faith in our ability to defeat Shulgi. As he knew our plans, our slaughter was preordained in a battle designed to turn the war in our favor. That massacre included the deaths of my wife and daughter as a punishment for my defiance and to break my spirit. They succeeded. I could not deal with the shock of what happened — so I ran away, eking out a living on the fringes for years until I crashed on your planet." Vocalizing these words rekindles the despair I once felt and causes my voice to crack. Adala reaches out to comfort me, but the table's width prevents her. I give a wan smile of gratitude.

"My so-called rescuers changed course to Eridu and when I realized what they were doing, they imprisoned me on their ship. As fortune had it, I turned the tables on them, imprisoning them instead and taking the ship to Santori, where I fulfilled my commitments to Queen Adala. I purchased a yacht for her while I was there — it's parked within this system. I named the craft the *Queen Rosalind* in honor of Queen Adala's mother."

Adala's eyes widen at this, and she shoots me a warm look of gratitude.

"I then traveled to Larsa, another planet in the empire, and it was there that I bumped into my past." I pause for a moment, but everyone is looking at me spellbound. I continue, "Let's just say that on Larsa, I realized I had a responsibility to continue the unfinished business to overthrow the emperor. So, I traveled to Eridu and rejoined the Resistance movement. We had minor success capturing armaments to add to the rebel's arsenal and made other incursions to frustrate the emperor. But our triumph came at a price: Shulgi noticed my re-emergence."

I pause a moment as painful memories resurface before continuing, "A traitor handed me over, and I was incarcerated in the palace. Shulgi tortured and humiliated me. In my semi-conscious state, I revealed the existence of Helheim — but not its location." I turn to glance at Lilith. "Lilith, Shulgi's daughter, helped secure my escape, placing herself at significant risk."

Everyone turns to look at Lilith, including Sentinel.

"Once I escaped, we embarked on a more ambitious and audacious strategy, securing the embryo of a space-based navy by stealing theirs."

"I bet that upset the emperor," interjects Sigmund, and there is a stir of amusement in the room.

"It did. I could not leave Lilith in harm's way after she had saved me. I had to take her from Shulgi's reach. So, I devised a plan to extract her from the palace. My scheme failed, and I was flung in prison a second time, along with Lilith, with the immediate prospect of my execution."

I hang my head in humility. "But I had more support than I realized. The Resistance organized a rescue, which succeeded, and I rejoined my fellow rebels in space. After a massive battle, which we narrowly won, we had no alternative but to move to safer grounds to regroup and devise further strategies for Shulgi's downfall."

Silence surrounds me as my words settle.

I continue, "But Shulgi will not rest until I am dead, and the rebels defeated. In coming here, I place you in grave danger. Please forgive my desperation. There are further reasons I desired to return here, other than my wish to reunite with you." My eyes linger on Adala. "I need to access the library. And you must prepare for war."

I have said my piece and await a reply from Adala. She stares at me, and then at Sentinel before offering, "I ... do not know what to say. Your suffering is beyond my understanding. Your war is beyond my grasp. How can I enter an altercation not of my making? How do I defend this planet, my loyal subjects, against ships and weapons we can't conceive or understand? We know nothing of the universe beyond our skies. You yourself told us, Halwende, that our armaments are primitive compared to yours. I can't place my realm at the mercy of your emperor. Tell me, how can we help you? How can we survive?" She looks straight at me with a dedicated ruler's passion in her eyes.

I look away. "I have no right to ask for your help. But I tell you, this war affects you more than you realize." I glance at Zabada, who gives a barely perceptible shake of his head in warning.

Adala rises, furious with me again. "Yes, you have no right. How many people have you imperiled with your games? I saw it in you the last time. You keep pushing until something breaks — usually you. I can't watch it ... I can't." Tears threaten to escape her eyes.

Her accusations slice into me. Her dedication to her realm humiliates me, and her love for me drowns me. I have nowhere to hide. Zabada's warning prevents me from revealing what I most want to reveal, and I don't yet know how Helheim can help me in this war.

"Enough of this," Ishtar, sitting next to me, blurts out. I stare at her in horror, aware of her intentions. "Halwende is like no one I know. The Resistance was made up of separate rebel bands before he came along. We were fighting more amongst ourselves than against the emperor. He united us. He rallied us to conduct the most audacious assaults, and we prevailed. We are stronger than ever. More desert the emperor and join us by the day. He is the hope we lacked."

"Then take your hope and your increased support," Adala replies with a venom I have never seen, "and fight your own war. Why involve us? I'm aware of Halwende's charisma. Helheim will not help you."

Adala and Ishtar glare across the table at each other while I gaze at the heavens, wondering how to salvage the situation and calm both sides.

To my surprise, Sentinel speaks. "If I may have a few words, my Queen." He glances at me and then at Adala. She nods her assent. "You are right to point out that we lack the weapons and technology to resist the power Halwende warns us we will face. My understanding from his report is that even his presence here has placed us in danger. His mention of our existence has endangered us, regardless of whether he stays or leaves.

"But it was when you threw the switch and rejoined the galaxy, Your Majesty, that you sealed our fate, whether you realized it or not at the time. I do not rue your decision or chastise you — it was the right decision. But with it, you sealed our fate. We now must decide if we will rise to the challenge."

All eyes are now on Sentinel and none more ardent than Lilith's.

"Left to ourselves, we will surely fall to Shulgi's might," Sentinel continues. "They are stronger than us. We will have no choice but to surrender to save our people. But with Halwende, there's a chance. He has proven this over and over. I don't know how yet, but I believe he will resist the coming onslaught. I would give Halwende an opportunity not only to show us the means of resisting this menace but to raise us to be a power of reckoning on a galactic scale."

It is my turn to fight back the tears. Sentinel's impassioned defense humbles me.

Adala's glare focuses on him before deflating into a sigh of resignation. "Oh, Ranulf, you're meant to defend me, not manipulate me." Sentinel gives a wry smile. Adala sits and looks at me, studying me with the laser-sharp emerald eyes I remember so well. She glances at Ishtar again before returning to me. "I will trust you, Halwende — for now. If you show us how we can defend ourselves, we will join your war, but I have grave fears for my people."

"I am humbled by Sentinel's words and your confidence. I will die before I disappoint you."

Adala glances away. "That's what frightens me."

AFTER THE INTENSE MEETING, and with no further commitments, I retire to my chambers to relax and recuperate. I walk to the window and peer out at the cherished view of Brandenfälle Waterfall, the sight of the torrent calming my mood. What right do I have to drag Helheim into my battles? What has overcome me to endanger Adala? Everything is evolving too fast. To digest the knowledge of my past and so my destiny is overwhelming. I desperately wish to enlighten Adala, but circumstances prevent me. I sigh as I watch the sun dip below the horizon.

A soft knock breaks the silence in the room, and I frown at the disturbance. After striding to the door, I open it. Sentinel stands there, wearing his usual somber expression. "May I enter?"

My frown lifts. "Sure, my friend." I step aside for his passage and close the door.

Before I can thank him for his support today, he says, "This news you bring is grim. It has upset Queen Adala no end."

"I'm aware of that. But why come to tell me this?"

"There are those who resist her reforms. They question the wisdom of reinstating the royal family after Egon's defeat. They want a governing body more malleable to their manipulations. This complication just adds fuel to their political goals." Sentinel paces beside the window, glancing my way often. He stops and confronts me. "But I know you. You haven't returned unaware of the danger or without a plan. So, what game are you playing?"

My tension eases. "I appreciate your honesty, Ranulf. I wasn't aware of Adala's troubles — she hasn't confided in me. To answer your question, I play a dangerous game with many potential pitfalls. I wish I could take you into my confidence, but that isn't possible yet. I will relate that I intertwine Adala's and my destinies in the deadliest of games. If I don't resolve this war, we won't have a tomorrow ... I won't. And I dare not contemplate Adala's future if I fail."

"This is dire news." With unexpected swiftness, Sentinel bridges the gap between us and grabs my shoulders. He drills his eyes into mine. "When we asked for aid, you assisted us. You sacrificed your life for us many times with no expectation of reward. Now it's my turn to help you. My loyalty will always be to Queen Adala, but I give my full support to your cause as far as I am able. I, too, sense a joining of destinies here. Ask what you need, and I will strive to offer it. This is the friendship I give you."

Sentinel's words overwhelm me, and I hug him to hide my tears. "You are a loyal friend. I cannot repay you."

Parted again, Sentinel replies, "My Queen's happiness is the only repayment I seek."

"And I, too, wish that."

I sense a tension dissolve, only to be replaced with a new one. Sentinel looks troubled, but I wait for him to speak his mind.

He glances at me and sighs. "What is it with this nymph that fawns after me whenever we meet?"

I roar with laughter. Sentinel stares, confused.

"Lilith? Can't you tell? She's infatuated with you."

"Well, inform her to cease it immediately. She makes me nervous."

"The great Sentinel unnerved by a woman?" I beam, feeling my worries draining from me for the moment.

"Stop making fun of me." He uses stern words, but good humor lies beneath them.

"You must understand by now, you can't deny womanly wiles. You'll just have to resolve your problem yourself."

"At least I know to avoid her at the banquet tonight."

I glance at my chronometer. "Speaking of which, I must prepare for it."

Sentinel moves to leave. "See you at the dinner."

He leaves, and I stare at the closed door, marveling at our friendship. His relationship trouble brings another snigger to my lips as I head for the bathroom.

2

A ROYAL BANQUET

Dressed, I check my appearance before a full-length mirror just as a second knock beckons me. A moment after opening it, I stagger two steps back, taking in the goddess Adala. She is as charming as I remember, her emerald dress complementing her green irises. A massive diamond dangles around her neck, sparkling in unison with her eyes. As the spell breaks, I stand without words until a wry smile develops. "You never knock."

"My regal etiquette has taught me a modicum of decorum." She smiles back.

"I liked it better when you were less decorous. You look stunning, as usual."

"Thank you." Her cheeks blush. "Shall I escort you to the dining room?"

"With pleasure."

We make our way to dinner and the festivities, arriving first so Adala can receive her guests.

I stand beside her in my Grand Chancellor role.

Sigmund and Freida arrive and greet us before taking the soft drinks offered to them by the staff. I marvel again at how much they have matured since the first day I met them. Sigmund has grown into a teenager and Freida into a young lady.

Sentinel arrives next. He is dressed in regal apparel, his hair groomed and plaited, but he looks nervous, and I grin as I guess the source of his nervousness. Generals Ernst and Tancred arrive on his tail and move over to join the others.

Mamagal and Zabada enter together, discussing matters between themselves in voices too low to overhear, before concentrating on their host.

"Welcome, Mamagal, Zabada," Adala says.

"The pleasure is ours," Mamagal replies.

Zabada gives Adala a piercing stare before responding, "You are twice as stunning as I've been told." He glances toward me. "You should have warned me. She could beguile even an old man."

I smile. "Where are your manners? You're discussing my Queen. I'm not sure if such language is permissible."

Adala glares at me as I turn to her, although I see mirth behind the glare. "A Queen requires compliments too." She returns her attention to Zabada. "You are most gracious, Zabada. Halwende is poor at describing people."

"Ah, but it's not Halwende who informed me."

Adala raises her eyebrows. "Well, enjoy the evening. We shall discuss this mysterious source later."

"At your pleasure." Zabada bows and moves over to join the others.

Lilith and Ishtar, who had arrived while we were talking with Zabada, now await our attention — although I notice Lilith craning her neck to find Sentinel.

Once Zabada leaves, they step forward to present themselves.

"Welcome, Lilith." Adala smiles as she greets her.

"Your Majesty, it's an honor to dine with you tonight." Lilith curtseys.

"No formalities, please. I hope you enjoy the evening and the company." Adala glances over at me and flashes a wicked smile.

I struggle to prevent a snigger from escaping my lips.

"I shall." Lilith drifts toward the other guests.

"Your Majesty." Ishtar bows her head.

"Ishtar. May your evening be enjoyable," Adala says in an icy tone.

Ishtar looks hurt by the frosty reception and glances at me for enlightenment before politely thanking Adala and moving to join the others, too.

"Why the terse welcome?" I whisper to Adala.

"What terse welcome?"

"Ishtar."

"I just greeted her as I did everyone else."

I don't believe her, and she knows it but won't elaborate. Her manner isn't typical.

We dine, interwoven with convivial small talk — although an underlying tension remains between Adala and Ishtar. I fear it will boil over at any moment, which disturbs and confuses me. What is Adala's problem?

Lilith, placed opposite Sentinel, much to his discomfort, tries to strike up a conversation with him, but he parries every attempt. I grin as I watch them. Lilith's frustration is plain, and eventually she resorts to talking with Frieda instead, despite the disparity in age.

Afterward, we mingle on the balcony overlooking the palace gardens. Adala and I have separated to converse with the guests. I notice Lilith has cornered Sentinel and won't let him escape as she talks with him. He glances over at me and signals with his eyes for help. I shrug and move on, grinning at his expense. I know I'll pay for it later.

Ishtar approaches me, looking troubled. "Your Queen is more aloof than you described her," she says quietly as she moves closer to me.

"She has much on her mind."

"But why is she hostile toward me? Did my defense of you in the meeting upset her?" Ishtar's manner shows Adala's rebuff has hurt her.

I glance over at Adala while Ishtar is talking, and her expression shocks me. She has the iciest glare I've seen from her. "I'm sure it's nothing to do with you," I say after regaining my composure.

Adala steps beside us moments later. "Is this a *private* conversation, or may I join you?"

The chill in her voice leaves me speechless for a second. "You're welcome to join us," I say, frowning.

"I see you and Halwende are friendly."

Ishtar attempts a cordial response. "We've developed a good working relationship on our assault campaigns. Halwende is a brilliant strategist."

"That he is. He gets distracted, though." She glares at me.

With no more words spoken, Adala moves away, leaving us both bewildered by her behavior. Her treating my friends in such a manner upsets me. I resolve to confront her later.

After everybody leaves and retires except Adala and me, she stares into the distance from the balcony, holding a glass of wine and remaining aloof. I watch her in confusion, my emotions in turmoil. As my temper rises, I can stand her iciness no longer.

"What is wrong with you?" I say, raising my voice higher than I intended.

Adala whirls to confront me. She glares at me with something that looks disturbingly like hatred in her eyes. Although underlying that emotion, I see fear, too. "Do you think I'm unaware of what's going on between you and Ishtar? Do you think I'm blind?"

I step back in shock and open my mouth, but no words emerge. Everything clicks into place. How could I be so obtuse? "You're jealous!"

"Don't flatter yourself." She turns to hide her emotions.

Unsure of what reception I'll receive, I draw closer and touch her. She shrugs me off and moves away.

"Adala, please. Nothing is happening between Ishtar and me. And nothing has happened either."

When Adala glances back at me, tears blemish her cheeks.

"I'll be frank — once, after Ishtar became intoxicated and before she knew my heart belonged to you, she attempted to be intimate. I explained matters to her, and she ran away, embarrassed by her behavior. Apart from that one incident, she has been a rock for me. She has saved my life many times, risking hers, as Sentinel would with you. She is my most valuable general, and that is the limit of our relationship."

The same child-like vulnerability she displayed when I initially refused her request for help crosses her face now. "You promise?" she whispers.

I step closer again, and this time she doesn't retreat. "I promise. My heart is yours forever."

Adala's cold facade shatters. Crying, she rushes to rest her head on my shoulder, spilling her drink over me. "I'm such a fool."

"Shh." I stroke her hair as I comfort her. "I've been slow-witted."

She hiccups a laugh between her sobs.

Once her tears subside, I lift her chin and kiss her. She responds and we part. "Remember, I love you."

She nods and moves to kiss me again before we hold each other in our arms.

"Forgive me."

"I do. It's Ishtar you owe an apology, but I'm not sure she'll get it."

"You consider me too proud to give it?"

"No. Too embarrassed maybe."

Adala gives a melancholic smile. "No. I must humble myself and apologize tomorrow."

I beam with delight. "That's one thing I love about you."

"One? What are the others?"

I clasp her hand. "If you're interested, I'll show you."

"I am."

3

A JOYRIDE IN THE QUEEN ROSALIND

I watch Adala trembling with excitement. I have promised to take her to the space yacht, the *Queen Rosalind*, for a joyride. Sailing her yacht on Lake Brandensee next to the palace is the extent of her yachting experience. She stands dressed in her red military uniform, which she wore when fighting to regain her throne from Egon. This was the uniform she was wearing when I first laid eyes on her, and it still takes my breath away.

Sentinel accompanies her with six guards. They have never traveled into space — they don't believe it exists. So, they stand in various degrees of apprehension, their sworn duty to protect Adala the only thing keeping them there. Even Sentinel paces nervously. Zabada tags along for his own reasons.

"Is everyone ready?" I ask.

Adala grabs my arm in anticipation. "Let's go."

We pile into the royal scooter, and the driver takes us to my landing shuttle, where we disembark from the scooter and get aboard the shuttle.

"Excuse the austerity of this vessel," I say. "It's not typical of the style of your yacht, Adala. The one that came with it had an unfortunate accident." I give a wry grin.

"I doubt I'd know."

"Oh, you will when you get there. Now, take a seat and we'll begin. Adala, sit up front at the helm with me if you wish."

"Please." Adala beams. "I want to see you fly this device."

"Is there another seat?" Sentinel asks. "Someone must protect the Queen."

I raise an eyebrow.

"From you," Sentinel adds.

With a laugh, I say, "Yes, there're more seats."

We buckle in and I fire up the drive. After checking the instrumentation, I lift the shuttle from the planet and ascend through the atmosphere.

Adala, sitting next to me in the copilot's seat, grabs my arm and stares out the front screen in wonder as the ground diminishes below her. "Have you seen a sight more amazing, Ranulf?" she asks him.

I glance around to catch his reaction. He is sitting in the auxiliary engineer's chair. "It's ... extraordinary," he admits, a nervous frown still covering his face. Even though the guards occupy a different cabin, their awed voices filter through to the helm as they watch the view displayed on a screen in front of them. I chuckle and concentrate on flying again.

We continue rising from the planet, and the orb's curvature emerges as the sky darkens, with the thinning atmosphere disappearing below us.

"Why are we not moving?" Adala asks.

"We are. Inertial dampeners counteract the acceleration." She frowns in confusion when I glance over at her. "A machine removes it from this cabin."

"I still don't understand."

Moments later, as we hurtle out into space, Adala bursts out, "Oh, look, Ranulf! See our planet. It's so tiny."

"I can't believe we live on that," Sentinel says in amazement.

Our trip to the yacht takes another twenty minutes as we traverse deep space. Just before I dock, I point out the other ships that accompanied me from Eridu, making up my rag-tag navy. They have congregated in a distant orbit around Helheim, near the *Queen Rosalind*.

I enter the shuttle bay on the ship and land, switching the controls off once we settle.

As I jump from my seat, I ask Adala, "Shall we?"

"Let's." She rises and follows my lead from the helm with Sentinel close behind her.

After opening the hatch, I escort the others out onto the yacht. They stare up at the roof as they disembark, the guards forgetting their duty for the moment. When they've had their fill, I escort them to the yacht interior proper and to the residential space, showcasing its opulence, ending with the royal cabin.

"These are your quarters, Adala."

Adala's eyes sparkle with delight, but then she frowns. "Someone's used it."

Evidence of my use lies scattered on the floor and elsewhere. I scratch the nape of my neck as I make an excuse. "I didn't think you'd mind." She places her fists on her hips. "I was going to clean up beforehand." I glance across to Sentinel for support.

He crosses his arms and gives one of his rare laughs. "You're on your own with this."

Forgetting her disapproval, Adala strolls around the spacious cabin, inspecting each room and nodding her approval. We return to the living space where she soon notices the locked safe. "What's in there?"

"Nothing," I say. I give a nervous smile, not wanting her to see the blue crystal or the box with the ring in it.

"Can you open it?"

"No."

Adala gives her trademark stern look again.

"There are items in there I can't divulge to anyone yet. I'll remove them to another location later." When I see her head tilt obstinately, I glance toward Zabada for help.

"Your Majesty," Zabada interjects in the smooth voice of reason, "Halwende keeps these items concealed at my insistence. I beg your forgiveness for not revealing them."

Adala switches between eying me and Zabada, not convinced, but lets the matter drop for now.

"Shall we tour the rest of the ship?" I ask.

Adala nods, and I continue the tour until we reach the helm. I see the yacht impresses them. The only areas I don't show them are the weapons spaces and the engineering compartment. They don't need to view the drives and reactor modifications.

"That's it," I say.

Adala grabs my arm. "Can we go somewhere?" she pleads like an excited child.

I glance at Sentinel. "How long do we have?"

"We have the rest of the day."

With a shrug, I reply, "OK, then."

After climbing into the captain's seat, I power up the controls and inform Argandea on the destroyer *Enzu* of my intentions. A star with uninhabitable planets lies nearby, which I point out to Adala and the others. I intend to travel there through hyperspace and return. It should take thirty minutes.

As I bank out of orbit, Adala gazes at the screen, watching her planet dwindle to a pinhead before disappearing as I jump into hyperspace. She screams in surprise.

"It's OK," I reassure her. "We just went into hyperspace to make the trip shorter."

"I got a funny feeling just then."

"It can happen when you go from normal space to hyperspace. You acclimatize to it."

Ten minutes later, I bring the ship back to dimensional space as we orbit the destination star. Once I stabilize my position, I point out where Helheim is. They stare in disbelief.

"This is impossible," a guard, congregated at the helm with the others, exclaims, forgetting protocol.

The senior officer admonishes the offender.

"That's OK," Adala comments. "We're overwhelmed at present. Can we leave this yacht?"

"Only if you put a spacesuit on," I tell her. "Otherwise, you won't survive. There's no air, and you'd freeze."

Adala rests her head in her hand, thinking. "Maybe that's why our scientists claim there's nothing here."

"I don't think so," I say. "I've considered their point of view, and it's an understandable one. When you live isolated in another dimension, it's possible to think there is nothing else. It was not possible for them to reach space, and they had no other frame of reference to disprove their beliefs."

"Hmm, possible. They had better find out." Adala sits in contemplation before speaking again. "If space is so vast, how will we ever see anyone attacking us?"

"You can't without sensor systems. I have our fleet scanning for intruding ships for now."

"We need our own, then."

"Yes."

Once they sate their curiosity here, I decide to extend the trip and set course for another star, a red giant, to impress them. We arrive after twenty minutes with the star filling the whole screen, to the terror of those on board except Zabada. The convolutions of the star's thermal currents are prominent, with a massive solar flare streaming out into space. Its performance is impressive, even to my eyes.

Adala and Sentinel have settled their fears, and the guards return to the cabin once again.

Zabada glances at Adala and asks, "What do you know of your heritage?"

Adala jumps in surprise. "We have a complete family tree back to our first king, King Alulim. And his father was King Alalgar, although reference to him is vague in folklore. No further information exists before that time. Not in our library. Why?"

"Oh, just curious."

Squinting and frowning in suspicion, Adala stares at him but doesn't interrogate him further.

"Had enough?" I ask to change the topic.

They say yes, so I set our coordinates for Helheim and head home.

4

A NIGHT ON THE TOWN

I spend the next few days discussing defensive strategies with Argandea and the others and developing practice maneuvers to defend the planet. They conduct exercises to keep their pilots and weapons personnel in training, too. Uneasiness accompanies me as I watch our meager number of fighting vessels. I wonder how we will protect Adala or where to source more ships. We can't buy them.

During one of my periods in space, I remove the flerovium and ring from the safe on the *Queen Rosalind* and store them in a secure spot in the portal room under the palace, since only I can access that crypt.

My relationship with Adala mends as we spend time together. We enjoy a peaceful afternoon on the lake in her yacht on a sunny day. She still has doubts and concerns for her people should space-based war come to Helheim.

My doubt and depression linger as images of my past failings return. But I have an unexpected break from my gloom one day as I sit in the palace gardens in a secluded spot as afternoon turns into evening. Voices drift over to me, distracting my reflections. Sentinel's voice pricks my curiosity, especially when the other one is female. As they come closer, I recognize the female's voice as Lilith's. I'm in a dilemma whether to linger and eavesdrop on their conversation or make my presence known, with potential embarrassment for everyone. Choosing the first option, I stay still, only to have them wander into a small alcove nearby where I can hear every word they say. Too late, I realize I can't leave now without them noticing and knowing I've overheard their intimate conversation. My awkwardness multiplies. I'd be furious if Sentinel were to do the same when Adala and I seclude ourselves.

Still, the knowledge that Sentinel might develop a deep relationship with someone warms my heart. Despite his stern presence and general gruff manner, I've always sensed a loneliness within him, as if he finds himself incomplete. We've been close friends from soon after we met, but since my rapport with Adala has deepened, our friendship has taken a back seat.

I chuckle noiselessly, replaying Lilith's infatuation with Sentinel. From the first moment she laid eyes on him I have delighted in watching his terror unfold.

They move off half an hour later, leaving me undiscovered, oblivious to my presence.

Later that evening, Sentinel corners me. He wants to visit our regular bar. Sensing something is on his mind, I accept, and we sit at a table sipping beers soon afterward. He seems distracted, only replying with succinct phrases to my attempts at conversation until my patience runs out.

"What's wrong?"

"Huh?" He looks puzzled as he glances up from staring at the tabletop. "Nothing. Why do you ask?"

"You beg me for a drinking session, and yet you haven't said two words since we sat down. What's on your mind?"

He blushes. "I'm confused."

"What's confusing you?"

A sheepish grin materializes as his reddening deepens, and he shuffles in his chair. "Lilith."

I give a shout of laughter, disturbing the entire bar before the patrons beam at us and return to their drinking. "Ohh ..." A tear escapes my eye, which I wipe away. Not wanting to relieve Sentinel of his awkwardness just yet, I ask, "And how does Lilith confuse you?"

It dawns on him that I'm having fun at his expense, and he frowns. "You are a real bastard sometimes." His frown converts to a beaming smile. "Have your moment of entertainment, then."

I reach over and pat him on the shoulder. "Sorry. I couldn't help it. I'll get serious then."

"Well ..." Sentinel gulps his beer as he stares at me. He glances over to the bar and, when he gets their attention, signals for two more beers, even though mine is still half-full. He peers back at me. "We've had private discussions."

"Aha ..." is all I say, amused at his formal way of putting it.

"She confuses me."

"So you've said. But in what way?"

"She ... stirs something in me. A kinship."

"Love?" I beam at him.

"Don't be ridiculous."

"What then? Does she distract your thoughts? Do you dream about her and want her presence?"

"Well ... yes. But don't read your own emotions into it."

"I'm reading nothing into it, my friend." I frown, knowing he's searching for advice and considering what to say. "You've never been in a relationship, have you?"

"No. Adala has always consumed my time. I couldn't afford to in case it lured me away from protecting her."

"But you haven't faced that predicament, either?"

"No. Any woman I've ever met has always fluttered her eyelashes at me, thinking I'll become her slave by the action. That's no disrespect to women in general, just those that attend royal functions. They tend to be scheming to catch a noble prince to advance their social status. I have the utmost respect for Lilith. She's as strong a personality as I've seen."

"She is that. I have complete faith in her myself. But Lilith did flutter her eyelashes at you when you first met."

"She did not! She may have fawned her eyes at me, but no fluttering of eyelashes took place."

His description of Lilith's initial behavior makes me smirk. "She did that. I stand by my original assessment, though." On seeing Sentinel move to protest, I hold my hand up to let me finish. "I'm not saying it's sappy. But you've found someone who interests you, and you want to explore where that relationship might lead. You're just having a healthy reaction to your circumstances. I'm happy for you, and I'm sure Adala would be too. In fact, it'd surprise me if she didn't suspect something. She's very observant, as you perceive."

"But she's the enemy's daughter."

"So? She saved my life. Does she behave like her father? My understanding is she loathes her father. She's lost, having no anchor to support her, given she's rejected the life her father intended for her." I grin again. "You're trying to find excuses."

"I am not." Sentinel stares into his ale before glancing at me and returning my smile. "It might be true."

"Of course I'm right."

"Well, don't just sit there puffing yourself up, you smugger! Are we going to drink or not?

"I thought you'd never ask." I pick up my beer and scull the contents, watching Sentinel do the same before we order another.

MY HEAD POUNDS with a mild hangover the next morning. After dressing, I stroll to the dining room for breakfast. Adala still lingers, finishing her meal, deep in reflection. She glances over when she hears someone entering and smiles on noticing my approach. I bend to kiss her and sit.

"I hear you had a night on the town with Ranulf."

"Not too wild. More of a counseling session."

"Oh?"

I grin. "Relationship issues."

"What's wrong?" Adala looks alarmed.

I snigger. "Not me, Sentinel."

"Oh. Oh ..." Adala grins. "What's he done now?"

"It's not what he's done. It's confusion about how he feels."

"I still don't understand." She frowns.

"For someone who prides herself on her observational skills, you can be slow in connecting the dots."

Adala picks up her coffee and sips while she stares at me, deep in deliberation. She then smiles. "Lilith."

I nod.

She chuckles. "I hope you advised him well."

"Not sure. Might need a queen's touch."

"It's not a regal matter. You're–"

My comm unit buzzes. I pull it from my pocket and check who's calling. With a frown, I answer. "What's the problem, Argandea?" I peer at Adala and shrug.

"We had a flotilla of vessels arrive during the night."

"They haven't come early?" I ask, alarmed.

"No. Civilian. Refugees looking for asylum. We can't keep them in orbit. There's not enough food. Can you talk to Queen Adala and see if she will allow them to settle on the planet?"

I glance at Adala again, frowning. "I can ask and see what she says. She's sitting with me now."

"We'd appreciate it. We have our own problems without having to look after refugees."

"Yeah, OK. I'll get back to you." I disconnect. After taking a moment to gather my thoughts, I look at Adala. "A flotilla of ships with exiles on board has arrived. Argandea was wondering if you'd let them settle here, beyond reach of the fighting."

Alarm crosses Adala's face. "We can't accommodate refugees in the city. There's no room."

"I'm not asking in the city. There must be plenty of vacant land somewhere they can use. They might need supplies at the start, but they'll keep to themselves otherwise. Let them acclimatize. Once they've settled, they may be a useful asset for you. I'm sure they've brought gadgets with them you've never seen."

Adala stares at me, uncertain. After several seconds, she sighs, her refusal melting. "It's the right thing to do. Ask them to nominate a spokesperson. I'll organize a coordinator to work with them."

"Thanks. They'll be grateful." After relaying the information back to Argandea, I get breakfast and sit again.

"Have you made any progress in how we'll defend ourselves against your emperor yet?" Adala asks.

"No," I say as I frown. "And it's worrying me. I need a game-changer — and I'm not getting one."

"I made a mistake in shutting off the cloaking." Adala sags in doubt.

I reach out and clasp her hand. "No, you didn't. I'll find a way. Have I ever disappointed you?"

Adala's eyebrows rise, her mouth ready to respond, but she desists in saying what she intended. Instead, she says, "No, you haven't."

"I want to talk to Mamagal today. He hides a wealth of information."

"Well, don't delay in finding a solution. I sense our time is short."

5

ASK THE LIBRARY

Mamagal is more elusive than expected. I eventually locate him in the palace gardens. He is in a typical Mamagal pose, meditating on a bench seat while gazing out over the lake and waterfall. He sits under the shade of an oak tree, oblivious to my approach until I'm atop of him. He glances up as I step forward.

"Halwende! It's wonderful to see you. I was just contemplating the machinations in play with our presence here."

"You're difficult to find." I sit on the bench next to him. "I need questions answered."

"And what questions perplex you?" Mamagal eyes me with mischief.

"You know this planet's history and the events causing the decision to isolate it from the universe."

"I have read the annals, yes."

"I can't believe that King Alalgar just abandoned the planet. He must have developed a contingency for the planet's re-emergence. Otherwise, he left them defenseless on purpose, and that's inconsistent with my knowledge of him."

"The text describes what King Alalgar did. It doesn't mention everything, but no history does. After so long, information dissipates or distorts to suit the purposes of the political powers, with distortion on distortion as eons elapse."

"That isn't an answer," I say, annoyed at his useless reply. His tendency to avoid straightforward responses irks me, a trait I prefer he lost.

"What do you wish me to tell you? You can read the histories as well as I."

"But you must have discovered the ancient original texts in your studies."

With an air of indecision, Mamagal eyes me, choosing his words with care. "Your mind has atrophied with your dalliance in trading. You had a sharper intelligence than this. Where did you receive your trusted intelligence while you were here?"

If that question intended quenching my rising temper with him, his old age must have dulled his intellect. But his remarks contain a kernel of truth. Whenever I needed information or guidance from antiquity, I found my way to the library. Its reluctance to offer the knowledge straightaway would frustrate me too, but that was because I didn't ask the right question. I stare at him, realizing my annoyance is abating, and end up giving him a wry smile. "I could strangle you sometimes. Why don't you ever give a straight answer? Why didn't you just say, 'ask the library.'"

"But your brain would've remained dormant if I had." Mamagal sits straighter. "I won't always be here and nor will Zabada. We are valuable advisers for you while we still live, but we won't hold your hand with actions you can undertake on your own. It's as if you've lost your nerve, your self-confidence. Prepare your moves, develop your strategies. We'll offer our thoughts if we consider your plans ill-conceived."

I chuckle. "I take that as a reprimand."

"You could say that. I prefer to call it judicious words from a trusted friend."

My next step known I turn to absorb the scenery myself. The view of the waterfall always calms and amazes me. It's so picturesque.

While sorting through my emotions, I settle on an inquiry that is troubling me. "What are your thoughts about these refugees arriving?"

Mamagal eyes me again for a moment but returns his gaze to the lake. "Their confidence in obtaining shelter here with you as their protector is noteworthy. They prefer their chances here instead of their life of repression under Shulgi. I sense it is but a bow wave of what's coming. Be wary, though. There may be those amongst them we can't trust."

"Spies?"

"Maybe. I was considering those whose personal interests are greater than the cause we fight. Queen Adala's position has enormous risk."

"She knows that. It terrifies her."

"She is wise, far wiser than she knows. I sometimes wonder what she finds in you."

I splutter as I stare in shock at him, but his grin leaves me with no choice but to swallow the implied slight. He meant to insult me. The frustrating thing is, I'm never sure what he truly thinks. There are always layers upon layers of meaning to his words. On pondering what he means, I ask, "Should I declare my identity?"

Silence sits between us for several seconds before Mamagal answers. "I cannot offer my advice on that." When I open my mouth to respond, he holds up his hand. "Only you will know the right moment. I do sense the time hasn't arrived yet. You place yourself in great danger when you announce your heritage to the empire, so have complete confidence when you do."

I nod, acknowledging his words. "I won't get any more guidance than that from you, then?" My smile placates his wary eyes when he turns.

With a chuckle, Mamagal says, "No, you won't."

I sigh. "This garden is relaxing, but I must attend to urgent matters. So, I thank you for your time and advice."

"Yes, the view is serene. A most refreshing place to sit in my old age. You're welcome."

After rising, I give Mamagal one last look before I return to the palace and the corridors leading to the library.

I TAKE a detour to the portal room on my route to the library. The door opens without hesitation and the vast switchboards for the city's force fields stretch before me. I switched most off after Adala rose to the throne. Flerovium crystals lie scattered on the floor, but my purpose lies on the shelves at the rear of the crypt.

The casket with the blazing Star of Rigel, the emblem of the House of Alalgar, sits on it. I pick it up and open the lid, revealing Alalgar's ring. As I pluck it from the box, I wonder if my time has arrived, but Mamagal's words still ring in my head, and I sense events have not yet brought fate to the crisis required for my reincarnation. Slipping the band on my finger is so tempting, so natural, but I resist the temptation and replace it in the box, returning it to the shelf for safekeeping. Are the dreams awakened by Mamagal and Zabada just that —or are they nightmares? I was not aware of my true identity until they told me a few weeks ago. Yet, I have suspected since childhood that I was born for a higher purpose.

I sigh and recall my original intention. I leave the portal room, heading for the library. The white illuminated library walls surround me ten minutes later, the questions I might ask flashing through my mind. I procrastinate, fearing the answers, but steel myself in the end and focus.

"Tell me of King Alalgar's activities on Helheim before he left," I speak into the vacant chamber, the words echoing off the sides.

Silence greets my demand before the library replies. "King Alalgar accomplished great undertakings before relinquishing control of Helheim to his son. He made preparations for his eventual return but concealed them. I can only divulge this information to a verified descendent of King Alalgar."

Not this avoidance again. The cantankerous nature of the library is really starting to grate on me. "I am the portal room's custodian. Doesn't that testify to my identity?"

"No, it does not."

"What does then?"

Seconds of silence elapse before the room says, "I cannot tell you."

I would throw an object if I had one. If I had a target, that is. With the ethereal voice saturating the room's space, nowhere exists to vent my anger. What in Eridu is the library demanding for proof? My thoughts swirl as I contemplate my conundrum until they gravitate to a solution. I rush to the portal room and grab the casket containing the ring and return to the library, holding the box up to the spiritual presence as if it's an offering.

"Is this evidence enough of my identity?" I ask in triumph.

"The royal chest proves nothing."

"Ahhh ...!" I fume, frustration clouding my reasoning. Once I vent my anger, I take several deep breaths and settle on only one solution. I open the box, the majestic ring beckoning me, the blazing Star of Rigel inscribed on the bevel. My hands shaking, I pull the band from it and slip it on my left forefinger. If I'm expecting an exalted blowing of trumpets, I am mistaken. And yet, a change engulfs me. My thoughts are clearer, and the space blazes in light, causing me to shade my eyes from the brightness. The star shines with the blue of flerovium.

"Welcome, Sargon, heir of Alalgar," the library intones.

Maybe now it will answer my questions. How does it know my royal name? I didn't even know it. "How do you recognize me?"

"The ring identifies you."

"But how do you know my name? Jewelry can't perceive my identity, and you existed in another dimension until recently. How could you gain that information?"

"I cannot answer that question."

It's a comfort to know that even the library isn't omniscient. "What did King Alalgar do to prepare for his return?"

"King Alalgar recognized the world would have changed when they lifted the cloaking. But he understood the temptations would persist, and he prepared for the planet's defense, considering that eventuality. He secreted a fleet of ships deep within the ground on Helheim."

"Why didn't he use them at the time?"

"Opponents and technology held equal sway during that period. King Alalgar realized the empire's inevitable decay into alternative, less powerful machinery without flerovium. It was for this purpose that he concealed the fleet, trusting in the wisdom of his descendants."

This could give us the edge if the ships are still working — although, after four hundred years of storage, they are probably degraded. "Where is this navy hidden?"

"That information inhabits a tome on the shelves."

I stride to the shelving. The portal room book still sits there, but I sense my search isn't in its pages. As I peruse the other volumes stored there, one stands out — one that just had a plain cover previously. It is black but has the Star of Rigel emblazoned on its spine where it once had nothing. I pull out the volume and sit cross-legged on the floor, cradling it in my lap. The title reads *The History and Geography of Ur*. I open the book and flip through the leaves until I reach a section detailing the geography of Helheim. I have seen no part of the planet except the region surrounding Heimstadt. The pages contain maps depicting the continents. Heimstadt sits on the continent of Elam. Another land mass lies nearby — Punt. Another, further out, is Phoenicia. And a high-lighted spot on this map beckons me. I frown as I turn the pages, seeking more details.

After scanning through the information about Elam and Punt, I find an enlargement of Phoenicia. On that chart, a circle draws my attention to a location. In its center is a waterfall called *The Falls of Destiny*. I look up and blink. It must be important since it's emphasized. But, as I flick through the rest of the tome, I detect no further mention of it. I must investigate these falls.

The ring on my finger is chafing my skin, so I remove it. As soon as it dislodges, the maps and writing in the book disappear. Unless Adala has these charts, I'll need to trace the details from the reference, since I can't wear my ring without revealing my true identity.

With renewed enthusiasm, I pack the book away and leave the library. I return the ring to the portal room and go in search of Adala.

"Do you have maps of Helheim?" I ask Adala as I barge in on her, much to her bodyguard's displeasure.

Adala glances up from her work at the desk in the royal office. She blinks and smiles in recognition. "Maps?"

As soon as I see her blank face, I realize I may have asked the wrong question. "Yeah, maps. Charts that describe your world beyond what you can see."

"I know what maps are." Adala's forehead crinkles in annoyance. "Doesn't the library have them?"

"No, it doesn't," I lie, despite suspecting Adala has picked up a hint of my deception, but she lets it drop.

"Why do you want them?"

"I discovered information that could help us in our predicament, but I need a map of the planet. I need it to direct us to a location on another continent."

"What's there?"

"I could stay here if I knew."

Adala frowns, distrusting me. "There may be maps in the cathedral. You could ask the bishop. I'll have Ranulf escort you there."

"No need to disturb him."

"Yes, there is — you must follow proper protocols."

"Ah, yes. Protocols."

"Stop teasing," Adala says as she grins.

Since she wants me to desist, I add, "I beg your forgiveness, Your Majesty."

"Oh ..." Adala searches for something on her desk to throw at me and finds nothing suitable, so she throws her stylus instead.

After making to dodge the missile, I catch it, noticing the guard is desperately trying to keep a blank expression. "Is she always so violent?" I ask him.

His chin quivers, but he regains control, avoiding any breach of procedures on his part.

I return the stylus to Adala's desk where she sits with crossed arms and a half-angry, half-amused expression. She breathes out her emotions. "What am I to do with you?"

I move to suggest an idea but defer my comment with the guard in earshot. "OK, I'll take Sentinel with me. Where is he?"

"I don't know. In his office, I presume."

"I'll see you later, then." I make to leave, but seeing the sentry, I face Adala again and bow as official protocol dictates. "Your Majesty."

"Leave me alone. Yes, we'll meet later, and you can tell me what you have found."

With that, I go in search of Sentinel.

I FIND him in his office and convince him to escort me to the cathedral to conduct a treasure hunt. We arrive a half-hour later and gain access to the bishop, who's busy in his bishopric. I'm unsure of his role, but he has more security surrounding him than Adala. When I lay eyes on him, I realize he is the person who officiated at

Adala's coronation ceremony. He is elderly, rotund, and balding. As he rises to greet us, he stoops, despite attempting to straighten his posture.

"Greetings," the bishop says. "It's rare I receive visitors from the palace. How may I help you?"

"It's gracious of you to see us," Sentinel says. "Halwende is searching for information that we hope might lie in the cathedral's vaults."

"Ah. And what information do you seek?"

"I want to locate a map of the planet," I say. "I wish to locate a waterfall called *The Falls of Destiny*."

The bishop's ears prick when I speak the phrase, so he has heard of it. "That name hasn't graced these walls in years." He peers into my eyes as if checking my integrity. "The original religious texts for Helheim reference the site as one that will release the wrath of God on the unbelievers and only the pure of heart may enter its chambers and live. Why seek such a fabled place?"

"I have knowledge suggesting it might be an actual location, but it's not on this continent. If you have any maps of the planet, I'd appreciate your permission to consult them."

"Hmm." The bishop scrutinizes me again before he reaches a decision. "Follow me."

We leave the bishop's office and walk up the cathedral's main aisle and through the left transept, where steps descend to a basement. The air is musty, and gloom engulfs the dim light. It's reminiscent of old horror films I watched as a child. The bishop leads us through several wrought-iron gates until we approach a crypt housing a sepulcher. The side walls contain stone inset shelving with ancient books and papers sitting on them.

"Whose tomb is this?" Sentinel asks.

"King Alulim, the first King of Helheim."

Both Sentinel and I gasp, recognizing the name.

"You have entered a place few know exists and fewer get to view."

I frown, wondering why people shouldn't be aware of their history. "Why is that? Why not open the crypt for public display?"

The bishop stares at me in horror. "It's sacrilege. I only bring you here because of Ranulf's royal heritage. Besides, the place is taboo for the general populace. Cursed, so the folklore resonates with the superstitious. Now, you may find what you seek on the ledges."

"We are indebted to you," Sentinel says.

"Well, just leave the relics undamaged. I shall let you delve into the documents at your leisure. Report your findings to me before you retire."

Left to ourselves, I sift through the myriad of material stacked on the shelves, searching for any document or book suggesting it could contain maps. Sentinel helps me. After twenty minutes, I chance on three parchments, each one-meter square once unfolded, with the outline of the world and the continents drawn on them. I point out Elam and Heimstadt. The other two landmasses, Punt and Phoenicia, complete the world chart. As I study the map of Phoenicia, I find the waterfall I seek.

"There," I tell Sentinel as I point to it.

"What's there?"

"The answer to our prayers, I hope. You interested in a joy ride?"

"Sure. I'm curious why this place interests you so much, especially since it's cursed."

"Not for the pure of heart."

Sentinel glances at me with skepticism. I laugh.

After taking photos of the maps with my tablet, we pack the parchments away and retrace our steps to the bishop's office. Eager to be on my way, I report our success and thank him for allowing us access to the ancient records.

6

THE FALLS OF DESTINY

My shuttle skims over the ocean as Sentinel and I speed toward the continent of Phoenicia. Cliffs loom before us, announcing the onset of land approaching. Once we cross the coast, I review the map on my screen and alter direction, searching for a river and the spot where the waterfalls should be.

After twenty minutes, the river, a vast and voluminous watercourse winding its way to the sea, finally comes into view. I turn our flight to follow the river upstream. Immense jungle hugs the riverbanks, and high cliffs appear in front of us on both sides as we penetrate a monstrous canyon. I retard the shuttle's speed once we enter the ravine, the precipices encroaching on our course. A sweeping bend looms ahead, the river disappearing behind the left cliff face, but mist escapes from beyond the clifftop. I am intrigued by the source of such a massive fog of particles. I have my question answered as we round the curve and the largest waterfalls that I've ever seen materialize before us from a hidden landscape. Their breadth is at least two thousand meters, with the water dropping five hundred meters from the elevated plateau.

As we approach the falls, I search for a place to land and discover a suitable spot near the base. When I open the hatch, a gargantuan roar confronts us, so loud that Sentinel and I cannot communicate with speech and must cover our ears to protect them. I rush back and find two sets of earmuffs, handing one to Sentinel. They have internal speakers and microphones so we can speak with each other.

"What now?" Sentinel asks, staring in astonishment at the sight before him.

"I'm not sure. Let's walk to the base and search for clues. Hope you don't mind a drenching."

We thread our way through the jungle and arrive at our destination an hour later. My stature reduces to that of an ant as I stand next to an incredible flow of water cascading past me. The noise is deafening, even with our earmuffs on. I scout for clues on why these falls are important or what may lie behind them. As my gaze rises higher, I notice a terrace carved into the cliff two hundred meters above us. I point to it and move to find a route to it. Sentinel nods, and after many false starts, we locate a path up to the platform. The mist makes us wipe our faces incessantly. When we reach it, the sight from the platform is beyond words as we stare out along the waterfalls and the river that winds to the bend.

Drawing my attention back to our purpose, I scan the wall of rock behind the falls. The moisture covers its flat granite surface with a glistening sheen. My eyes search across the face for non-uniformities or signs of a vault entrance, but find none, despite the writing suggesting the contrary. My enthusiasm wanes as my venture threatens to end in futility. Sentinel scans the wall with me but is fruitless too.

"What's that?" Sentinel shouts at me above the roar of the waterfall, his voice barely audible through the muffs we wear.

He points to a discrepancy further under the falls. The smallest of indentations shimmers from the wet surface. The rock platform where we stand is wide, but it tapers away as it disappears behind the cascade of water, becoming a mere ledge barely wide enough for one person at the anomaly's position. I make to step closer, but Sentinel restrains me, fear spreading across his face.

"I'll be careful," I reassure him.

He frowns his skepticism but then shakes his head and lets me go.

I shuffle along the wet slippery rocks as I near my destination, not daring to look over the edge to the base of the falls below me. The cascading water threatens to engulf me as I wipe my hands across the wall surface, searching for the indentation we saw. I locate it and lean backward to view its shape — a hand imprinted with the Star of Rigel embossed in the center. I glance at Sentinel and nod, gesturing to him that I have found something. My hand fits in the outline and I press, but nothing happens. Disappointment fills me as I prepare to return to Sentinel. But as I take my first step, a groan and creak emanate from the rock, and a doorway slides open, making me smile. I signal to Sentinel to join me as I enter the dark interior.

With a deep intake of breath, I stride through into darkness. Sentinel comes through moments later. The noise abates tenfold with the wall between us and the waterfall. After removing my muffs, I wipe my face and wring out my hair. Sentinel does likewise and then he reaches inside a bag he brought along, drawing out a flashlight and turning it on. We both stand flabbergasted as he waves the flashlight across the immensity of the cavern, the light illuminating glistening metallic surfaces.

7

KING ALALGAR'S HIDDEN FLEET

We stare at each other, the view leaving us speechless. I retrieve my flashlight and shine it around, searching for steps to descend to the cavern floor. When I illuminate the entrance wall, I notice a matching palm print. I touch it and the door closes, dropping us into darkness. Without warning, the whole chamber ignites into brilliance, revealing its expanse. Warships line the floor in both directions. Who carved this hole, and why deposit these ships inside it? The library's words come to mind. This is King Alalgar's hidden fleet.

"Let's explore," I say as I continue to search for stairs to the cavern floor.

I find them nearby and lead our descent, Sentinel close behind and following in silence. The only noise we hear is the echo of our footsteps. As we reach the base, the monstrous size of the ships dwarfs us, turning us into minute insects in comparison.

"Impressive," Sentinel says in a laconic tone as he holds his head back.

I gape at him and then burst out laughing. "Yeah, impressive. Let's discover an entrance to the ships." I walk to the nearest vessel, searching for an opening. The ship's front shuttle bay doors are an obvious entry point but have no personnel airlock, so I stride to the side and find a hatch halfway along it. The entrance has a panel positioned next to it, but it's dead with no lights as evidence the ship still possesses power. If these are Alalgar's fleet, they must be over four hundred years old. With nothing to lose, I touch the activation switch. To my surprise, the board lights up, and the hatch opens. I glance at Sentinel.

"What should we do?"

Sentinel shrugs. "Let's look inside then since you opened it."

Not disagreeing with his logic, I step into the ship with Sentinel close behind and press the button to shut the outer hatch. After a delay, the inner hatch opens, giving us access to the interior. The corridor is dark until we breach the airlock threshold. Lights blaze along the passageway. A blank screen sits opposite us, so I stride to it and bring it to life with a press of my finger. The language is old Eriduan, but I can read it. With several presses, a map of the ship displays. Once I find an elevator to the helm deck, I wave for Sentinel to follow me. When I glance at him, he resembles an awestruck child. My heart goes out to him. Apart from his flight on the *Queen Rosalind*, it's his first experience of a spaceship. It must be terrifying him.

We use the elevator and march along the helm deck until we reach the helm itself. I come to a halt. What I see takes even my breath away. The technology is unlike modern vessels. Even the modern ships are nothing in comparison. It's incredible, and to think it's from so long ago. How did the galaxy degenerate so much? The helm comprises the captain's seat, with the first officer's seat next to it, in the center of the compartment and elevated two meters above the main floor. Mounted at the captain's eye level is a massive full-width screen. Below the captain's seat, the pilot sits behind navigation and drive controls, and the astrogator is next to him. On their left are the engineering screens, and communications are next to that. To the pilot's right are two weapons-control positions. A mezzanine corridor extends across the ship at the captain's level and behind him. Three other doorways penetrate the walls of this walkway.

I plod along the floor and check out these doors. The first accommodates a meeting room capable of seating twenty people at an oval conference table. The next door leads into the captain's cabin, plush and fitted out with essentials and luxuries without being opulent. And the final doorway leads to another corridor.

With the exits from the helm identified, I go to the captain's chair and sit. Sentinel, still in a fantasy world, sits in the first officer's seat.

"You know how to fly this?" Sentinel asks.

"No. I'm not even sure it can still fly. Let's see if I can start it up first." I flick the captain's screen into position in front of me and begin tapping, delving into the layers and sub-layers of menus to familiarize myself with the ship's systems. Despite the ship's age and the sophistication of its controls, I discover that its means of control are little different from any other vessel from our era. So, I press buttons to energize the ship's power-up sequence. A screen comes forward, requiring authorization before the sequence can progress. I stare at it, wondering what identification it wants.

"Snag?" Sentinel asks.

I glance at him. "Maybe." I press the button on the display, and a hand outline shows. So, I place my palm within the print, after which the sequence continues, and we hear drives and other controls starting.

"May I ask another question?" Sentinel asks.

"What?"

"If you're going to fly this ship, how do we exit this cavern? I presume it can't pass through walls."

I chuckle. "Good question. Let's get things running first, and we'll see what happens next." Once the startup sequence has finished, I consider what I should do. Should I check the engineering compartment or start working through the different controls here to figure out what's functioning? I decide on the former because I want to discover the ship's power source and the reserve available. I prefer not getting halfway off the planet and having the generators cut out on me. "Follow me."

We retrace our steps and enter the engineering compartment twenty minutes later. My sense of awe at the ship's technology has worn off, allowing me to scan the room's equipment with a more impartial mien. The power reactors and generators are massive, though.

"Touch nothing," I caution. "You could kill both of us."

Sentinel nods as he strolls along the equipment aisles. I make my way to the main reactors to satisfy my curiosity about the ship's energy source. After making sure that Sentinel can't see me, I open a maintenance panel on one reactor and peek inside. A human hand-sized flerovium crystal shines blue within, as I suspected. Given that knowledge, I have no doubt the power supply can cater to the ship's needs for many years. I close the door and stride to the engineering screen. Bringing up the power supply screen, I confirm there's still ninety-nine percent of the full energy capacity available.

"We have enough power here for what we need," I tell Sentinel. "Let's return to the helm and resolve how this hangar opens."

We weave our way back, Sentinel striding beside me. It feels good having him with me as if we are a team in this unlikely alliance of the long-lost sons of Alalgar.

"Is this what you want?" Sentinel asks.

"Yes." I glance at him. "If these vessels work, we have a chance of defeating Shulgi."

"You forget one thing."

"What's that?"

"Qualified people to run these monsters."

"You wanted your military to have something to occupy them other than their bickering. Between us and them, we'll have enough. Whether we can train them in time is another matter."

Sentinel chuckles.

After reaching the helm, I head for the captain's chair and flick through the pages of information, searching for clues for opening this vast vault to escape to the freedom of space. I find nothing and scratch my chin in frustration. Are we on the wrong vessel? Is there a unique fleet flagship? But we'd have to search the entire armada until we found it. That could take days. No, I can't believe they'd restrict it to one ship. I rise and pace the aisle behind me, considering a potential line of thought. My eyes settle on the door to the captain's quarters. If it's on the captain's console, they might hide it in his quarters on a need-to-know basis. Sentinel sits in the first officer's chair, observing my deliberations in silence.

"I'm going to search the captain's quarters," I say.

"As you wish. I can't think of any brilliant ideas to aid you."

With that, I stride to the captain's cabin and eye its contents. The main living and sleeping sections are separate from the office. In front of me stands a desk and chair with three other chairs nearby for the captain's subordinates to use when meeting there. The wall has a cabinet attached with a small side table underneath. A food dispenser complete with a water unit rests on top. I round the desk and sit, bringing the captain's screen before me and pouring over it. It demands the same identification procedure as the one at the helm. On activating it, I search the console for more clues but find none. I slap the screen away in frustration. I don't believe only one ship controls the means of escaping the hangar. There must be a clue here.

There are few draws in the captain's desk, but I rifle through them. They are empty. The captain must own a safe somewhere for his classified documents, but I can't fathom its hiding spot. "Sentinel!"

After several seconds, Sentinel shows up at the door. "Yeah?"

"You look capable of finding a secret compartment. Help me search this office for a concealed safe."

Sentinel raises his eyebrow. "Are you calling me a thief?"

"Of course not." I snigger. "Why did you jump to that conclusion?"

"No reason. You implied I have secretive behaviors."

"You do, don't you?"

"Only when receiving strangers."

"Well, help me look."

Sentinel steps inside the room and starts opening everything he can find and wiping his fingers over concealed surfaces in search of clues. After ten minutes, he says, "Found something." His hand is half-hidden behind a wall screen. A click unlocks the screen, and it hinges sideways, revealing a safe. "Is this it?"

"Maybe." I stride over to him and examine the safe for a means of opening it. A handle sits flush with the door, but its opening mechanism confounds me. With no other choice, I rotate the handle and it moves a few degrees before it clicks but doesn't open. Another panel opens with a hand and retinal scanner. I place my hand in the handprint and position my eye before the scanner. After a few seconds, I hear another click and the door opens. "Now, we might get somewhere."

The safe holds just one item — a data tablet. I extract it and activate it. Despite its age, it boots up with no trouble. "This is it," I say as I glance at Sentinel.

He leans against the doorframe, staring at me.

"What?"

"You call me a thief. Why then, does everything open when you touch it?"

I shrug. "Lucky fingers." I push past him and return to the captain's seat at the helm with Sentinel in tow. After working through the screens, I find the information I need. "Let's see what this does." I press a button on the screen.

With a massive screech, the wall of stone before us rises. Three minutes later, the entire barrier has disappeared, and the relentless pouring waterfall stands as a curtain before us. The streaked lens of water distorts our view of the exterior landscape. "We get a free shipwash included." Sentinel shakes his head in amusement when I look at him. I beam a smile.

Renewing my concentration on the ship, I power up the drives and lift the monstrous vessel from the cavern floor, inching toward the cascading water. The vessel jerks downward when it enters the falls but adjusts from the unexpected thrust, continuing its progress from the hangar, the ship creeping out into the daylight after centuries in darkness. Once the entire ship is outside and away from the water, I grab the tablet and activate the close button. The shadow of the wall descends behind the waterfall again. "Don't want anyone snooping around finding this."

I inch from the waterfalls and toward our shuttle. When I reach it, I land the ship, the incredible weight indenting the ground where it settles. Not wanting to leave our shuttle behind, I bring it inside the bay. With everything settled, I increase power to the drives and speed, angling the ship up and into space. Once I break through the atmosphere, I receive a communications message.

"Unidentified ship, please announce your identity." It's Argandea's voice.

I fumble for the communication page on the screen. "Can you find out how to answer that?" I ask Sentinel.

He retreats to the communications console and looks for a means of replying.

"Unidentified ship, please name yourself, or we shall take defensive actions against you."

Touchy.

"Found it," Sentinel says. He presses a button. "Um ..." He glances at me, his eyes asking for help with the words he should say.

"Tell him who you are before he shoots us," I yell at him.

"Oh ... um ... Ranulf speaking. I'm with Halwende. We're just testing a ship we found."

I force myself not to laugh.

Argandea can barely contain himself. "Where on Eridu did you discover that ship?"

"Um ... long story. I'll let Halwende enlighten you at a later date. We're busy right now. Mind if we contact you later?"

"Yeah, fine. But next time don't give me a heart attack. You'd better have a good story, Halwende."

With that said, Sentinel and Argandea cut communication, and I return to concentrating on flying the ship to the asteroid belt and finding a suitable site for target practice.

Targets come into view an hour afterward, and I park the vessel. Flicking over to the weapons screen on the captain's console, I review my choices, but then glance across to Sentinel parked with his feet on a console and his eyes closed, taking a nap.

"Interested in learning the weapons systems?" I ask.

"Huh ...?" Sentinel lashes out to prevent himself from falling from his seat as he wakes from his daydream. He peers over at me.

"Want to try shooting at an asteroid?"

"Why not? Beats sitting here doing nothing."

"Let's get you set up then."

I walk Sentinel over to the weapons console and turn on the screen. The specialized station has many more features than my captain's screen. After stepping him through the weapons setup and locking in his target, I have him practice the procedures. A grin plasters his face as if he's playing a game. Afterward, I set the power level for the maser cannon at twenty percent and ask him to blast an asteroid I select. I'm unsure what damage the energy release will inflict, but this will enlighten us. Once Sentinel locks in the target, he presses the fire button, and the asteroid vanishes in a cloud of dust. The ease with which the blast destroys the asteroid even makes me gasp in astonishment. Sentinel figuratively falls off his seat. I'd hate to see what full power inflicted on its target. When I sit back in my captain's chair and contemplate it, I realize it shouldn't have surprised me. The modification I made to the yacht's weapons has the same lethal capacity when I connected the flerovium to its power source. I let Sentinel continue practicing for another half an hour before packing the weapons away and returning to Helheim, descending to the planet's surface, and landing in a vast field next to the city. Goggle-eyed observers stare at the warship as we exit the hatch and head back to the palace.

8

ADALA'S ULTIMATUM

Sentinel and I stand before Adala in the palace's official conference room. Her siblings and generals occupy the table with her. I can't read her face. It's as if she is hiding her true feelings from me, afraid of my reaction. Whatever the reason, I will find out soon.

She eyes me, enquiring and uncertain before she signals to the guard to close the door so that she can start the meeting.

"What is that monstrosity in the fields?" she begins.

"It's a warship from our ancestors," I respond, unsure why she asks or where she intends to lead the conversation. "They placed it and many others in storage for the time you brought Helheim back into the galaxy and needed to defend yourselves. Today is the day."

"And you saw this?" Adala's eyes dart to Sentinel.

"I did."

As she stares in front of her at nothing in particular, she continues. "Is this what we've unleashed? Another war? Over what? What of value does your emperor want? Why should we fight? Why not become an ally with your ruler? Isn't this empire of yours living in peace and prosperity?"

"Peace maybe," I say. "But certainly not prosperous. Those

pandering to the emperor are the ones who profit. Others live in fear with a grueling demand for taxes to help pay for military expansion. Shulgi maintains unity with force. The emperor is not interested in an alliance. I know him well. He will expect nothing short of complete absorption of Helheim into his empire, as he has done to many other similar realms."

I can't fathom why Adala appears to have altered her stance on our course of action. I gaze across at the rest of the attendees, hoping for enlightenment. Sigmund's and Freida's expressions show nothing beyond keen interest. The generals stare straight ahead, their expressions inscrutable.

"Your reasons are not good enough." Adala brings my attention back to her.

"What has changed since we last talked?" I ask her.

"*That!*" Adala points in the warship's direction. "*That* has changed. While we relied on you and the Resistance forces for our protection, we had nothing with which to defend ourselves. Now, with that ship and the others, people whisper discontent. They question why we should accept your help when we own our own defenses."

The reason for the change in perspective becomes obvious. I glance again at the generals. "Do you believe you don't need our aid?"

General Tancred and General Ernst look at each other before Tancred speaks. "We are still of the opinion that we need you. These vessels' capabilities are unknown to us. We will need months of training to achieve competency in their use. Yet, officers within the upper ranks of our military believe otherwise. I've seen this before — a lust for power and self-promotion is forever simmering in the hearts of our elite. Egon had it and now others covet it. They caution Queen Adala, and ... they have outlined choices for her consideration."

As I internalize Tancred's words, I realize these 'others' have threatened a coup if she doesn't agree to their demands. I challenge her. "They have blackmailed you?"

"They offered their considered opinions," Adala says with a stony face.

Something bothers me. It doesn't come to the forefront of my consciousness at once, but I understand its source. "Who forwarded information of these ships to these generals?"

I sense Sentinel shuffling beside me, so I turn to him, raising a questioning eyebrow.

He gazes at the floor. "It is my fault. When we met earlier, I mentioned these ships. I spoke in good faith, wanting immediate plans developed to train our military in their use. A contingent of my direct reports now has their own ideas for their service. Forgive me, Halwende."

"Your intentions were pure." I scratch my head as I pace, thinking. I need these ships and Adala's armed forces to defeat Shulgi. But I can't dictate terms to Adala and her citizens. They have no loyalty to me. I stare at Adala. "And you intend caving in to this blackmail?"

Adala's resolve wavers. "I must consider the welfare of my people. We cannot fight another civil war after our suffering under Egon."

"And these ships? How will you use them? How will you train in them when you do not know space-based warfare? And how will you even activate them without my help?"

"Is it you that now blackmails us?" Adala asks, gritting her teeth.

"Of course not." My anger rises, but I know losing it will serve no purpose, for me or for Adala and her realm. How have matters degenerated to this bickering? How have we allowed the ambitions of a few people to dictate our cause? "Where does that leave me?"

"We demand that your Resistance forces withdraw from our planet in peace, and that includes the refugees who arrived seeking safety here." Adala's hard expression cracks slightly as she intones the words, pain radiating from her eyes.

I open my mouth, but nothing comes out. Her words stab me. These people do not comprehend the implications of her ultimatum — Shulgi will arrive and enslave them. He will have come of his own accord without my presence alerting him to this planet. I stare at Adala, pleading with my eyes and searching the others for any crack in their resolve. I can sense Sentinel's disagreement, but he can't move against Adala, his Queen. And so, he stands at attention, silent. This is too much for me.

"Protect yourselves then!"

I storm off before I say any more that I may regret. I'm finished reasoning with them.

After packing, I rush to the portal room to collect my ring before boarding the warship and heading for the Resistance forces with the news and to prepare for departure.

9

RECONCILIATION

My current state of mind makes me unpleasant to be around. I feel rejected and betrayed by Helheim. What breaks my heart more, though, is the sense of being forsaken by Adala. We cannot win the battle that I know is coming without these warships, but they are being denied me by those who heralded me as a hero when I won their war. I claim equal ownership of them, but I cannot divulge my true identity — it is not yet the time.

I walk the decks of the ships in despair, lost in the fires of Hades. Everyone avoids me, limiting our encounters to those necessary for planning and training. Ishtar and the others display a shell of optimism and resolve, but their eyes mirror defeat even before we fire the first shot. My plans always fail. I always disappoint those I love. And now, the one I cherish the most has abandoned me.

Not wanting company, I retire to my captain's quarters on the retrieved warship and lie on the bed, staring at the ceiling, wondering where everything went wrong. My comm blinks an incoming call from the planet's surface. I ignore it for a moment, but the constant buzzing draws me back to it. Sighing, I answer. "Yes," I blurt out, harsher than I intend.

"Hi. I want to talk, if you're willing to listen," Sentinel says, his words restrained as if he is uncertain of the reception he'll receive.

I raise myself and sit. "There's not much to discuss. Adala has made her views plain."

"These are not her desires."

"Then why does she demand them?"

"I am at odds in talking to you. My position is in jeopardy if the military discovers this conversation. This stance isn't uniting the realm. It's tearing it apart, and I suspect that is the instigators' intent. Queen Adala has lost her enthusiasm for ruling the kingdom. She sits and mopes instead of concentrating on her tasks."

"What is that to me? I have a fleet to disperse and a war to wage."

"Please come to the planet. Talk to her. For the sake of our friendship."

My petulance wavers with Sentinel's personal plea. We have been through too much together for my pride to destroy our friendship. "OK, I'll see her. I don't know how circumstances have brought us to this. Nothing will repair the damage if we refuse to communicate. I'll be there soon."

"Thank you." Sentinel breaks the call.

I sit staring at the comm for ages before I break the spell and prepare to leave for the planet.

Before I can exit my quarters, a knock resounds on the door. "Enter," I say, and Zabada shuffles his aging frame into the office section of my accommodation. "How did you get on the ship? What can I do for you?"

Ignoring my first question, he says, "I sense an understanding friend may be in order." Zabada moves to a chair, and there is a heavy thump as his rear hits the seat.

I chuckle as I sit next to him. "I have more friends than I realize wishing to counsel me."

"No one is above friendly advice."

"Mention that to Adala."

Zabada scrutinizes me with anxious eyes. "This is what I want to discuss, amongst other matters."

"Drink?"

"A refreshing beer?"

I retire to the bar and extract two bottles, handing one to Zabada, then sit. After taking a gulp, I peer at him, searching for useful words to say. "And to what do I owe this fatherly chat?"

"I am concerned."

"So am I. Everyone is. But I have no choice. Adala has decided."

"Has she? She might need a reason to change her mind. You didn't improve matters by storming off as you did."

I splutter the liquid from my mouth. "Me? Storming off made things worse? She's the one who ordered us, ordered me, off the planet."

"You helped her keep her resolve that it's the right course of action."

Zabada's remark pierces me like a spear through my stomach. I blush and stare at the floor. "I'm at a loss, though. They will defeat us without these ships, and ..."

"And?" he prompted when I paused.

"And I miss her." I did not intend to voice those words. They just slipped out, but I know they are true. "Sentinel informs me the whole aim may be to cause discontent within her realm."

"Give her a reason to change her mind."

"I considered revealing my identity to her, but now isn't the time."

"I'm glad you see sense there."

"But what else can I do?"

"Offer her help. Tell her she has your support."

"But she's ordered me to leave."

"When have you ever obeyed orders not to your liking?"

I burst into laughter. "Checkmate."

Zabada frowns. "That was no joke."

I shake my head as I regain my composure. "No, it wasn't. But you got me where you wanted me, didn't you?"

"Maybe." A wisp of a smile crosses Zabada's face.

I gulp my beer. "Well, I was on my way to her when you interrupted me. But I'm glad you came. You've helped me sort through my options and emotions over the matter and over Adala."

"At least I'm good for something in my old age."

"Your wisdom is always welcome. Whether I listen is on my head."

"I'd better not keep you waiting then." Zabada rose, placed his half-drunk beer on the desk and left. I gulped the rest of mine and prepared to do likewise.

Two hours later, I walk toward Adala's office, nervous and unsure of the reception I'll receive. The guard stands motionless at the entrance until I arrive. With a glance, he steps aside, allowing me to knock.

A sigh filters through the door. "Enter."

My stomach knots as I open the door and gaze at Adala sitting at a small table by the window, staring into the palace gardens. "May I enter?"

Adala freezes, her muscles taut, before turning her head toward me. Despair and fear radiate from her eyes when our eyes lock. "Shut the door." Her voice is soft and meek.

I oblige and stride at a slow pace toward her, unsure even now of what reception I am to receive. *She hasn't told me to leave.* When I reach the table, I sit in a chair opposite her. "Hi."

Tears threaten to escape her eyes, but she resists her emotions. "Hi."

"We need to talk."

Adala nods.

"I ... was rash in rushing off as I did. I should have persisted in negotiating an acceptable solution."

"No other resolution is open to us." Adala squeezes her hands together so tight they are white as they grip the tabletop. "They give me no choice."

"Why? Who is restraining you?"

"A monarch cannot do as she pleases."

"That's not what you keep telling me."

Adala offers a wan smile. "I have learned the limitations of my power."

My nerves melt as I watch Adala. She exhibits the same scared-child look she had when we first met and I refused to help her. "I have heard rumors." We sit in silence. I divert my eyes to the gardens and wonder what tack I should take with her. As I consider my choices, I conclude I must be direct. It will allow us both to jump this hurdle in our relationship. I turn my attention back to her. "I don't want to lose you." Adala's chin quivers. "And I won't."

Unable to control her emotions any longer, Adala places her face in her hands and sobs. I yearn to remove the table that separates us to comfort her but resist the temptation. Her bout of weeping wanes, and she sniffs and wipes her tears away. "I'm at the mercy of others and in despair."

Suddenly, I know what to say. "I was in your position. When they murdered my family and our cause was crushed, I felt as I presume you do now. I had no more reason to continue. But, to my shame, I was a coward. I was too afraid to fight and ineffectual in ending my suffering forever. So, I hid and became a trader to escape the pain. It was only when I crashed on Helheim and met you and helped you in your battle that I realized the prospect of improving your life is always possible. You gave me hope and purpose again. Let me help you now as you helped me." I want to be completely honest with it, so I add, "My motives are not entirely altruistic. I need you. I need Helheim and your people to defeat Shulgi, and I must have those ships to overthrow Shulgi. But most importantly, I need you by my side. I am not complete without you."

"Oh, Halwende." Adala sobs before she gathers her strength and squares her shoulders. "What can we do?"

Now is the time. I stand and round the table. As I clasp her hand, I pull her up to my level, and her eyes lock on mine. She shakes. I wrap my arms around her and hug her, feeling her warmth. It sends a shiver of ecstasy through me. "We must stand together."

We part, still holding each other. Adala's strength returns and grows with each second that passes. "Walk with me in the garden."

"Is that an order?" I give a lopsided smile.

Adala smiles. "Yes."

I move and open the French doors, allowing Adala to exit first. I follow and close the doors behind us. We hold hands again and stroll along the path leading to the lake. I don't look behind, but I know guards attend at a discreet distance. We stay silent as we walk, enjoying the sunshine and a gentle breeze brushing across our faces. Oaks bordering the pathway mottle the sunlight as we pass under their mighty boughs.

When we reach the lake's edge where waves lap the shoreline, Adala turns to me. "How do I crush this insurrection?"

"Who is leading it?"

"Generals that were loyal to Egon."

I gaze out toward the waterfall, watching its torrent cascade to the lake below, as I consider Adala's options. "Do they demand your replacement or just want to keep you on a leash?"

"They want to keep me on a leash. Egon was a special case. He wielded much more influence. They want to control me."

"For what purpose?"

"Power and wealth. What else do people lust after?"

"There's limited scope for achieving that under normal circumstances, so they must crave their share of any prosperity generated from trade with the empire. Even alliances with military benefactors. You could negotiate with them."

"What arrangement? I'd be giving in to them."

I raise my eyebrows. "Isn't that what you're doing now?"

Adala gives a wry smile.

"I'm unsure what Sentinel has told you of what we discovered. You saw just one of many ships. I must use them to defeat Shulgi. But they are powerful. Much too potent to allow these generals to control them."

"Where did these vessels originate? Why were they buried?"

"This is our legacy, our contingency. Keep this a secret for now. Before King Alalgar left Helheim, he placed those ships in storage for his heirs for when the planet came out of its cloaking in case they needed them for the planet's defense. Both of his descendants. I had to arrive to access the portal room."

"But why are you doing this? I can't believe it's just for revenge for your family." Adala looks puzzled.

"I can't divulge my reasons yet, even to you. The knowledge is too dangerous. But the time of revelation is soon. Besides, the people of the empire wallow in slavery, serving Shulgi and his cronies. They need freedom. I've become a focal point to lead this battle for liberation. I'm their game-changer."

Adala grins. "That's a familiar saying. I, too, saw that ... something in you. It's hard to describe, but you have a charisma that naturally encourages others to follow you."

"Unfortunately, it means people die for me, too, and that weighs on my shoulders." My head drops as I remember those deaths, and we descend into silence.

Adala breaks the silence with, "So, how do these ships solve my problem with these generals?"

"By limiting their control over the battleships so they can't use them against us. And, with the knowledge I have, I believe I can do that. Only I can activate the ships. There's a fail-safe in their usage. At the least, experienced people must command these vessels to prevent power from going to these generals' heads. Offer them these ships to help re-enter the galaxy. But they stay under my control."

"They'll enjoy these new toys to play with, but they won't take kindly to taking orders from you."

I scratch my head. "I have no other suggestion."

We stand side by side, gazing out across the lake, our discussion exhausted for now.

"I found you," came a voice from behind us. We turn to see

Sentinel running toward us. He bows, puffing. "I need to exercise more."

"What brings you here, Ranulf?" Adala asks, frowning.

"Grave news, Your Majesty. Ishtar contacted me when she couldn't raise Halwende."

"My comm's on your desk. I didn't want us to be disturbed," I say. "What message does Ishtar have?"

"General Barak is amassing a large naval force to annihilate you, Halwende."

Both Adala and I turn to each other, her alarm reflecting mine.

I turn back to Sentinel. "Did she say how much time we have?"

"Ten days. And they have orders to conquer Helheim."

I turn to Adala. "This may encourage your recalcitrant generals to follow my direction."

10

TRAINING FOR WAR

With the news of Barak's imminent arrival, time has no meaning for me. Sleep is a luxury I can't afford, despite the pleas of others. Ishtar organizes pilots and other crew to help me activate the new ships and prepare them for battle once we have them orbiting around Helheim.

Two days after the announcement, I assemble a war council at the palace in the afternoon, with Resistance and Helheim military members attending.

Adala and I sit at the head of the table. Ishtar, Lugal, Argandea, Ninsar, and Lilith sit to our left, and Sentinel, General Tancred, and General Ernst are on our right. Zabada and Mamagal are present, too. I wait for Adala to start proceedings.

"Let us begin," Adala says. The others fall silent and give her their full attention. "News has arrived of an impending attack on our planet from an unknown empire. We could apportion blame for forcing us into this predicament, but that doesn't remove the threat." Adala shoots a quick glance at me. "Fortunately, the Resistance forces from Eridu can offer support for our defense. An unexpected supply of ships is available, too, thanks to Halwende. But these vessels need crews of trained personnel within a week. In one respect, we face an impossible task, but we must do our best. I will have Halwende continue this discussion."

I barely stop myself yawning as fatigue threatens to overcome me. "Thank you, Your Majesty. This morning I handed Sentinel a list of personnel needed to crew the new ships or help with assignments on our existing battleships, replacing those transferred to the new vessels as experienced space combat troops. I know it's not much time, Sentinel, but could you give an update on progress?"

Sentinel frowns. "We have difficulties in filling these positions. Maybe I'll hand over to General Tancred to explain why."

He surprises General Tancred by putting him on the spot, but Tancred recovers and clears his throat. "I stand by the bravery of our military, but to be frank, they are terrified of being sent into space. In fact, they insist it doesn't exist and they will die if forced to travel beyond the limits of our existing vehicles."

"Can't you explain the Resistance forces come from Eridu," I say, pointing at Ishtar and the others, "and they need not worry?"

"They believe these people are foreigners from our planet."

"And the warships?"

"Carriers for ground-based assaults."

"Is this fear being fermented by my dissenting generals?" Adala asks.

"No. They're as frustrated as we are. I expect they want use of their newfound toys — on what or who is a different question." Tancred frowns.

"How can we convince these people?" Argandea asks. "We need to train at once."

"Would the Queen flying into space herself and broadcasting a message to the military reassure them it's safe?" I ask.

Tancred glances at Ernst and turns back to me. "It is worth a try. I'm at a loss how to persuade them."

"I'm sure I need not worry," Sentinel says, "but what are your attitudes toward space?"

Fear flashes across Tancred's and Ernst's faces before their stoic mien reappears.

"We ... admit we are apprehensive. But we will do what we must."

"So, you would go with Queen Adala into space for the broadcast?"

After rubbing his finger under his collar, Ernst says, "Yes, we will undertake what is necessary. I must gain control of my fear."

"My guards went with me when I ventured up there. We could get them to discuss their experience," Adala suggests.

Sentinel smirks. "Most had their eyes closed."

"Oh, Ranulf."

"Just an observation." Sentinel shrugs.

"You must do something and fast," Lilith interjects. "General Barak comes with his full force. He won't care about your people's superstitions. He'll eradicate those who dissent. The fate of Halwende's family is testimony to that."

"We'll try this then," Adala says. "Please manage it, Halwende."

I'm nervous about my impending order, but I'm too busy to arrange the event. "Ishtar can organize the itinerary." Both women stiffen but stay civil.

"As you wish," Ishtar says.

"Let's get to it then."

Adala brings the meeting to a close, and everyone leaves but Adala and me.

"You won't fight with her, will you?"

Adala smiles. "Not if she behaves herself."

I laugh. "We'd better move."

"Please rest sometime."

"I will." We both know I won't.

Ishtar organizes Adala's flight into space, accompanied by Ernst and Tancred, and coordinates her broadcast with Sentinel. They announce the event and detour to my command ship. Adala enters my captain's conference room, where data tablets and other information are spread over the table.

I look up at her. "How did it go?"

Dejected, Adala flops into a seat, a frown expressing her reply.

"That good?"

She smiles. "They just won't believe in such a thing as space. They think we were transmitting from a secret studio in the capital."

"Oh." I lower the stylus I hold to the tabletop. "Stubborn adherence to their lifelong instruction. I suppose I can understand that."

"How do we break their mindset, though?"

"I don't know."

"Have you rested?"

"A little."

"Have you?"

I shrug.

Adala stands and, despite the guard accompanying her, she rounds the conference table to give me a shoulder massage. I groan before I remember we're not alone and glance at the sentry. He remains impassive, but a wisp of a smile crosses his face.

"You make life difficult for me," I say.

"Who are you talking to, me or the guard?"

I grin. "Both."

Adala sniggers. She looks at the officer and winks. "You'll just have to bear it."

The massage is soothing, but it allows me to mull over the problem.

"We have a proverb, ah ... ahhh." The stress-relieving deftness of Adala's hands presses on my shoulder muscles. "If King Alalgar won't come to the mountain, we'll bring the mountain to King Alalgar."

Adala stops massaging. "What are you mumbling?"

"Please continue." I glance at Adala, who grins at me and starts massaging again. "If your people are too scared to fly into space of their own volition, we'll load them into a transport vessel and transfer them there before they realize what's happening. They'll then understand space exists, and it's safe."

"You can't do that!"

"You got any better ideas?"

"No."

MY IDEA WORKS. In the end, fifty Helheim soldiers accept the possibility of space, despite their fears. I split the Helheim people up amongst our own for the instruction and give them ships with which to familiarize themselves. The first tutoring of the Helheim personnel is tedious. Their experience in flying troop-carrying scooters on the surface has limited value in the freedom of space, where direction is relative.

I split my day between overseeing the training and spells planet-side, discussing defense plans with Adala. Sleep is a luxury I cannot afford, but Adala insists I rest as part of my visits with her.

On the sixth day of exercises, I take part in the maneuvers to witness their progress for myself. We intend to chase a group of minute asteroids with disposable drives attached to them, mimicking enemy destroyers and corvettes. Our fleet comprises ten destroyers from Alalgar's recommissioned cache.

"Are we ready?" I ask Conrad, the captain of my ship. I act as admiral of the squadron for the exercise.

"Yes, sir."

"Begin."

Conrad relays the instructions to the rest, and we move forward in a ragged formation toward the asteroid field where the decoys hide. To make the exercise more realistic, I ask Argandea to arrange fighters to simulate dog fights as distractions for our recruits. I cringe when I see how loose the arrangement is.

"Keep things tight," I order over the navy comm channel.

Even though I receive acknowledgments, the vessels fair no better, making me sigh in disappointment.

The forward ship tactical officer spots the fake enemy vessels first and relays their position to the rest, the trainee squadron increasing speed to engage. The faster we move, the more nervous I get, as the ships often move alarmingly near each other. I'm glad they relegated us to the rear of the formation and stay apart from the others.

"Split and surround the enemy," I command.

The fleet bisects and one-half change vector to trap the adversary in a box arrangement, cutting off their escape. The opposition, controlled by Resistance fighters on the Nergal battlecruiser, sees us and maneuvers to flee. We increase our speed to cut off their move. The chatter rises across our ships as the soldiers smell blood and want to get in on the kill, resulting in the design drifting apart, threatening to offer gaps for the foe to exploit. I caution the warships to tighten their formation, but they obey with frustration and reluctance.

A fake destroyer breaks off from the rest and makes a run for freedom. Two Helheim destroyers break off to give chase. In doing so, they forget to check their relative positions and vectors. In just moments, they crash into each other like bouncing billiard balls. I grit my teeth, and Conrad glances in my direction, unimpressed with his compatriots' performance. I respect him. He is subordinate to General Tancred and shows much promise.

Despite the collision, the vessels recover and continue the chase, even though we recall one several times to return to the main formation. They resist our demands to obey orders, so I allow them their minor victory, knowing the outcome for the overall exercise.

With two ships out of position and the other arm of our squadron still encircling them, the enemy powers into the vacant space, eager to escape our net before it's too late. The ease with which they achieve their goal is humiliating, and we lose any chance to capture them within minutes. I call the fleet to disengage and end the assault.

I turn and go to my cabin, staying silent, too furious to risk my thoughts escaping into words. It was a straightforward exercise, and they failed miserably. How will they behave when they must fight the real enemy?

A soft knock raps on my door. "Enter," I say. I'm not in the mood for conversation, but I can't sit and simmer in my disappointment.

Conrad enters and salutes.

"At ease. Please take a seat."

He sits opposite me around the small meeting table.

I stare at him for several seconds, making him nervous. "Drink?" slips from my mouth.

Conrad fidgets, uneasy with the question. "It's early, sir."

"May as well consume something to dull our dismal failure."

"If it settles you, I'll join you. I see you're agitated."

"You need not be diplomatic. I'm not disturbed. I'm furious." I rise, pour two shots of whisky, hand him one, and return to my seat.

After taking a sip, Conrad glances at me. "Sir, I will speak freely. I'm disappointed too. Please consider the history of these recruits. They've never flown or taken a spaceship into battle. Hell, we've never been in space. Most didn't believe it existed, and the notion still terrifies them. I'm not making excuses, but it's only been six days. Don't you think you're being harsh with them?"

As I sip, I glare at Conrad. My gaze then softens. "I know, and you're right. It's a mammoth step your people have taken. But the Rigel navy will arrive soon, and they won't go easy just because we aren't ready. It frightens me. I'm sending these soldiers into battle, many to their deaths, and that weighs on my conscience no end."

"We volunteered, despite the unexpected turn of events." A wisp of a smile covers his face. "We have sworn to protect Queen Adala with our lives. We may not have expected the arena in which we must play, but our oaths still stand."

"General Tancred has chosen well." I extend my glass to Conrad in recognition. "I should change his rank to admiral."

"General Tancred is content with general and wishes to stay on solid soil."

I burst into laughter. "Well said. I believe you're right. So, what should we do?"

Conrad shakes his head. "It is difficult." He rubs the nape of his neck. "We must continue practicing. That is a given. But we can't afford to exhaust them either. Otherwise, they'll be too fatigued to fight.

"Understand, these soldiers — that's what they are — haven't fought many battles, their only conflict being the battle for the throne. We trained them in ground-based fighting. And they are excellent in that arena. They need time to adjust to the terrain of space. They must temper their eagerness to enter the fray, too. Once we discipline them to shed their egos and their passion for firing weapons regardless of established plans, you'll own an elite navy, sir."

"And if they're not ready?"

"They must be. The shock of engaging in an actual battle will cause them to resort to their training, too. How good are these ships?"

"They'll crush everything the empire can throw at us, but they aren't invincible. And I can't allow Barak to capture one of them."

Conrad finishes his whisky and stands. "I'd better get back and start debriefing. Thanks for the drink and the talk, sir."

"Thank you. Keep pushing them." I frown and rub my chin before glancing at him. "How are you integrating with the Resistance?"

"We have our differences. They like to remind us that they're more experienced astrogators, and we point out we're trained soldiers. I believe it's working OK, though. Your people are taking my orders without fuss."

"Tell me of any issues."

"Will do, sir." Conrad leaves.

Maybe I am expecting too much too quickly from them. I'd prefer to give them a fighting chance, though. While I continue my contemplation and depressed outlook, I find solace in knowing Adala supports me.

My comm chimes, disturbing my melancholic reverie. "Halwende here."

"Ishtar. I have an update on Barak. Disturbances closer to home delay him."

"What do you mean?"

"We have started a trend. According to the intel I'm getting, citizens are doing more than voicing their disapproval. A group on Larsa is rebelling, and there are even large-scale demonstrations on Eridu. Barak needs to put these fires out before he returns his concentration to us."

"That's a relief. After what I saw today, these people still need extensive training."

"Don't relax too much. We're only talking days, not months."

"I know, but every day counts."

"Just thought you should know."

"Thanks."

I allow myself a wry smile as I wonder who's causing trouble on the Eridu end. I can't believe it's a coincidence that conflict within the empire is increasing at the same time as Barak intends to deploy most of his fleet to defeat me. As I recline in my chair, I rest my head and contemplate my next moves.

11

LOOKING FOR ANSWERS

Time away from drills seems a waste of opportunity for me, but Adala pleads with me to return to Helheim, so I relent and descend to the planet. Once I'm on the ground, I realize I've been looking forward to a break and time with Adala more than I allowed myself to consider. So, instead of the restless distraction of training, I resolve to forget my frustrations for a moment and appreciate the rest with Adala. But I refrain from sitting when I meet her at the palace. She whisks me off into the underground tunnels and to the secluded garden that is her haven.

Once the door closes and we leave the guards behind, she wraps her arms around me and gives me a passionate kiss before I comprehend what has happened. When we break, I push her to arm's length and search her eyes, wondering over her intentions.

"What is it?" I ask.

"You need to relax."

"What's for dessert?"

Adala laughs, and I realize I haven't heard a laugh of joy for so long. But her joyfulness is infectious, and I join in moments later. I bring her to me and hug her, then kiss her and embrace her again, reveling in the moment, forgetting the dangers that hang over us.

We break and stroll through the garden, enjoying the sunshine filtering through the trees as we approach the waterfall.

"Do you still relax here often, now that you're Queen?" I ask.

"Yes. I find it more relaxing and peaceful than anywhere else. And no one else comes here, so I'm alone without worry of being disturbed."

"I can appreciate that. If only I had such a retreat."

"You can use it any time."

"I know. But it's your haven. I wish I had a secret place of my own."

"You do, don't you?"

Her question confuses me. "What do you mean?"

"There are secrets here." She points to my heart. "You won't let anyone see them."

"There are innumerable things there. Few are peaceful. Significant pain still lingers."

"Your family?"

"Yes." I lower my gaze as I remember my loss.

"I can't imagine the feeling. Or maybe I can. I miss my mother, even after these many years." She pauses in silence. "But you have other secrets, too."

I raise my eyes and search hers. "Yes, I do. Ones I must not confess yet."

"But why not? Why can't you share the burden with me?"

"You have enough on your plate." I give a wry smile, then frown. "They are still too dangerous for you. I will tell you when it's right. I wish I didn't have to keep these secrets from you, but I must."

"You are a stubborn man." Adala grins. "Let's sit."

As we have come to her favorite bench seat, we both recline and enjoy the view in silence. I contemplate my good fortune in finding Adala, and warmth fills me.

"We walk a delicate path," I say, letting my thoughts filter out to Adala.

She turns and frowns. "What do you mean?"

"This war — we have little leeway for error or uncertainty. One minor mistake could change our destiny forever."

"I don't understand. I know that whatever happens, our meeting has changed the world." Adala searches me for my feelings.

A tear escapes my eye and trickles down my cheek. Adala reaches over and captures it with her tongue as if performing a ritual. The intimacy of the motion overpowers me, and I move closer to kiss her. She reacts. We part and gasp, staring into each other's eyes before voicing joyful laughter and kissing again.

Afterward, I lean my head against hers and sigh. "I must go."

"I'll cherish this moment," Adala says.

"So will I." I rise, and she copies me.

We stroll back to the entrance but hear noises as we near it. We both frown as the noise crystallizes into shouting. When Adala opens the door, we see Ishtar struggling with Adala's royal guards, attempting to enter the gardens. The conflict stops when they see us.

"At last," Ishtar says. "I was considering blasting these two if they refused my passage any longer."

"Why? What's happened?" A sense of alarm constricts my stomach.

"The new ships. They've lost power."

"What?"

"They have no power. They're dead in the vacuum, and no one knows what's wrong with them."

I sigh and turn to Adala. "Forgive me. I must leave."

"I know." She gives a resigned smile. "Stay safe and return soon."

"I will." After a moment's indecision, I give her a quick peck, disregarding any protocol for royal decorum.

Adala blushes, but the move delights her.

"Let's go," I say, turning to Ishtar. We leave, but I get one last glimpse of Adala before she disappears as we round a corner.

"I wasn't interrupting, was I?" Ishtar asks, giving a wry smile.

"Would it have mattered if I said you were?"

"No."

"Then, you didn't. Now let's inspect these ships."

Ishtar leads me to a waiting shuttle, and we ascend to my destroyer, which is in the same trouble as the rest of them. Zabada and Mamagal stand with Conrad awaiting me as I enter the helm. The lights are dim and the stations blank.

Conrad salutes. "Sir."

I salute back, understanding the need to maintain naval protocols. "Update me, please."

"We were moving into position for another formation practice when all power, but emergency power, tripped. Our engineers can't solve the problem, except they inform me the primary power supply has failed."

I glance at Zabada and Mamagal and back at Conrad. "I see." A million options rush through my head, but I resolve them to one course of action. "You two," I look at Zabada and Mamagal, "follow me." I lead them to my cabin, and Ishtar attempts to enter, too. "No," I say. "We must keep this private for now. I'm sorry."

Ishtar halts, shocked by the exclusion, resentful of the implications. "As you wish." She turns and takes a seat at the helm.

I close the door and stare at them. "What does this mean? We can't have depleted the crystals."

Zabada and Mamagal glance at each other. Mamagal speaks. "They should not be depleted. They established the crystal's potency in the days before they hid Ur. And you confirmed their power yourself."

"But I've only been using them for a short period." I scratch my chin. "Could their storage for so long have affected them? Or the cloaking?"

"It shouldn't have. Why don't you check their status first? How did you get the ships functioning?"

"I used the startup sequence, although it required me to prove my identity before it activated. I'll see if it will repeat it." Fortunately, there's a duplicate of the captain's controls in my cabin. So, I grab the screen and start the sequence. But nothing happens when I complete my identification. It perplexes me, as the crystal checked out with ninety-nine percent capacity. "I need to check the engineering compartment."

When I go to leave, Zabada grabs my arm. I stop and look at him. "What?"

"You mustn't divulge the crystal's secrets to the others."

"How am I going to avoid it? There's a ship full of crew, and we'll have to tell them sometime."

"The knowledge is too dangerous at present."

"He speaks the truth," Mamagal says.

"But I need these ships. Without them, our cause is hopeless."

"We understand," Zabada says. "But you must solve the problem without revealing this secret."

I stare at him and then at Mamagal, furious with their demand but realizing they are right. We can't allow Barak and Shulgi to gain knowledge of the crystals. Relenting, I shake my head. "OK. I'll find a way. Let's go."

I open the door. Ishtar still sits at the helm. "Stay here," I instruct her.

She stares at me like a spoiled child being refused a treat, but she complies.

I leave the helm with Zabada and Mamagal and enter the engineering compartment five minutes later. After instructing the personnel to take a break, I stride to the power supply reactor and open it.

The crystal still shines, as on earlier occasions. I check out the engineering screen. Scrutinizing the contents doesn't enlighten me on the cause of the problem. I scratch my head and move back to the reactor, sorting through the wiring. After a time, it becomes plain I do not know what I'm doing without proper circuitry diagrams. They aren't in the ship's records. I restore the covers and return to my cabin, accessing my data chip for clues. But there are no clues.

"The information I need isn't here. I have to go to the palace library," I tell Zabada and Mamagal, who cling to me like orbiting satellites. "You can stay here."

"We'd prefer to go with you," Zabada says.

"As you wish."

We leave my cabin, where Ishtar still sits and waits. She raises her eyebrows as I pass her and glance her way.

I stop and shrug. "Come along then. The more, the merrier."

My party goes to the shuttle bay and uses one of the shuttles to return to Helheim. We enter the palace an hour later, where I leave Ishtar, much to her indignation, and continue to the library after popping in on Adala to inform her of my presence. We descend to the lower levels and enter the library, Zabada and Mamagal for the first time.

They gape at the sparseness with fascination.

"Talk to it," I tell them. "Just ask any question you want, and it'll answer you if it can. But be specific. It's temperamental. I have other writings to consult."

I stride to the shelves and pull out the portal room volume. After making myself comfortable on the floor, I flick through the pages, searching for connection diagrams for power supplies to use for troubleshooting our problem. Half an hour later, I slam the book closed, disgusted by the lack of information.

I watch the others and smile. They prance around the room, asking the library questions, neither of them satisfied with the answers they get. "Having difficulties communicating?"

"You're right about its temperament," Zabada complains.

"Well, I need to use it, if you don't mind."

"Be our guest," Mamagal says.

"Library, please display data on flerovium power supply connection circuits."

Silence fills the room while the library consults its databases.

"No such information exists in my files."

"Damn!" I rise, the sudden blood flow to my feet making me feel faint. "Where can I access that knowledge?"

"My records specify they stored that intelligence in a repository on Larsa."

"What?"

"My re–"

"I heard you." My attention focuses on Mamagal. "Did you know?"

"I knew they kept information and crystals there but was unaware of the details."

"Stands to reason now that I consider it, given the pricelessness of the contents of the vault. I'm going on a trip to Larsa. Nothing beats waltzing into the lion's den."

12

BACK TO LARSA

"I must travel back to the Rigel Empire to retrieve vital information on our ships," I explain to a gaping-mouthed Adala. She displays a calm exterior, but I know she's fuming.

"So you can get captured again? Or worse?" she asks once she regains her composure.

"It's the only way. We need those vessels, and I must fix them. The information is on Larsa."

"Why can't you send someone else? Ishtar or another? Why must it be you? Why must I suffer again?"

I sigh. "It must be me. No one else can access the vault. The sooner I go, the earlier I return. And I have to borrow your yacht."

Adala paces her office, tears threatening to escape. "You must take Ranulf then."

"But I ..."

"There will be no argument." She stamps her foot, much to my internal amusement. "Either he goes with you, or I won't give you the yacht."

"But—"

Adala glares at me, arms folded, obstinate in her demand.

"OK, OK. I'll take him. I don't understand why you're worried."

"You don't understand why! They captured and tortured you last time ... twice. And I didn't know what happened to you. You just disappeared."

"OK." I wince and glance at her bodyguard. I know he's laughing, but he hides it well. After I close the distance between us, I peer back at the guard, undecided about my course of action. "I'll return before you know it," I say, turning to Adala.

"You'd better," she says, tempering her emotions to touch my shoulder.

Before I react, she has me in her arms, gazing into my eyes. "Come back."

I nod and rest my forehead on hers. "It makes me nervous to leave, but I must."

"Just return." She gives me a quick peck and releases me. "Now go, before I change my mind."

I need no encouragement, so I move and chase up Sentinel, informing him of our impending trip.

His eyes light up at the prospect of excitement, and he quickly collects what he needs, including the arms he has accumulated after having known me — a significant arsenal.

When he arrives at the scooter to ferry us to the shuttle, I eye his baggage. "Expecting trouble?"

"I'm traveling with you, aren't I?"

I burst out laughing. "Let's get going then."

Zabada, Mamagal, and Ishtar tag along, and together we return to the destroyer.

After discussing my plans with them, we decide Ishtar will go with Sentinel and me. Ishtar does not hide her fury over my returning to Larsa, but she knows I won't change my mind.

We board the *Queen Rosalind* two hours later, its familiarity calming my nerves, and head for Larsa with due haste.

∽

∽

⌇

LARSA LOOKS peaceful as though it's business as usual. I park the yacht well away from surveillance systems, as the planetary security will have the *Rosalind* earmarked. We get on the shuttle and descend to the surface. To lessen our time on the planet, I bypass the spaceport and head straight for the crypt, angling the shuttle to a landing site near the entrance and settling it on the ground.

We egress and start our short hike to the cavern entry doorway, Sentinel laden with weapons of every description.

"Do you intend to use those, or are you just bragging?" Ishtar says to him.

After an extended resigned stare, Sentinel replies. "You can never be over-prepared when you're traveling with Halwende. I've had experience."

Ishtar glances at me and back at Sentinel. "I know what you mean."

"You're both overreacting," I complain.

They both glare at me.

"Let's keep moving," I say.

We arrive at the doorway after twenty minutes, and I soon locate the access panel. The door opens and we go in, Sentinel eying the space with excitement. When we enter the bowels of the crypt, they both gape at their surroundings. As I've seen it before, I waste no time gaping. I head for the shelves with the data chip storage and begin searching for any information on the ship's energy supply design.

After reviewing several chips, I find one that looks promising. I study it and confirm the circuitry differs in subtle detail from the destroyer's circuitry. A detail easily missed. But I wonder why my inclusion of the crystal in the yacht's power supply succeeded. Deciding it's irrelevant, I slide the chip into my pocket and pack up the rest into the bag I have. While Sentinel and Ishtar busy themselves exploring the crypt and talking, I slip over to the cabinets and grab two more crystals.

"I'm ready," I say, once I have the stones hidden away.

"That was quick," Sentinel comments.

"The information wasn't hard to locate. It's just a pain we had to travel so far to get it. Let's return before something else happens."

The others nod and we head back to the entrance. The door opens and we freeze. Six security guards are standing nearby talking. When they see the door's movement, they turn toward it and us.

On seeing strangers, the guards go for their weapons. But Sentinel's quicker than they are and, hefting a maser rifle into his arms, he mows them down before they can gather their thoughts.

"Let's get moving," I say. "There's bound to be other troops nearby."

We leave and jog back to the shuttle with our guns ready for further surprises from the enemy.

As we approach the shuttle, I hear voices. I gesture for the others to stop. We hide behind boulders near the stream path we follow. I chance a peek and spot three guards up ahead. A scan of the surroundings reveals more lurking further afield. We can't just blast the ones we see and hope to make it to the shuttle before someone else arrives.

"Any ideas?" I ask.

Sentinel hazards his own glance and scans the surrounding terrain before answering. "I'll scout around them and try approaching from their rear."

Ishtar raises an eyebrow. "Risky."

"You got any better suggestions?"

"No." She shakes her head.

"You two stay here." Sentinel disappears before I can object.

As I wait, my mind tortures itself, devising every scenario of us being caught or killed and fulfilling Adala's worst nightmare. I can't let this happen. I look at my chronometer, thinking Sentinel's taking a long time.

"Come out unless you want to see your friend die," someone yells from beyond the boulders.

I cuss as I realize they've captured Sentinel.

"It's no good, Ishtar," Sentinel calls. "They know you're there. You might as well surrender."

Ishtar and I stare at each other.

"Sounds like they think it's only you," I say.

"Yeah." Ishtar gulps as she prepares to surrender.

I clutch her shoulder. "You can't."

"They'll kill Sentinel if I don't. You've got a chance of escaping if I do."

"Or I can devise another plan."

Ishtar shakes her head. "No. You must escape and return, or we've lost." She takes a deep breath. "I'm coming out," she calls.

I let go, guilt-ridden over the sacrifices being made on my behalf.

I watch Ishtar disappear with her hands in the air. This mustn't happen. I must do something. Searching for a vantage point, I grab the weapons bag Sentinel left with us, retreat a short distance, and climb up to the top of the ravine. As I scan the ground below, I see Sentinel and Ishtar, both cuffed and sitting, two guards surrounding them. I count five others scouting the terrain and attempting to gain entry to the shuttle. Fortunately, they haven't interrogated either Sentinel or Ishtar about the lock since it's locked to my DNA biometrics.

I scratch my chin and stare at the sack of deadly devices while considering my options. After pulling the bag open, I scrounge through its contents until I find a gadget that gives me an idea. A rabbit grenade is a simple device — you pull the pin, but instead of throwing it, you let it hop in the direction you point it until the timer ticks out and it explodes. Unsophisticated and often ineffective if the enemy knows how it operates. But I'm counting on these guards never having seen one. So, I scramble closer, set the timer, and allow the rabbit to do its job as it hops toward the two guards.

Their astonishment and jovial disinterest tell me they do not realize their peril. After several more seconds, it times out and explodes. I jump out and blast the other three guards, using the explosion's dust cloud to hide me. With them disposed of, I rush for Sentinel, Ishtar, and their two captors. Before the captors comprehend what has just happened, they're dead with maser blast holes through them. Not convinced others don't lurk out of view, I hide behind nearby boulders and wait, searching the surrounds for danger.

"Can you move?" I call out to Sentinel and Ishtar.

"Not sure," Sentinel responds.

Shuffles and scrapings rasp through to me while I continue surveying the surroundings. I hear ouches.

"We can't move," Ishtar confirms. "They've placed a mobile force field around us."

"Give me a minute," I say.

After five minutes, I relax, comfortable that it is safe to venture toward Sentinel and Ishtar again. I check the surroundings and the dead, searching for the force field control box. I find it in one of the dead guard's pockets. Once I extract it, I turn off the controls. Sentinel and Ishtar are both shackled with magnetic restraints, but I locate that key, too, and release them.

"That was close," Sentinel says.

"Too close." I nod in agreement.

"Let's get out of here, shall we?" Ishtar looks miffed at the whole debacle.

I nod, and we jog the short distance to the shuttle.

Within minutes, I lift the vessel in the air and rocket from the atmosphere. Having escaped, I relax as I set course for the yacht, eager to return to Helheim.

"We've got company," Ishtar says.

"Where?" My eyes widen in alarm.

"Three fighters coming in from Larsa Platform 1 headed straight for us."

"Must be desperate," Sentinel says.

"We only have two masers to defend ourselves." I glance at the others. "Get on them and scare them off while I dodge their fire."

Sentinel and Ishtar seize the weapons consoles and target the approaching fighters, starting evasive maneuvers once the fighters come into range.

The shuttle rocks as it takes a maser hit to the hull. I curse and begin weaving. It's impossible to evade three fighters at once. I hope the others destroy at least one before long. As if Ishtar reads my thoughts, she fires off a maser blast and strikes a fighter with a direct hit. It's not destroyed, but it peels off its pursuit, the damage making any further attack pointless.

Another blast shudders through the frame, and alarms light up my screen. Our hull has been breached, and the automatic bulkhead emergency sealing mechanism activates to stop the atmosphere from bleeding into space. Before long, seals isolate the damaged section and we're safe from asphyxiation, but we can't afford too many more hits.

"You need to do something about them," I yell to the others as I watch the fighters dogfight us on another approach.

Sentinel fires his maser and shouts in triumph seconds later when a fighter breaks off its attack, smoke trailing from the drives.

My confidence in our escape increases, just as the shuttle shakes violently. As I gaze at the screen, my hopes shatter. Our primary drive is unusable. We are dead in the vacuum of space, far from the yacht and safety. The others stare at me, fear ricocheting between us. A destroyer arrives, headed straight our way.

I breathe a heavy sigh. "You may as well stop. We can do nothing. They might just destroy us if you continue firing."

"We can't concede," Ishtar says.

"You got any better ideas? The drive's shot, and we're too distant from the yacht." My body language says the rest.

"But the ships and Helheim. We can't surrender. We have to do something."

I glance over at Sentinel. He looks as devastated as I feel. Ishtar's mention of the ships reminds me of the data chip and the flerovium I have with me. I must not allow it to slip into the empire's hands. I can't space it either, not the chip. Ideas of escape flash through my head, but I find none that'll enable our escape without risk of renewed capture or death. I'd prefer to stay alive, but I must hide the data chip. There's no point in hiding it on the ship, as I can't guarantee ever returning to it. I have only one choice.

"We can't surrender without a fight," Sentinel protests.

"As much as I agree with you, you'll just die for no gain. I'd choose to yield for now and hope for an idea later," I say.

Ishtar nods. "I hate it too, Sentinel, but I agree."

"Prepare for being boarded. I must do something before they arrive." I rush from my seat, grab the bag, and head for the medical booth.

After grabbing the chip, I place it in a miniature non-evasive pouch. I scrounge for a scalpel and lower my trousers, cutting a small incision in my leg, behind my knee. As I grimace, I slip the chip beneath the skin and use surgical stitching salve to rejoin the dermis and start the rapid-heal reaction. The incision will be invisible when it heals.

With the chip secure, I rush to the airlock, place the bag in it and eject it and the flerovium into space. It will float to the Larsa star as gravity pulls at it over the eons. The others stare at me when I return.

"I just needed to hide the chip. It's safe for now. What's happening?"

"We're being pulled into the destroyer shuttle bay," Ishtar says. She slouches in her seat, defeat in her eyes.

"Let's see how this plays out."

Twenty minutes later, the airlock opens, and troopers storm into the shuttle. A squad enters the helm and surrounds us, a captain striding in behind them. He nods to the staff sergeant, who gives a hand movement to his soldiers. They move forward and knock us to the deck.

13

CAPTURED

I wake alone in the destroyer's brig. My head throbs and I wince as I touch my scalp. A sticky lump sits proud of my hair. Blood covers my fingers when I remove them. My last memory is being hit with the butt of a soldier's maser rifle.

As I sit alone wallowing in my misery, I speculate whether my captors have any idea who they've caught. A sudden dread overpowers me, and I reach for the space behind my knee. Relief floods through me as my finger traces the chip's outline.

Sentinel and Ishtar lie in separate cells near me and take longer to regain consciousness. I know they are awake when I hear them moan. After that, we just sit, chatting and waiting for what comes next.

Two hours later, guards enter and march us to a shuttle — not ours, unfortunately. They strap us in, and we descend to the Larsa surface, ending our trip jailed in a military base's security compound on the planet. With no consideration of our injuries, they march us roughly into separate interrogation rooms. That's where I am now, waiting for whoever will talk to me.

The door opens, and a general and two guards enter. The sentries stand straddling the doorway as the commander rounds the table and takes a seat facing me. He glares at me, but I give him an innocent look in reply.

"What is your name?"

I nod at the name tag he wears. "I see yours is General Tuge."

"Answer the question."

"No." He obviously doesn't know who I am, and I'm not telling him.

Tuge nods. A guard steps forward, smashes his rifle into my ribs, and steps back. The sound fills the room as the weapon hits, and I buckle over in pain, my breathing labored.

"Not so hard next time," Tuge says to the soldier. "I still need him talking." He returns his attention to me. "What is your name?" he repeats.

"Tuge."

Tuge jams his jaw shut and flushes red. His hands tighten into fists. He then relaxes. "You think this is funny? I can have you shot for treason. I know you're a member of the Resistance, but you're new to Larsa. We thought we'd uncovered everyone. Ever since that renegade, Halwende, started prancing around thinking he's a leader and damaging our orbital platforms with his foolishness, you people have considered yourselves invincible. Your pathetic little escapade isn't even worth putting in the paperwork."

It's hard to keep a straight face when Tuge mentions my name. I fully intend escaping this predicament and how foolish he'll feel when he realizes he had the empire's nemesis in his hands. When Barak and Shulgi find out, he will be lucky to escape with only a court-martial.

Since he thinks I'm a lowly Resistance fighter, I may as well amuse myself. "I came from a remote base a few weeks ago," I offer, pretending he has worn me down.

"Where were you going in the shuttle?" He seems willing to forego knowing my name for now.

"Back to our headquarters."

"Which is where?"

"I don't know. I'm new to Larsa. Everything's still strange to me."

Tuge eyes me as he judges the truth of my words.

"What's your leader's name?"

"They don't tell a novice those secrets. I just follow orders."

After staring at me, Tuge stands and strides to the door. "Watch him," he barks to the guards before he walks out.

I can't believe the gullibility of this man. If escaping is as easy as telling him my lies, we'll leave before nightfall. My problem is that I don't know the base's layout or how to hijack a shuttle. I turn to check out the sentries, but they look competent and inclined to inflict pain, as my agonizing rib tells me.

Seconds tick by into minutes and then hours before Tuge returns. He wears a smug smile and makes sure I notice it as he sits. "At least your female companion's willing to talk. It's amazing what ... well, let's skip the details."

I grit my teeth. If he's done to Ishtar what he infers, he's dead. I'll destroy this base.

"Now we will chat ... Halwende. I have caught a big fish, haven't I?"

Oh, Ishtar. I can't imagine the barbarity they inflicted on her to extract my name. My facade drains away, but I won't give him any further information. He can kill me if he wants. Shulgi was going to do that, anyway. I wonder what they've done to Sentinel.

"Where have you been hiding?"

I stay silent.

"Refusing to respond to my questions is pointless. We are informing General Barak as I speak. He'll be ecstatic to have you in his clutches again. And I'll receive a huge reward for capturing you. So, reply to my question."

That's your hope ... a promotion and a commendation. You'll get your bonus when Barak finds out I've escaped. I stay silent.

"Answer me!" Tuge smashes his fist on the desk, but I preserve my silence, unflinching. He glares at me.

Tuge stands. "Bring him with me." He walks out the door.

The guards lift me and march me between them as we follow Tuge to our destination. Tuge arrives at a doorway but waits before he opens it and waves us through, a smug smile plastered across his face. The room is painted white and lit by glaring lights from the ceiling. A force field dissects the room. When I turn to check the layout, I stop and gasp.

Ishtar lies on the floor, naked, bruised, and bleeding. It's obvious they've abused and violated her repeatedly. She looks dead until she coughs, blood and saliva dribbling from her mouth. As if she's aware of someone else in the room, her eyelids flutter into slits, despair weeping from them. "I'm sorry," she croaks as she gazes at me dully.

I gulp as tears escape my eyes. Why do people resort to such barbarity? A knot of anger and rage ignites in my stomach and rises within me as I turn my attention to Tuge. "You're dead. You will burn in hell before I leave."

Tuge chuckles, but even he grimaces when he peers at his torturer's handiwork. "I don't think so. Now, where is your base?"

"Out toward Santori." I haven't lied, but there's an enormous space between here and Santori. I wish him luck in finding it if he's gullible enough to believe me.

"There isn't much out that way. It shouldn't be difficult to find." Tuge smiles. "General Barak will reward me well if I discover the headquarters for him."

Good luck with that.

"Take him back to the cells." He turns to go but stops. "And clean her up and clothe her. Put her in her cell, too. Make sure Halwende can see her." With his instructions issued, he leaves, whistling as he goes.

The guards roughly move me forward. I turn my head as we leave. "We're leaving this place soon and burning it to the ground," I tell Ishtar just before she disappears behind the doorframe.

After the guard shoves me into my cell, I sprawl onto the floor, the force field locking me inside. I pace the prison, devising and evaluating ideas for escape, but none gives enough chance of success to risk the effort.

They deposit Ishtar in her cage thirty minutes afterward, too weak to walk. She crawls to her bed and collapses onto it. I leave her to recuperate for now, as it's pointless disturbing her.

Sentinel's cell is still vacant, which worries me. Either he's getting the same treatment as Ishtar, or he's dead. I'm in two minds over which outcome I hope for him.

Conscious of my fidgeting, I sit on my bunk and recline against the wall, filled with regret. Why does trouble always follow me wherever I go? It's as if I'm a magnet for it. My thoughts spiral into depression until I shake myself from them and consider options for freedom again. It must be possible to escape.

"Halwende," Ishtar says, croaking just loud enough for me to hear.

I rise and walk closer to her. "Yes?"

"I'm sorry. I couldn't take it anymore."

"Everyone has their breaking point. Judging by the looks of you, yours is exceptional. Don't apologize. You withstood the pain to your limit. Remember, Tuge and his cronies will burn in hell when we leave. I promise."

After coughing and spluttering — traces of blood still tinge her spittle — Ishtar turns her head and stares with puffy eyes. "Any ideas?"

"No. But I'm working on it."

"There's little time before Barak arrives."

"I know, but Sentinel's missing. We can't leave without him."

"I can't help you yet."

"Just rest and be ready when we get our chance."

We fall silent, and I return to my bed. I wish Sentinel would come back but wishing won't bring him to me any faster.

An hour later, a noise of distant maser fire filters through the passages of our prison block. My ears prick when I realize it's coming closer. Ishtar has heard it too, and she props herself up on her bed, eyes glued to the doorway. She glances at me. I shrug, and she looks at the exit again. We wait as the commotion grows louder.

The door bursts open ten minutes later, and two people enter backward, battling the guards. I grunt when I recognize Sentinel. There I was fretting he was being tortured, and he doesn't appear to have a scratch on him.

"Open the cells," Sentinel tells his accomplice, who is wearing a guard's uniform. I just make out that she's holding a force-field shield, protecting them both from enemy fire. She reaches out to the control panel and punches the code to switch the force-field barriers off.

Sentinel hazards a quick glance at me. "Hi." He smiles as if we're meeting for drinks.

If our plight wasn't so serious, I'd laugh. "Good to see you. You can tell me how you stayed unharmed later. And I take it you have a plan for our escape. Do you have a weapon for me?"

The woman throws a handgun at me, which I snatch from the air. She looks at me. "I'm Tiamat."

I nod and focus my attention on the people shooting at us, returning their fire. In between shots, I see Ishtar has stood, although she's crouched over and in obvious pain.

She shuffles over to us. "Got another one?" A second pistol materializes, and she grabs it and contributes to our defense.

Between blasts, Sentinel looks at Ishtar. "What happened to you?"

"What didn't happen?" Ishtar replies as she fires, a scream echoing back to us moments later.

"Oh."

"We must pay Tuge a visit before we leave," I say. "I've got a present for him."

Tiamat glances at me with alarm. "That's going to be difficult."

"I promised him." My jaw tenses with determination.

"Let's push these back then," Tiamat suggests as she intensifies her shooting and inches forward, the shield deflecting most shots coming at us.

Because of the corridor's confined nature, few assailants can attack us before they interfere with each other, swinging the odds in our favor. We make steady progress along the passageway, stepping over deceased guards as we go. Tiamat puts another shot in each to make sure they're dead. We don't want someone waking and coming up behind us.

After ten minutes, we reach a tee junction. We're on the branch, so we must fend off attacks from both directions. Tiamat gives me a flashbang. "Here, throw this." She points to our left.

I prime it and toss it around one corner. A flare and explosion report back to us. Without hesitation, Tiamat rushes forward, firing her maser at any movement. Her skill astounds me. Before long, we have our tee of the junction in our possession and retreat along it. Ishtar and I keep a vigil ahead as we move forward while Tiamat and Sentinel protect us from the onslaught behind us. Our progress speeds up as we keep running.

"What's the plan?" I ask.

Between shots, Tiamat peers behind her at me and outlines her plan. "You crave Tuge. It's risky to go after him, but it's also true no one will shoot us if we have him. And he's too much of a coward to risk dying by acting the hero. So, we kidnap him and use him to escape to a shuttle. After that, do with him what you will."

"Bold move, but won't he have guards surrounding him?"

"Despite what you've seen, few soldiers protect this base. We don't expect trouble here. They'll have second thoughts after this." She keeps shooting.

It could be my imagination, but the resistance to our flight seems to be waning as if they're running out of troopers. We move faster and turn several corners before entering a corridor with offices. Tiamat blasts the doors off as we go ahead, checking the rooms for occupants. With one door left, she opens it the usual way and peers through the doorway. The office is larger and more lavish than the others but looks empty.

"He must have fled," Tiamat says and adds, "Protect our rear, Halwende." She makes a thorough scan of the office and begins gesturing for us to leave when we hear a sob coming from behind the desk. Tiamat wears a grin when I glance at her. She enters the room and creeps to the desk, her maser ready. "Come out, Tuge."

"Don't shoot." Tuge whimpers and crawls from his hiding spot. He remains on his knees with his arms raised.

"Get up, you poor excuse for a general," Tiamat says, kicking his torso. Fearful, Tuge rises, and Tiamat grabs his collar. "You're going to lead us to a shuttle. And if you try any tricks, you'll fry. Got it?"

Tuge nods with too much enthusiasm.

"Now go." Tiamat shoves her pistol muzzle into his spine and moves.

They leave the office with Sentinel, Ishtar, and me covering them from the front and behind us. Resistance to our movement is minimal, and we arrive at the shuttle compound with only minor skirmishes along the way. Tiamat is right — the risk of Tuge becoming collateral damage is going in our favor.

Tiamat opens the shuttle access hatch and glances at me. "What do we do with him?" She nods at Tuge.

"Let me handle him," Ishtar says, her jaw clenched and eyes hard.

After adjusting the power of her maser to a mid-range value, she shoves Tuge aside, aims and fires. He screams as he burns and cooks, Ishtar keeping her finger on the trigger until he continues his combustion without an external stimulus.

I grimace as I imagine the painful death, although I have no sympathy for him.

"Dramatic," I say.

Ishtar glares at me. "You said he'd burn. I made sure he did."

"Let's get going before the base realizes Tuge is dead and decides to kill us," Tiamat says as she enters the vessel. We follow and I close the hatch.

Jumping into the pilot's seat, I start the drives and prepare to take off a minute later. Tiamat sits next to me. With the lights green, I pour power into the drive and launch the shuttle into the atmosphere.

I notice the shuttle is heavily armed. I glance over at Tiamat. "You chose this vessel for a reason."

"Sure did. Fly a lap of the base, will you?" Tiamat grins.

I obey her and veer off my course to sweep the compound. She launches five missiles, and the post explodes in a pyrotechnic display of destruction.

After adjusting to my original flight path, we leave Larsa and not a moment too soon.

14

RETURN TO HELHEIM

We encounter no further obstacles to our departure and return to Helheim. Once there, I insist Ishtar have a thorough checkup by the Resistance medical team before returning to service, ignoring her protests. I am motivated not only by my concern for her. After her traumatic ordeal at the hands of Tuge, I can't afford for her psychological stamina to fail in the fight ahead.

After removing the chip from my leg, I visit the stranded ships and change their power circuits, getting them re-energized one at a time, to my immense relief. With training restarted, I take a brief rest on Helheim with Adala.

"About time you came to say hello." Adala raises her head from her work and glares chastisement at me when I enter her study in the late afternoon.

I smile as her enchantment wraps around me, warming me. "Do you do anything apart from sitting behind your desk?"

Adala stretches backward as she peers at me, giving herself time to plan a reply. "If I had a full-time Grand Chancellor, I could conduct other duties." She smiles with a challenging expression.

"Ouch! That's below the belt." I move closer.

"But true." She stands and rounds the desk to hug me. "I missed you. And I hear your trip wasn't uneventful."

"I didn't realize Sentinel was a snitch."

Adala laughs. "It wasn't easy to draw it from him, believe me. But I could see his reticence over the matter."

I nod. "Was he happy to be back?"

"What do you ...? Oh, yes, he was. He rushed off to Lilith before even greeting me. What lack of protocol."

With a shout of laughter, I withdraw from Adala, shaking my head as I gaze out the window of her office. After a moment's thought, I turn and glance at her, solemn. "It was a lucky escape. Except for help from within, we mightn't be here. Ishtar had a most traumatic experience."

Adala draws near me. "Why keep placing yourself in such danger?"

"It's in my nature. I'm repenting of my cowardice."

"You must forgive yourself. You can't carry this constant guilt forever."

"I'll try." I wrap my arms around Adala's waist and direct my gaze to the outside view.

"Can you stay for dinner?" Adala asks.

"Yes."

"Good."

The way Adala says the word draws my attention to it, and I glance at her. She wears a wicked smile.

THE NEXT MORNING, I arrive back on my command destroyer

refreshed, despite last evening's after-dinner activities. "How are preparations progressing?" I ask Conrad.

"Well, sir. We should be ready for the training exercise in thirty minutes." Conrad replies, saluting.

"Good. I'll be in my cabin while I wait."

"As you wish, sir."

I stride to my cabin and close the door, immediately opening my tablet to retrieve the mock battle plans. They're basic maneuvers, but I'm nervous about the outcome after last time's effort. A knock disturbs my contemplations. "Enter."

Conrad strides into the room. "The simulation is ready, sir. Admiral Ishtar wishes to speak with you beforehand."

"OK. I'll be out in a minute." Conrad leaves. I smile to myself as I recall his addressing Ishtar by her new title. Ishtar's call comes through to me. "Admiral Ishtar. What can I do for you?"

Ishtar frowns. "Why are you being so formal? I just wanted to wish you well in the battle."

"Indeed? I suggest you keep your eyes on your own vessels. They will be pseudo-destroyed soon."

"As you please." Ishtar cuts her connection.

Ishtar and I are opposing commanders in the mock confrontation. She controls half the fleet, including half the Helheim ships, and I control the other half. As we only have one fighter carrier, we share it and have half the fighters each at our disposal.

The starting time arrives, so I rise and head for the helm. After acknowledging those present, I command a connection to the ships' captains in our mock fleet on the main screen. They appear one minute later. The faces staring back at me are both enthusiastic and tense. I'm the only one not in uniform, but that's been my trademark.

"Captains, welcome to my battle fleet. You've trained together as a unit and should be familiar with each other's peculiarities. Use your training in the fighting ahead and we'll gain victory. If you keep your formations and positions in the firing runs, we will win this exercise. It won't be perfect. There will be room for improvement. That's the purpose of these exercises. We debrief afterward. Good luck and I'll be watching."

"Sir," a chorus of captains shout through the comm before they sign off and the screen blanks.

I find my seat and wait for the conflict to begin.

The opposing fleet lines up, and I announce the start of the mock battle. My flotilla moves into their attack formations, and Ishtar's ships do the same. I see her tactics at once and send a message to my captains announcing a change to compensate for her intended assault. Within a few seconds, I realize my mistake. The ships I lead drift into nonsensical positions. One could only describe it as utter chaos. They were so intent on practicing for our trained maneuvers that they couldn't change formation in a disciplined manner. While I'm bringing my ships back into position, Ishtar's fleet starts its battle run. I groan as I expect the outcome before the fighting begins.

To my surprise, the two captains in charge of their squadrons understand my directions and start barking orders to the vessels under their command, placing them into position and driving them forward to meet the attack. Once the ships return to order, I nod, appreciating the effort they made in achieving the result, despite the unnecessary chaos.

Mock firing transpires as the ships pass each other. To make fighting fair, I have my found ships' firepower changed to mirror the others. The opposing vessels complete their run and turn to come at us again. Several vessels show simulated damage, but we have destroyed none so far.

While the major battle continues, I watch the fighters attack each other as they duck and weave in between the corvettes and destroyers. As I study the conflict, one fighter attracts my scrutiny. The pilot's maneuverability is excellent, and he puts several fighters out of action while I pay attention.

I turn to Conrad. "Who's flying fighter FH-107?"

"Let me check, sir." After several seconds, Conrad returns a reply. "I'm uncertain, sir. There was a last-minute change in pilot allocations. I've asked for an update."

"When we finish, tell that pilot to come see me."

"Will do, sir."

I redirect my mind to the battle. I should have remained undistracted. The following attack runs degenerate into disaster after disaster. Two ships even collide, causing significant damage to them both. Later I learn that three people died in the collision. My intervention with orders has no effect as stressed captains try to obey them while commanding their ships and making sure they don't collide with each other. I groan at the exercise's confusion and am glad when it's complete.

"Admirals and captains to the main debriefing hall on my ship in one hour," I bark over the communication channel.

While I wait, I retire to my quarters. A knock raps the door and I tell the person to enter. I don't look up straight away, so I don't know who enters the cabin. I just see legs and shoes in the periphery of my vision. When I peer up, my mouth drops. "Why are you here, Rickshaw?"

"They ordered me to present myself, sir." My old friend Rickshaw is undecided on whether to stand to attention or offer a casual stance of familiarity. As a result, it's somewhere in between, his expression hovering between a grin and a solemn frown.

I frown in confusion. His presence then clicks. "*You're* the pilot?"

"Yes."

"Why?"

"Want to do my bit, sir. It's exciting."

"You're very good."

"Thank you, sir."

"Well, keep up the good work." I wink. "And we'll have a drink sometime."

"Thank you, sir." Rickshaw grins. "I'll hold you to that promise."

"Get out before I change my mind."

As Rickshaw hesitates, he can't decide whether to salute. In the end, he gives a perfunctory salute and leaves. I stare at his back, still amazed at his flying skills.

The meeting time arrives, and I take the short walk to the hall, where I reprimand the captains for their poor performance. "We'd have had no chance of surviving, never mind winning, a proper battle based on today's exercise," I tell them unequivocally. After an open discussion of their shortcomings and plans for improvement, I dismiss them.

Left alone, I stand in an empty room, wondering whether we have any likelihood of victory in a real battle.

15

TREACHERY

Our preparations for Barak's arrival are a disaster — no other word can describe the fleet's performance during the trials. I recognize similarities between now and my last catastrophic battle, the thought sending me into yet another depression, and this one I can't seem to shake. I return to my cabin after the meeting and lock the latch. I don't want anyone witnessing me in this state. Several calls come in, but I leave them unanswered. My only solace is the warmth Adala brings me when my thoughts drift to her. But even that has a dark edge. It's like I'm endangering her simply by calling her to mind.

A rap on the door disturbs me. "Halwende, I know you're in there." It's Ishtar.

"Go away."

"No."

I glare at the entrance as if Ishtar will balk at the black thoughts that I push through to her.

"I'm waiting."

After considering leaving her standing there, I sigh. I'm being ridiculous. Caving in, I unlock the door and open it, revealing a pickle-faced Ishtar with her arms folded in frustration. "Come in then."

Ishtar enters slowly. "What's eating you?"

"You saw the disaster that happened. How can that shambles win a battle?"

Although she's in my cabin, she goes straight to the drinks cabinet without asking me and pours us both a whisky, slamming mine on my desk. "Drink!"

I glare at her but skull my shot, the fiery liquid burning my throat. She does the same. I stay silent, waiting for her to say what's on her mind.

Ishtar sits, still studying me. "You're a strange man." She gives me a wry smile. "One moment you display a strength of disposition and an optimism I've never seen in anyone and the next you're a wreck as if the world is closing in on you."

"Maybe the universe is destroying me. Barak is coming here for one reason only. To capture or kill me. I'm sure he'd choose to seize me so he and Shulgi can execute me at their leisure, entertaining themselves as they do so."

"Well, aren't you important then?" she mocks. "Wake up to yourself and stop wallowing in self-pity! They don't care. They'd much prefer you running away and hiding, so you stay out of their hair. It's the charisma and ability to rally people to your cause they want to kill. And besides, they have a planet on their doorstep that isn't under their control. They can't allow that."

I realize Ishtar is right. But it doesn't help us in our current predicament. "You can't protect a whole planet with our pathetic fleet," I point out.

"What do you suggest, then? Go ask Barak for more ships so the battle is more evenly balanced?"

"Don't be ridiculous." If only she knew my identity. After a pause, I murmur like a spoilt child, "I'm more important than you realize."

With a bemused grin, Ishtar says, "Really? Enlighten me."

Damn! I shouldn't have said that. "It's nothing. You're right — I have an inflated ego." I smile at her to deflect her curiosity.

But Ishtar's smile turns to a frown. "No. You meant something with that comment. Tell me."

"It's not relevant. Now go! I must consider pressing matters, and you have a fleet to belt into shape."

I haven't convinced her, but I see she will not pursue the discussion — for now.

"Alright then. You're an enigma. I can never read you, but I'll let you be."

"Don't concern yourself with me. I'll snap out of this soon enough."

"You'd better. We're counting on you." Ishtar rises and leaves, with me watching her back as the door closes.

Our conversation hasn't improved my mood. If anything, it's worse. But I know she's right. I must rid myself of this depression. After more consideration, I decide to return to Helheim and visit the portal room. There is no sane reason I should frequent that chamber, but an instinct draws me to it, so I make ready my shuttle and descend to the planet.

Still in no fit condition to see Adala, I divert my path into the depths of the palace and to the portal room, but my effort is in vain. I barely avoid bumping into her as I round a corner.

"What are you doing here?" I bark. It's a stupid question, but they're the first words that come to me.

"I live here, remember?" Adala gives me an enquiring stare. "I've just visited the library. Why are you here?"

"No reason. I'm in a hurry if you don't mind."

"Hurry for what?"

"Nothing."

"You won't even say hello?"

"Just let me be!" I rush off, knowing I've humiliated myself and left Adala hurt and confused. But I must have my solitude in the portal room.

Without glancing back, I continue to the chamber and enter it, exhaling a sigh of relief once I'm out of reach of everyone. My world was becoming claustrophobic, but, for an unknown reason, I feel this room will relieve the hysteria rising in me.

I find a seat and close my eyes, calming myself with rhythmic breathing until the tension leaves and relaxation replaces it. As I open my eyelids, I cast them over the machinery, realizing for the first time the foresight my ancestors had in creating it. And not only the room's contents, but the vast store of information and relics left in the crypts across many worlds show immense planning as if they foresaw the empire deteriorating and their reign waning. The blue light of the flerovium reflecting from the ceiling calms me further. I wonder if the purpose of this room is to provide a refuge in times of doubt.

On closing my eyes again, my mind wanders and returns to the disastrous exercise. Could these people be any more incompetent? Argandea, Ishtar, Lugal, and the others have fighting skills. They've disciplined their followers for years, and experienced pilots fly their ships. How did they allow their vessels to become so disorganized? Is the inclusion of the Helheim Military the problem? That argument doesn't fit either. Despite the inexperienced crews on the vessels, the pilots still had experience. But what other reason could there be?

I rise and pace the floor, letting the steady rhythm of my steps calm the ruminations of my mind. The portrayed incompetence is too great. Sabotage is the only other conceivable basis for the debacle. Someone is undermining my efforts, but who? And why?

Does a Shulgi mole hide amongst the defecting vessels or the refugees following us? Or are there other enemies wanting me to fail? Adala's dissenting generals want me off the planet and away from her, as if I'm a pariah they must banish from their presence. They have no power or understanding to disrupt the spaceship fleet in training, though. Their experience couldn't offer the knowledge to undertake such a disruption unless they have found supporters among my rebels. These revelations trouble me if they are true. And yet no other reason exists.

One thing's for sure. Barak will annihilate us if I don't discover who these people are.

16

TAKING CHARGE

As my mood improves, I realize I have damaged my relationship with Adala, and I must repair it. I leave the portal room and go searching for her. I find her in her office, busy with her duties.

Adala glances up as I enter but returns to her obligations without acknowledging my presence. I close the door and stand, waiting for her to deign to give me her attention. I deserve her snub, so I wait in silence. After five more minutes, she finishes her task and raises her eyes, her hands folded and body tense. Tears glisten in her eyes. "Yes?"

"I'm sorry." My head hangs in shame. "I don't know what I was thinking. My world is unraveling, and I needed time to myself. But it's no excuse for my rudeness."

Adala turns to her bodyguard. "Can you leave us for a moment?"

"Your Majesty." The guard clicks his heels and exits the room.

Adala stands and rounds her desk, facing me. "What you did was hurtful."

"I know, and I'm sorry. I wasn't myself. Sometimes I focus and exclude everything else, forgetting the people around me." I approach Adala and caress her face, her warmth infusing my palm.

"Why are you so depressed?" Her piercing eyes transfix me.

"The fighting exercise was a total disaster. If they fight Barak as they did today, we'll lose the battle before it starts."

"That terrible?"

"That's the point. I've realized they can't be that terrible. Not even with your military mixed in with the Resistance fighters."

She raises her eyebrows, and I add quickly, "I'm not doubting your soldiers' fighting abilities, just pointing out their inexperience."

"So, what are you trying to say?" Adala frowns.

"I think there's deliberate sabotage."

"But how?"

"I don't know."

Adala drifts away and my arm drops. She walks to the window and gazes out toward the gardens before turning and glancing at me. "Come." After opening the French doors, she steps outside, and I join her. We walk a short distance from the buildings. Once we've moved fifty meters away, she stops and says, "Stay facing the lake. I fear someone spies on me and can read lips."

I look at her in alarm. "Are you in danger?"

Adala gives an amused smile. "Only you endanger me."

I chuckle.

"Ranulf's informants tell him of a dissenting general in my ranks. He's influential. Almost as powerful as Egon was. I suspect he has his own designs on the realm and our relationship with your dictator. From your assessment, your emperor would welcome another groveler."

"But how could he disrupt my operations?"

"I don't know. Maybe he has befriended people in your organization."

"Who can I depend on, then?"

Adala turns to me, one eyebrow raised.

I turn my lips into a crooked smile. "Apart from you."

Satisfaction spreads across Adala's face. "Ranulf ... and Ishtar."

Her mention of Ishtar's name surprises me.

"Yes. Even though I dare not trust her alone with you, I have confidence in her loyalty to you."

Her frankness makes me laugh. But then I sober my thoughts. "That's it? Just two people?"

"There's Sigmund and Frieda, but they are still young and easily manipulated to divulge information. Tancred and Ernst could have pressure placed on them, too. As for your compatriots, only you can decide whom you trust."

As I consider Adala's words, I realize only three friends have my complete confidence — Zabada and Mamagal and, to my surprise given our brief history, Ishtar. I can't even be sure of Argandea, Lugal, and my other close friends. I do not count on any of the deserting commanders. "We need to meet to discuss this. But where is a safe place? Anywhere in the palace is suspect, since you believe eavesdroppers overhear our personal conversations. And the ships are prone to spying."

"My underground domain. I can seal it from anyone snooping for information."

"I'll tell Ishtar, Zabada, and Mamagal to come. You fetch Sentinel and we'll meet. We must converse as a matter of urgency."

Within two hours, we assemble around Adala's large conference table, which is still in place in her underground rebel fortress used during Egon's coup. I stride in with Adala, and we sit together at the head of the table. The others stare at us, especially at me.

I search each person's eyes before I speak. "You are here for one reason. You are the only people both Adala and I trust completely."

A mumble and subdued questions circle the table, each person confused by my revelation.

"Only the four of us?" Sentinel asks.

"With regret, yes." I wave Ishtar to silence. "Yes, we work with the Resistance. But search within yourselves. Do you trust them with your lives? Even you, Ishtar, succumbed to divulging more than you should have under extreme torture."

Ishtar blushes. "Forgive me."

"There's nothing to forgive. No one should have to suffer what you did. Regardless, you are the people we trust. Now, I will divulge the reason we are here. I suspect a mole in our ranks, one who is obstructing the outcome of training exercises."

Everyone but Adala stares at me in disbelief.

"How is this possible?" Ishtar asks. "Too many people are involved. To disrupt the exercise, the person must control every battleship."

"Not every ship," Mamagal interjects. "Just enough to cause chaos. One ship out of position can change the outcome of an assault." I study Mamagal, whose quickness astounds me. A thoughtful frown accompanies his words.

"As Mamagal said, they only need one or a few strategically placed ships within the battle formation to disrupt and destroy the entire fleet." I watch the others.

"This is a difficult allegation to believe," Ishtar says, glancing at me pensively.

Sentinel moves in his seat, making to speak, but unsure of articulating his thoughts. Finally, he says, "If this issue is amongst your people, how are we affected?" He gazes at me and then at Adala.

I turn to Adala to answer.

"It's a good question, Ranulf," she says. "On the surface, no connection might exist. Is it a coincidence, though, that I have problems controlling my military force?"

Sentinel stares at Adala for an extended period. "No, coincidences like that don't happen."

"General Klaus is vocal in his opposition to Halwende and the rebels," Adala says. "He has significant backing within the armed forces and in society. His pressure on me for reform is mounting. What better way to drive home his point than to show the fleet's incompetence in fighting any battle? Does he have sympathizers among Halwende's people with similar intentions or other ambitions?"

"But you have only trained with us for a short period," Ishtar says.

"It doesn't take long to negotiate alliances. What's preventing Klaus from infiltrating our recruits and his spies sourcing like-minded people within the Resistance?"

I notice Zabada has sat in silence, observing us. "What are your thoughts, Zabada?"

"I can offer no opinions that others haven't expressed. This intrigue disturbs me, though. If our defense is so easily infiltrated and nullified, how will we repulse the enemy when we must fight?"

"Halwende must accept direct control of the navy," Ishtar says.

"Don't I offer my leadership now?"

"That's just it. You contribute. But your influence is fluid, and we take orders from too many sources. The line of command is undefined. It's time our fighters not only see you as our leader but for you to be our commander and the ultimate authority we rely on for direction."

Ishtar's words sting me. Not only because they imply a dereliction of duty on my part, but because her demand reminds me of years ago when I held a similar position and failed my subordinates. And most tragically, I failed my family. Tears prick my eyes. "I've failed in past endeavors."

"Not from what I've heard. And I've unearthed much more than you think. You can't have expected Barak's betrayal. Barak was the one person you trusted who knew of your plans and your troop positions. No wonder he annihilated you. That wasn't your fault."

"Then why do I feel so guilty?" I say too loudly. I look away but quickly regain control and turn back to Ishtar.

"Because you care," she whispers. She stares at me, her intensity drilling into my soul.

Adala reaches across and squeezes my hand in support.

A knock raps the door.

Adala frowns. "I left explicit instructions we were not to be disturbed."

"I will check who interrupts us," Sentinel offers as he rises and strides to the entrance. He cracks it open and conducts a whispered conversation with the person on the other side. After a minute, he closes the door and glances at us, his expression one of concern. He returns to the table but remains standing.

"We have a problem." He looks at Adala and then at me. "Fighting has broken out between the Resistance forces and our military."

17

EXILE

I groan while the others stare at Sentinel in alarm. My plans are unraveling at an ever-quickening pace. How could fighting even start with Helheim's people and mine mixed?

Ishtar jolts up and paces from the table bent on contacting the fleet for an update of events. My eyes search her for information as she barks words into her comm, her frown deepening. I must wait until she finishes her conversation and reports.

I break contact with Ishtar and turn to Adala. Her concern reflects mine as I reach across and hold her hand.

"Klaus has a part in this. I know it," Adala whispers.

My attention returns to Ishtar as she ends her communication and glances at me. She strides back to us. "They have destroyed three corvettes. A destroyer fired on them when they lowered their shields. Argandea is attempting to regain control of the fleet, but a contingent of five destroyers refuses our demands to desist. The status of the Resistance personnel on those ships is unknown."

My teeth clench so hard my jaw hurts. "This is unacceptable. At least I downgraded the firepower on the new vessels for now. If one of those had used full weapons power, they could have wiped out the

whole fleet. I must return to my ship and force sense into these rene-
gades before they do further damage."

"Wait," Zabada says, his wise eyes arresting me.

"For what? For the people to destroy my entire fleet?"

"What can you do in your current state of mind?"

"I can increase my ship's firepower and blast those ships."

"And what will that achieve?"

My temper abates as I understand what Zabada is implying. My
anger could cost me another five essential ships. I turn to Ishtar. "Has
anyone tried to contact them?"

"They won't respond."

"What are they trying to gain, then?"

"Could it be a diversion?" Sentinel suggests.

My attention focuses on him. "Diversion for what?"

"For something to happen here." He gazes at Adala.

"Is Klaus so coordinated so fast?" Adala asks, alarmed.

Sentinel shrugs. "There's no point in this happening in isolation.
It must be part of a larger plan."

I stare at Sentinel, deep in contemplation. He makes a compelling
argument, but what else could Klaus instigate to intensify the esca-
lated tension? My thoughts drift. "I must contact my ship — if it still
obeys me."

I leave the table and dial Conrad.

"Captain Conrad here."

"So, Conrad, do you still support me?"

"You are my commander, sir. My loyalty is binding until I am
relieved of that duty."

"And the rest of the crew?"

"We serve you."

"So, you are aware of current events within the fleet?"

"Yes, sir. I have remained neutral awaiting your orders."

"You're an excellent captain, Conrad. Just wait for my
instructions."

"Thank you, sir."

At least I have one ship loyal to me. But why did the ships mutiny, and who instigated it? I stroll back, pondering the conundrum until I return to the table and glance at Adala. "What now?"

"I do not know. Ranulf, can you suggest a course of action?"

Sentinel stares at me and then Adala. "Your Majesty, we must find the perpetrator of these events. If Klaus isn't behind it, we must discover who is."

"And how do we do that?" Adala looks at me while staying seated. Her hands knit together on the tabletop so tightly that her knuckles whiten.

"I'll talk to him," I say. "It should be simple enough to figure out if he's lying and hiding something."

We decide on that strategy while awaiting the outcome of the standoff between the fleet and the mutiny of ships. The meeting ends, and we disperse to our respective duties.

AN HOUR LATER, General Klaus sits across from me in the palace with a proud and smug smile. He is in his fifties, has gray hair, and carries too much weight without being obese. He wears a full military uniform, and his eyes watch me with a predator's stare, waiting for the right moment to pounce.

"Are you loyal to Queen Adala?" I begin.

"You have no right to ask me that question."

"I am the Grand Chancellor."

"You are an impostor from another planet."

"What harm is there in answering such a basic question?"

Klaus scrutinizes me. I sense he's weighing up where my line of questioning may lead. "Very well. I will give you the pleasure. My allegiance lies with Queen Adala as long as her loyalty remains with her subjects."

My eyes widen at the openness of his admission. "And is she loyal to her people?"

"That is a difficult question to answer. Her attention wanders from her regal duties. She fraternizes with unsavory characters instead of considering the continuity of the royal pedigree."

His words anger me. "She isn't a baby factory to carry out the people's bidding." His chauvinistic attitude is monstrous.

"Ah, but she is. And she must learn that and cease this obsession with space before we find ourselves annexed. We have everything we want here."

"You cannot avoid the rest of the universe forever."

"We have you to thank for that, don't we? Meddling in other people's business. It must end."

"And how will you stop it?" I grin inside as I believe I have trapped him into admitting his complicity in the fighting above us.

"I wish to say nothing else on the matter." He folds his arms and smirks as if he has me defeated.

Which he has unless I can get him to continue talking. "So, you did orchestrate it?"

Klaus remains silent.

As I can't force him to speak, I tell him to leave. He opens the door, and instantly a riotous roar blasts through to me. Klaus turns one last time and beams a devious smirk at me before he departs. I stand and stride to the window, craning my neck to find the source of the noise, but the palace's walls block my view. Frustrated, I rush to the elevator, intent on gaining access to the roof balcony.

A gust of wind pummels my face as the elevator door opens and I step onto the open-air roof. The crowd's roar increases as I approach the forward balustrade, but I can't decipher the words. Once I round the structures, I see Adala standing near the railing, her back to me, staring at the mob below her.

"What's happening?" I ask as I stride up to her.

Tears fill her eyes when she turns to me. "They're demanding you leave us."

"This is Klaus's doing." I grit my teeth, seething at his manipulations.

"We have no proof. Regardless, the protest is becoming violent. I fear they may fight and die soon."

As if on cue, the noise from below increases, and shots ring out with accompanying screams of pain and anguish. I cannot answer this. It pains me that these are the same people who showered me with accolades when I returned the throne to Adala's father before he abdicated it to her.

I gaze over the crowd that grows as more protestors thread their way to the palace. Military gunships hover overhead, but that doesn't deter them, and the gunships are reluctant to open fire on the throng. That is something that pleases me. We can't have more carnage from trigger-happy troopers. Adala wraps an arm around me, seeking support. I can only offer her one solution, which we don't want.

As I stand there, my mind wanders to Eridu and my defeat and devastation. Are the desires of this crowd any different from my supporters? Why shouldn't we listen to them? And yet a distinction exists. In my case, the objectors fed their loyalty from the ground up, each desiring a life devoid of tyranny. Here, these leaders feed the protestors their poison to control them.

A few minutes later, Sentinel joins us. He glances at us both before directing his gaze at the crowd. "This is being orchestrated by a few ringleaders," he reports. "But they remain elusive."

"This is Klaus's doing," I say.

"I agree, but we have no proof."

"What do they say I've done to upset them?"

"They say you've brought warfare for your own glorification. Before you came, we had no interference from outsiders. Now, we're being ordered to obey with no recourse. They want to know whether their queen will resist and remove you from the planet. They conveniently forget the years of civil war we endured with Egon and the servitude they suffered under him."

Sentinel's words sting me like a knife piercing my heart. Unable to tolerate the hatred any longer, I rush from the roof, not looking back even when I hear Adala's pitiful pleas rising above the noise of the crowd. I use the elevator to descend to the basement levels, finding refuge in the portal room a short time later, my chest heaving with emotion.

My stay in the room, staring at the walls and machines, is time-less. Unsuccessfully, I try to dispel the dire incident from my mind. This isn't fair to Adala. She is involved in a power game that I am unsure she has the experience to fight. Then again, I should acknowl-edge Adala's strength. I contemplate revealing my identity but realize it will not influence her people. They know nothing of Sargon and the Rigel Empire. After further self-examination, I know what I must do, despite fearing what will inevitably proceed from my action and dreading telling Adala my decision.

With a heavy heart, I stand and retrace my steps to the main palace corridors in search of Adala. When I find her, I can tell she knows what I will say.

As I clasp her hands, I gaze into her eyes. "I must go."

"No! You cannot leave me here alone." Adala shakes, tears streaming from her face.

"There is no other way."

∽

∽

∽

Once Adala has wept her distress away, we leave to tell Sentinel and the others my decision. If I had tears to shed, I would join her, my heart in tatters yet again. After another hour, our friends assemble in the meeting room, their faces somber.

I gaze at each of them, but Sentinel in particular, before I speak. "I must leave the planet and remove any basis for continual conflict. While I stay, this friction will continue and cause irreparable damage to Adala's reputation."

Sentinel nods and glances at Adala before turning to me. "The riots are escalating, and looting has begun. But the orchestrators elude us. It saddens my heart to see you leave. I know we continue in great peril in the future, a danger only your fleet and courage can avert. But our circumstances cannot change, and we must be patient until the dice rolls and events unfold in our favor. I will protect and care for Queen Adala as best I can until you come back. I am confident of your return. You will come to our rescue in our greatest need."

His speech inflicts me with pangs of sadness. "I am made a better person for having known you, Sentinel."

He nods in acknowledgment of our friendship.

I search my compatriots for their thoughts or disagreements, but they have none to offer.

With no further discussion, the others go, discreetly leaving Adala and me alone to say our farewells.

I comb a loose tress clinging to her cheek back into position with my fingers and gaze into her mesmerizing emerald eyes. "Until I return," I say.

"I will wait for you."

No words can express our feelings. So, with a heavy heart and one last kiss, I turn from her and walk out of the room.

Spotting Sentinel, I pace over to him, embracing him as well. "Look after her."

"I will."

"Let's go," I say as I glance at Ishtar and the others. We ride from the halls of the palace on a waiting scooter that ferries us to my shuttle. In no time, we are lifting and ascending into orbit and my ship.

After landing on my destroyer, I stride to the helm. "What is the status of the fighting?" I ask Conrad.

"They're at a stalemate at present. The mutineers don't wish to attack, and we don't want to destroy our ships without cause."

"Any word of the state of our remaining loyal personnel on these ships?"

"None, sir."

I chew my cheek in thought. Ishtar stands next to me, awaiting orders. But I gain the communications officer's attention. "Try contacting a ship again. Tell them I demand to talk to them."

She nods and gets to work. Ten minutes later, she signals me. "One has responded, sir."

"Put the person on the screen." I sit in the captain's chair and wait.

An unkempt visage fills the screen, someone I've never seen before. He looks left and right before realizing I'm watching him and freezes. After adjusting his uniform and attempting to comb his hair with his fingers, he stares at the camera. "Hello. This is Captain Erik."

I study him for a moment before I reply. "This is Halwende. I take it you're not a true captain."

Erik straightens his shoulders as if he's offended by my accusation. "I'm the senior person on this ship."

"That isn't being held captive."

"I didn't agree to talk with you to discuss rank," Erik says, becoming agitated.

"Do you speak for every mutineer?"

"Yes, I do."

"Well, I left Helheim and don't intend to return to it. The reason for this conflict escapes me, but if I've resolved the issue, relinquish my ships to me. If not, why did you mutiny?"

"We do not have confirmation of your permanent departure from the planet. Once we receive that, we will land our ships and you can be on your way."

"You are not taking my ships. And you're definitely not keeping my personnel."

"How will you stop us? Blast us? If that was your intent, you would've attempted it already. And if you decide to try now, we'll start executing people until you see reason." Erik gives a smug smile.

He has me there. I can't destroy the vessels without killing innocent people, but I can't prevent the mutineers from landing either unless I send raiding parties to each vessel, which might be more costly than giving them what they want. I don't want to lose those ships. My only comfort is these ships aren't the ones I retrieved from the cave. "So, if I allow you to land, will you release my people?"

"Once we're back safe on Helheim."

"There's no guarantee, though, is there?"

"You'll just have to trust us."

"Forgive me if I find it hard to do so at present. I'll confirm my decision when you receive word that I've left."

"Very well, until then." Erik cuts the communication.

I heave a huge sigh to release the rage threatening to explode within me.

"You restrained yourself marvelously," Ishtar says from the sidelines.

"What else can I do without endangering the lives of the prisoners?"

"A raid?"

"Difficult to coordinate for six vessels without significant casualties."

Ishtar sits next to me. "I get your point. So, are you just going to let them take your ships?"

"Unless you have a better plan."

Ishtar shakes her head.

I must wait an excruciating hour before I receive confirmation that I've left Helheim and the mutineers' superiors convince themselves to end the standoff. We haven't thought of any options for rescuing our people in the meantime. With regret, I give my word they won't come to any harm by returning to the planet's surface with the ships. My one hope is that I can wipe the smile from Erik's face soon.

Sentinel sends news that the rioting has ceased too, leaving me to stew in my anger. Later that day, I hear they have transported the imprisoned crew back to the fleet.

This drama has deflected our attention from our preparations for Barak's arrival, which I know I must now do.

18

DESPAIR

To forget Adala, I throw myself into training at a frantic pace and have the fleet rostered to practice maneuvers twenty-four hours a day. Lack of sleep takes its toll and contributes to my spiraling depression. The bags under my eyes darken daily.

To my surprise, not every Helheim recruit returns to the planet when we split ties with it. A high proportion wants to continue serving on the ships to help protect Helheim when the time comes. A few, Rickshaw included, even enjoy the challenge. And Klaus hasn't forced Adala to order their return either.

Conrad tries to deflect queries forwarded to me as best he can, but my authority requires my being kept in the chain of command. Ishtar chastises me for neglecting my personal grooming, but my full concentration is on ensuring we're ready for Barak.

The constant pressure takes its toll on my mental health, though. My disposition becomes more and more gloomy, and I lock myself in my cabin on ever-increasing occasions. My mood is unhealthy, but I don't care anymore. After three days, this depression is so immense that I can barely think. In fact, the others make decisions for me and pretend I'm making them.

Zabada finds me moping in such a state, my despair too thick to negotiate. I am staring at the wall, unaware of my surroundings when I hear a knock on the door. My mind is in no condition to react.

"... Halwende, Halwende?" Zabada shakes me.

My mind's fog dissipates, and my consciousness awakens and becomes responsive to Zabada's incessant demands. I blink as my concentration diverts from the wall to him. "Yes?"

"At last, you've returned. I've been trying to get your attention for ages."

"What's the time?" I glance at my chronometer and gasp. "The next training session is due to start. You must excuse–"

"You'll just have to miss it," Zabada interrupts, his voice firm.

"But we need to train."

"They can exercise without you for one practice."

I make to argue with him, but words won't form. They swirl in my brain but don't coalesce into any shape to use as sentences. Unable to even achieve that, my shoulders slump in exhaustion.

"You need to take care of yourself better. You can't keep pushing yourself this way."

"Why? My purpose is to prepare for war and hopefully an end to this miserable existence."

Zabada frowns with fists on hips, standing before me, speechless for several seconds. "Is this your solution? Self-pity? You've lost a minor battle, and now you lock yourself away."

"A minor battle!" I shout at Zabada. "I've surrendered everything that has any meaning to me. Without Adala, there's no point. I prepare the others for war out of duty. Any other motivation is pointless."

"I don't believe this. You've taken leave of your senses. Do you expect your absence from Queen Adala will last forever? Have you yielded to a fate you can change? Wake up, Halwende!"

I glare at him, but I know he speaks the truth. I have given up too easily, but I find no alternative to my predicament. With a major effort, I force myself to think calmly. "Maybe I should declare myself to the planet."

"No, don't do that. Not yet, and especially not in your present state."

"What else is there?"

Zabada finds a chair and sits opposite me. "Your instincts are true. You must fight this upcoming battle with Barak first. Remove his threat. You can then concentrate on regaining the favor of the Helheim population. But you need rest, or you'll be no use to anyone."

I study Zabada for so long I suspect he fears I have fallen asleep in my seat. And sleep would be pleasant. Re-assessing my actions over recent days, I acknowledge I've micro-managed the fleet by not allowing them to judge for themselves, a fatal error that could lead to defeat. They will have no confidence in their abilities if I don't allow them to make their own decisions. That was one of my past flaws, leading to my last downfall. "You're right."

Zabada nods, pleased with himself.

"But this fleet isn't enough. If we just come at him with our current setup, we'll fail. Barak will find a way of destroying even my deadliest destroyers."

"What do you suggest, then?"

My mind swims in the murkiness of sleep deprivation as I consider my options. "We need an elite squadron."

Zabada nods his approval. "But first, you must rest."

19

UR FORCE ALPHA

I return to consciousness after waking from my Zabada-enforced sleep. My senses are refreshed and ready to continue normal functions. Despite weariness still weighing heavily on me, I'm at least capable of sane thought and reasoned judgments again. I dress and attend the galley to eat with the crew before entering the helm.

"Morning, sir," Conrad greets me as he comes to attention.

"Morning, Conrad. It's amazing what a good night's sleep can do."

"Yes, sir."

"What's on the agenda today?"

"More practice maneuvers — the usual routine."

"How long since the last mock battle?"

Conrad thinks. "A week."

"Let's have one now. Tell the others we'll begin in two hours, the conventional division of ships."

"Yes, sir."

I leave Conrad to organize the mock conflict while I return to my cabin to catch up on any issues that occurred overnight. While I flick through the reports on my tablet, a call buzzes at me. I accept, and Ishtar's face flashes on the screen.

"What's with this emergency battle?" she asks, pretending anger, but I see her underlying smirk.

I grin. "Thought you needed mental stimulation."

"Pleased to have you back."

"Glad to be here. Can you shove my head out the airlock for a few seconds the next time I'm stupid?"

"Can't do that, Halwende. We'd leave it there."

I make to throw something at Ishtar — and if she were physically present, I would have — before I break out laughing.

"So, do you have a problem organizing the battle?" I ask her.

"No. I just wanted to say I'm pleased you're back."

"Why are you wasting our time, then? Go prepare yourself and show me you can defend yourselves."

Ishtar smiles. "Will do." She cuts the connection.

I continue with my work until someone raps on the door. I open it.

Conrad stands there. "We're ready, sir."

"Good." I close my tablet and stride into the helm to watch proceedings.

The mock battle starts, and the simulated fighting unfolds much better than on earlier occasions. With both sides performing efficient attack and defensive maneuvers, the combatants' performances balance. By the end of the exercise, neither side holds obvious superiority. For the first time since we arrived, I can smile over the fleet's capabilities.

Still, something is missing. We lack a special striking ability, but the specific role escapes me. Once I give my concern more thought, I realize that I need to offer more leverage in the upcoming battle with Barak. I turn to Conrad. "Inform the admiralty to meet on the *Dagan* in one hour."

"Yes, sir."

I leave to power up my shuttle and fly the short distance to the fighter carrier.

～

As I REST against the main conference room wall on the *Dagan*, sipping strong coffee, I wait for my subordinates to arrive. I am in a reflective mood. My ideas have crystallized into a full-scale plan to present to the others for their reactions.

Ishtar enters, surveys the place, nods a greeting to me, and strides over to the coffee machine. She returns to me with a steaming drink in her hands. "What's with this rush meeting?"

I smile. "You'll find out along with everyone else."

She gives a mock pout and takes a sip. "We performed much better this time."

"Yes. I'm pleased. After the other efforts, I started wondering if we should just surrender when Barak arrives."

Ishtar chokes on her coffee, and I chuckle at her response.

Argandea, Lugal, Ninsar, and Yarla arrive five minutes after Ishtar. They voice their greetings and sit at the conference table where Ishtar and I join them. They all watch me expectantly.

As I know they're busy people, I don't waste any time getting started. "The exercise we just conducted went much better than prior ones. You've done well in bringing the crew's performance to battle standard." I gaze at each of my friends, who acknowledge the praise. "But I fear it's not enough to give us confidence in defeating Barak, even with the increased firepower of the vessels I unearthed."

"You have something in mind," Argandea says. "What do you suggest?"

"I want to form a squadron of six new ships as an elite strike force. They will attack when and where needed to produce weaknesses in Barak's fleet for our main navy to exploit."

Heads nod at me as I scan for a response.

"Who'll lead this squad?" Lugal asks.

"I would lead it myself ..."

I see mouths start opening in protest, so I wave them into silence again, "... but I know you'll object to my leading such a vulnerable unit."

"You got that right," Ninsar says.

"I want Ishtar to lead it," I say.

Ishtar stares at me in surprise. The others do likewise, but on reflection, they soon agree with my choice.

"Who'll be around to keep you out of trouble?" Ishtar protests.

"I have plenty of you looking after me."

After a moment's contemplation, Ishtar continues. "It's an honor to lead this unit, Halwende."

"Its formation must stay a secret, though. I don't want word spreading that could leak to Barak."

"It's going to be hard to train unnoticed."

"You'll find a way. You can select anyone for your crew, except anyone from my ship."

Ishtar nods. "You have a squadron name in mind?"

"Ur Force Alpha."

The others chuckle.

"Isn't Ur the fabled planet that disappeared?" Argandea asks.

"Yes," I say with a knowing grin.

"Why that designation, then?"

"Has a nice ring to it."

No further questions arise on the matter, and the meeting breaks up. Ishtar remains with me.

"Any reason you chose me?" Ishtar asks, inquisitive.

"You're the most devious. A devious strategist needs to lead the squad."

"I'm not sure whether I am flattered or insulted."

I smile. "You should go. You have a squadron to organize." I watch Ishtar leave, knowing she'll do a great job.

Now I've set that in motion, I can sleep better. Their presence will surprise Barak the first time they're used. I hope it'll give me enough leverage to tip the fulcrum in my favor.

20

ASSASSINATION ATTEMPT

I carry out my usual duties over the next few days, visiting as many ships as I can to inspect them and encourage the crews. The Resistance fighters from Eridu and elsewhere in the Rigel Empire show signs of confidence, more so than I. I don't dampen their enthusiasm because they will need it for the coming battle. It is clear they foresee an end to Shulgi's tyrannical reign of terror. Their one wish is to raise their families in peace and certainty for the future.

The fighters from Helheim are a different matter. I sense confusion in why they stay with the fleet. It's not their war, and yet they risk as much. Once Barak defeats us, he will subjugate the planet to Shulgi and enslave us all.

Once I land in the shuttle bay of the battlecruiser *Nergal*, I prepare to disembark to inspect the ship. Yarla is in command of the vessel, and I can see he takes pride in running a tight crew. The hatch opens and I stroll out. An honorary guard awaits me as I descend the steps to the deck. Yarla stands to attention next to the stairs.

When I reach him, I salute him. "At ease, Yarla."

Yarla smiles and strikes a casual pose. "We're honored by your presence, sir."

I return his warmth. "Pleased you could accommodate me on such short notice. I haven't caused too much disruption to your schedule?"

"If we can't adapt for our admiral, what hope do we have when the enemy surprises us?"

I chuckle. "Well said. Let's continue with the inspection."

Yarla gestures for me to lead and inspect his honor guard. I step past each crew member, nodding and having a few words. What impresses me is I see a sense of pride in their eyes as I converse with them. From my observations of his training, Yarla has worked well in molding his team into an efficient unit, and my inspection confirms his performance.

Once I've greeted everybody, Yarla leads me to the elevator and up to the main physical exercise hall. A consignment of the crew practice marching formations as I watch. We then head to the helm, where everyone but one officer breaks from their activities and salutes me. The unresponsiveness of the one still working intrigues me, so I stride over to her. She is busy taking a communications message. A bead of sweat sits on the side of her brow as she keeps her focus on the task.

As soon as she finishes, the officer jumps up and stands to attention, worry radiating from her and more beads dotting her forehead.

I take a step back in surprise but smile. "At ease, Officer."

"Thank you, sir." She changes her position and becomes more relaxed.

"And what was so important that you couldn't salute my presence?"

Fear returns to her as her eyes glance at Yarla before returning to me. "I had an urgent message from the *Dagan*, sir, detailing positions for the next hour. Delaying the communication could have caused confusion within the fleet formation and delayed an attack run."

I nod, impressed by the reply. "What is your name, Officer?"

She shuffles, believing I will berate her. "Corporal Ruth, sir."

"Well, Corporal Ruth, Captain Yarla should be proud to

command an officer who places duty above ceremony. We need people of your caliber if we are to win the upcoming battle."

Corporal Ruth's face beams with pride. "Thank you, sir. I'm honored, sir."

I nod. "As you were." I look around the deck. "That goes for the rest of you. Continue with your duties."

After several sirs, the others return to their tasks, and I stride to Yarla. "I think she shat herself," I whisper.

With some difficulty, Yarla stops himself from laughing. "She's an excellent officer. As you said, she did the right thing, despite the self-imposed stress she placed herself under in thinking she'd get into trouble. They're a good team."

I stroll across the helm, craning over people's shoulders to inspect their tasks and chat before satisfying myself and returning to Yarla.

"If you can spare the time, I have arranged drinks with the off-duty personnel."

"I can manage that."

We leave the helm and head to a large assembly hall massed with people talking and laughing, both officers and crew. The noise stops when we enter, and they come to attention and salute. I salute in return. "At ease and continue with what you were doing," I say.

A steward approaches us and offers a drink. I select a beer and mingle with the crowd, intent on engaging with as many as I can during my stay.

A group of four of the ship's crew catches my scrutiny. They stand separately and don't display the others' jovial mien. Their behavior is so out of synch with the others that I decide to approach them. One glances my way as I near the group, his expression conveying an air of hostility. As I come within arm's length of them, they open their tight cluster.

I lower my gaze and, too late to react, see that the one facing me, hidden beforehand, is holding a laser pistol at waist height. Alarm tears through me as I dive sideways, a red flash ripping into my torso before I can complete the defensive movement. Pain radiates through me as shock and outrage from the attack penetrate my senses. As if in slow motion, I drop to the floor. Blue maser flashes annihilate the group in an instant as others rush toward me, Yarla in front.

"Medics!" Yarla yells as he kneels to check my condition.

My eyes glaze as I lie on the deck, staring at the ceiling. The pain is all I can think of.

"Forgive me, Halwende. This shouldn't have happened. We'll get you patched and on your feet."

I wave my arm haphazardly and mumble, "Not your fault," just before I lapse into unconsciousness.

21

A VISIT

Light filters through my eyelids as I return to consciousness. At first, my predicament confuses me. When I open my eyes, infirmary white surrounds me, and the beep of several machines attached to my arm and body like cyborg attachments echo throughout the room. A numb pain pulses from my side. Memory returns as I recall the events just before I blacked out.

The group. Why were they there? They weren't part of the crew, and they had a hostile disposition from the first time I spotted them. It would be easy to take them for Helheim spies dispatched by Klaus to assassinate me, but that presumed too much. Nothing showed their origin. They might have been planted in the Resistance by Barak. Sleepers sent to end my influence before he arrives. I will wait to talk with Yarla before I attempt to assess their motives.

No windows offer a view outside, but the stale air tang that only a spaceship has tells me I must still be on the *Nergal*. I turn my head and see I'm alone at present. I try to rise, which ends in failure as pain shoots up my body. My movement sets off an alert, and a man in a white coat enters, tall and thin with friendly eyes. He identifies himself as one of the ship's medical officers.

"You're awake," he says as if telling me something I don't know.

"I considered getting out of bed but realized what a lousy idea it was as soon as I tried."

The officer chuckles. "You won't be going anywhere for a while. That's a nasty wound. It's amazing you're alive. You must have feline genes." He busies himself, checking my vital statistics and recording them.

"Feline genes?"

"Yes. You know. Cats have nine lives, as the saying goes."

"No, I've never heard that saying. I doubt my luck will last that long, though."

"You've survived so far, from what they inform me."

"Who told you that?"

He stops his work and glances at me with a smile. "I may have said too much."

"You can't leave me hanging."

"Sorry. The good news is you're recovering well, so lie back and relax. I'll arrange food and drink for you." He leaves me alone except for the constant beep of the machines.

I sigh and consider what I should do. It would be disastrous if Barak arrived now. How I wish I could see Adala.

Moments later, Ishtar enters the medical unit. "It's time you woke. I can't trust you to go anywhere without you getting yourself into trouble."

I grin. "If I recall correctly, you're with me most of those times."

"You can't look after yourself. Someone has to clean up the mess."

The room fills with cheer as our banter continues. How our relationship has changed since I first met her.

Ishtar sobers her mood and sits. "How are you feeling?"

"Could be better. I'm not the greatest hospital patient."

Ishtar smiles. "Yeah."

"Has anyone checked up on who my would-be assassins were?"

"We've been trying, but they're an enigma at present."

"Is there evidence they originated from Helheim or Eridu?"

"No. No one recognizes them. I've been in contact with Sentinel–"

"Is Adala aware of my injury?" I interrupt.

With a frown, Ishtar shrugs. "I don't know. As I was saying, I talked to Sentinel, so I presume he passed the news on to her. He's chasing up on any likelihood they came from Helheim or whether Klaus knows them, but I haven't heard from him yet."

My mood sours as I regret the distress that I'm causing Adala. "What else is happening?"

"Training progresses. And before you ask, here is something for you to read." Ishtar reaches into her pocket and removes a scrap of plasto-paper, a novel and rare material in this age. She unfolds it and hands it to me.

I read the scrawled handwriting, raising my eyebrows twice but nodding when I've finished reading.

"I felt it best to keep knowledge of that part of our strategy away from normal communication channels," Ishtar says.

"Wise move. Can we trust no one?"

"It's not about who we can trust. It's about not letting anyone we can't trust, and we don't know who they are, access that information. We can't have that intelligence leak to Barak."

"No, we can't. You have an excellent team there."

"Yes. We'll make you proud when the time comes."

"I am confident you will, though I'm hoping you won't need to."

"I'd better be going. Someone has to keep things running while you nap."

I smile. "Great seeing you."

"Take care." Ishtar leaves.

Her concern over spies in our organization worries me, but she's right to take the precautions she has. Such an influx of refugees has joined our movement that the possibility of Barak's agents being amongst them shouldn't surprise me.

My recuperation drags on for several days, during which time my senior officers visit me with well-wishes for my recovery and updates on progress in preparations. They disconnect the machines, giving me freedom of movement and permitting me to sit in a chair.

With no forewarning and no information about my destination, I'm taken to a shuttle, and we fly to another ship. As the cabin I occupy has no windows or screens, I cannot see which vessel but, as soon as I'm pushed through the hatch in my gravity chair, I recognize the familiar surroundings of Adala's yacht.

"Why are we here?" I ask my nurse, the same man attending my recovery since my injury.

"I don't know. They just told me to take you to the shuttle."

As there's no further forewarning of the purpose of our trip or anyone to ask, I sit back and wait for whatever unfolds. The nurse walks me through the yacht's corridors until we reach the luxury cabin in the ship, the one reserved for Adala when she visits.

I frown. "They don't need to pamper and hide me."

"I don't know what's happening either," the nurse says.

The door opens, and the nurse pushes me inside the suite. My mouth gapes in surprise, but no words come out.

Adala stands to the side, tears threatening to burst from her eyes as she looks at me.

Seeing the unfolding scenario, the nurse says, "I might leave you two alone," and retires through the doorway again.

Once the door closes, Adala rushes to me and hugs me so tight I choke. As she realizes the hug's intensity, she releases me and wipes tears from her face.

"I may not need assassins to kill me with you around," I joke.

"Don't mock me ... this ..."

"I'm trying hard to stop myself from descending into your condition." I glance away. "And it's impossible." I look back at her. Even in her distress, she has the look of an angel.

Adala moves to me, gentler with her pressure as she enwraps my shoulders with her arms again.

After an eternity of time that I wish would never end, we part. "Can you push me over to the table and sit, too?"

She obeys me.

"Did you come alone?"

Adala shakes her head. "Ranulf is here and my usual bodyguards. They're nearby but made themselves scarce for our reunion."

I chuckle. "Sentinel's doing?"

She nods. "When he told me the news, I was so distressed I started tearing the palace apart." Adala half smiles and half sobs. "I dragged Klaus in for interrogations, positive he was behind the attack."

"And was he?"

"I don't think so. Even though he'd shed no tears to see you dead, I'm now convinced he wouldn't go that far to remove you from our presence."

We descend into silence.

"How is your injury?"

"Mending. I wish they'd rid me of this chair so I can continue with my life."

Adala gives a sympathetic smile. "You must listen to the doctor's advice."

"What do the doctors know of war?"

"Enough to keep you alive so we can win it."

"I hate this waiting." My eyes wander to the viewing screen and watch the ships scattered in the reflecting sunlight, imitating miniature stars across the cosmos.

"I wish I could do more."

"Just stay safe and check Klaus and his cohort."

Adala reaches out to hold my hand, stroking it with her thumb. "I'm afraid," she admits.

"So am I."

"What will happen if Barak defeats you?" She searches my eyes as she asks.

"You will become part of the Rigel Empire and live in servitude to Shulgi. He either executes people like Klaus or they turn into sycophants. You ... will lose your kingdom and likely marry Shulgi to consummate the union."

"Please don't let that come to pass."

"I won't. While I breathe, I will fight for Shulgi's downfall."

We sit gazing at each other, content to soak up each other's company for eternity. But we both realize we have other responsibilities. We sigh and kiss before Adala permits her guards to attend to her security and the servants to offer refreshments.

Minutes later, Sentinel enters. "You'll do anything to gain sympathy," he says.

"I won't get any from you."

He gazes at me with concern. "That was a lucky escape. You must take more care of yourself."

I nod. "I presume I'll have a bodyguard now."

Sentinel changes his attention to Adala. "We need to return before they miss you. Or more to the point, they suspect your movements and the reason."

Adala nods. "You're right. Give me a minute alone with Halwende."

Sentinel chases the others out so Adala and I can spend a few more precious moments together before we must separate. We gaze at each other, neither one of us wanting to speak first.

"Take care," Adala finally says before pulling away from me with reluctance.

"You too." I pull my chair around the table and sit next to her. As I twist, I touch her cheek and turn her head to mine, kissing her again, the warmth of her lips infusing me with strength for the ordeals to come.

We can't bear to say another word, so Adala rises and leaves, giving me one last glance before she disappears. My eyes linger, watching the opening long after she's gone while wondering when — if — I will see her again.

22

ARRIVAL OF BARAK

My convalescence drags on, much to my frustration, as well as my nurse's. But I finally receive the advice I can return to duties with the proviso that I don't overexert myself. Telling me to stop thinking of Adala would have as little effect.

I go back to my destroyer, and Conrad brings me up to date on the fleet's preparations for the approaching battle. We still lack news of Barak's arrival with his armada, but we know he will come. I present too dangerous a threat to Shulgi for him to forget about me. Ishtar gives regular updates on her progress with our clandestine squad of destroyers, using the same secure manual means of exchanging information.

I rest in the commander's chair on my destroyer as I watch another mock battle. At its completion, no more suggestions come to mind on improving our fleet's performance other than to continue regular training to preserve their skill level. We are ready, or at least as ready as we can be under the circumstances.

Five days later, our wait is over as I wake to the blare of a general alert and battle stations. I dress and rush to the helm. "Report," I command Conrad.

"Barak has arrived," he states. When I glance at him, his eyes and expression combine to convey both fear and eagerness.

I lick my lips as I gaze at the main screen. A twinkling of lights spreads across it like a galaxy of stars — Barak's fleet. He hasn't disappointed me in its size. He has most of the empire's navy here. My hotchpotch of battleships looks pathetic in comparison, but they must do. Barak is unaware of the extra fighting power of the Helheim ships, which I hope will give me at least the advantage of surprise.

A communication pings throughout the fleet, and it's my duty to answer it. "Open the channels," I tell the communications officer.

Barak's face comes on the screen, looking grim. But when he sees me, he breaks into a wide smile. "So, you are here. Good. It wouldn't be a battle without knowing you're watching your fleet being annihilated. Is what I see your navy's extent?"

"I can't say it's a pleasure to see you. There are still a few civilian ships amongst the fleet. I hope you'll give me the courtesy of removing them before you decide to start."

"You have one hour. Anyone left will become fodder for my weapons."

With that reply, I gesture to the communications officer to cut the transmission, and the screen goes blank before returning to the starfield. I ask Conrad to get a general alert out to the civilian ships to fly to safer locations beyond the battle arena. After that, I say, "I'll be in my cabin discussing tactics with the rest of the fleet."

Conrad nods and turns to conduct his business as I leave.

I sit and place a call through to Argandea. He connects, and I see he has connected Lugal, Ninsar, and Yarla. Fear and resolution line their faces.

"Morning," I say.

They greet me in return.

"I can't contact Ishtar," Argandea says.

"She has her orders. We must continue without her." They look puzzled by my words but don't comment further.

"So, what should we do in preparation?" Lugal asks.

"Lugal, Yarla, and Ninsar are to form an arrow formation with

Lugal's division in front. Argandea will gather his carrier and defensive craft at the rear, but the fighters will assemble, ready for engagement."

The others nod.

"When Barak moves, we will engage the center of his fleet, destroying his vessels on the way through, and then reassemble at his back."

"Will we last that long?" Ninsar asks.

"The Helheim ships will line the vanguard. I have recalibrated their shields and weapons for full power. They'll make Barak think twice when they unleash their firepower. Now prepare for battle." I disconnect and recline in thought.

I get hold of Ishtar. "Are you in position?"

"Yes. Where we agreed."

"Good. Stay hidden until I tell you."

"I will."

With my preparations made, I put a call through to Sentinel on Helheim.

"Hello, Halwende. To what do I owe the pleasure?"

"Just informing you Barak has arrived, and the battle is imminent."

"Oh. Should I inform Queen Adala?"

I bite my cheek as I consider my reply. Telling her will make her worry, but she needs to be prepared for the worst. "Yes. But tell her not to try contacting me. She will know soon enough the outcome of the next few hours. I shall contact you again when I have news."

"Godspeed, my friend."

I nod. "Pray we will be alive when this day is done." I break the connection.

My stomach tightens as the hour's reprieve nears its end, nerves quickening my pulse as my adrenaline surges through me. I rise and go to my safe, opening it. Extracting the box with the royal insignia on it, I open the lid and remove the ring, my ring of identity. I twirl it in my fingers, intrigued by the delicacy of its design. Resisting a temptation to slip it on my finger, I sigh and replace it in the container, which I return to the safe. I cannot divulge my secret yet. I return to the helm.

Conrad turns when he hears me enter. "The noncombatants have separated from the fleet, sir."

"Good." I stand and watch the screen as the unarmed ships continue their flight to a safe location.

Before the allocated time and surprising me, a squadron of fighters breaks off from Barak's forces and heads straight for the civilians.

"Sir?" Conrad appeals to me in horror.

Dismay smothers me as I wait for the inevitable slaughter, knowing there's nothing I can do. I can't afford to have my fighters engage with the others, sacrificing my resources for little gain.

The civilian ships start scattering as they realize their peril. Minutes later, the fighters fly in amongst them, destroying each ship with ease, murdering a multitude of men, women, and children.

My jaws clench as I rage at Barak's barbarity. There are no other words for it.

"Get Barak on the comms!" I shout at the shocked officer.

Barak's face materializes on the screen.

"Why did you do that? They were innocent people."

He smirks. "They were traitors. I just needed you to herd them away from your fleet to execute them as the treasonous scum they were."

He's trying to anger me into making a rash move so he can discern my tactics. "You will pay for this."

"Oh, I doubt it. Not with the poor effort I see in front of me."

I get the comms officer to cut the connection. I rage as what remains of the civilian ships disperse through space. They trusted me, and I failed them, as I always fail people. I breathe out to release my pent-up tension as I gauge our plight. Despite Barak's gouging, I wait for him to move first, and I know it won't be long.

23

BATTLE STATIONS

Two squadrons of five corvettes and one destroyer separate from Barak's fleet, scouting our outskirts, one on each flank. Barak wants me to weaken my primary force by chasing these with my ships. I suspect he will then begin his main attack. I order two of my Helheim vessels out to test the exploring party's resolve. The meager defense sent against his squads must amuse Barak, but he'll get a shock. I don't want to use my lethal firepower yet, but I may have no choice now.

Flanked by the corvettes, the destroyers fire missiles at my ships. They dispatch the weapons with efficiency but wait before retaliating. I smile at the familiar tactic I instilled into the crews. It's so tempting to unleash the full wrath of your weaponry. Both Barak's squadrons and my ships stay facing each other while each decides on the next move. Barak's destroyers send off another volley of missiles, and we dispose of them, too.

Movement comes from Barak's main armada, and they cruise into formations.

I get my navy on the comm. "This is it, men and women. Fight well. Fight bravely. But above all, fight with honor."

I hear shouts of defiance over the speaker and amongst the crew of my ship. Pride in my people envelopes me with hope.

Barak's fleet charges in a phalanx formation. Our fleet shoots forward in the agreed arrow to pierce through the enemy and cause as much damage as possible. One plus of Barak's tactics is that few missiles launch for fear of hitting his own vessels once they entangle us in the melee of battle.

I have the Helheim ships on the outer edges of my formation to protect the rest of the fleet. The fighter carrier remains behind with its own squadron to defend it.

As soon as the main fleet leaves the carrier, the two scouting squadrons try to move in to destroy it, effectively leaving us without fighters. But when these ships move, mine open fire, the masers destroying the shields of the destroyers and then ruining their drives before the reactors blow. The remaining corvettes halt while taking check of the change in circumstances. My vessels show no mercy and sustain their barrage of maser fire, targeting one corvette at a time, reducing each squadron to three corvettes until the rest retreat.

Meanwhile, the two fleets approach each other, and barrages of missiles fire from Barak's ships. Hundreds of them streak our way and I know we won't stop them, but we must continue regardless now. I order my barrage of missiles fired. With each fleet preoccupied destroying missiles, Barak has the outer edges of his attack shed from the primary assault to our flank, hoping to surround us.

I tell my navy to keep their nerve and stay with the plan.

Before long, the missile attacks have run their course. I have lost ten corvettes and three destroyers, but none of the Helheim vessels. Losing life upsets me. Our missiles have inflicted similar carnage on the enemy, but it only scratches the surface of their numbers.

Time runs out for the second barrage of missiles as we clash with Barak's fleet. Maser cannon-fire streaks from ship to ship. My Helheim ships inflict the most damage, as they should, carving through destroyers and battlecruisers as if they are unprotected yachts.

The fighting hasn't gone completely our own way, though. They have destroyed more of my ships, including a Helheim destroyer. They overpowered it, the enemy surrounding it until its shields failed. My only consolation is it took out several of Barak's vessels when it exploded.

Once our fleets pierce through the other, a squadron of my ships break off and heads for Barak's four fighter carriers. I hope to take out at least one of them. The primary force of my navy turns for a return attack.

I can tell by the less-than-perfect formation of Barak's armada that we took them by surprise with their losses. A smile sneaks onto my face before being replaced with absolute focus on the battle.

To mirror my intent, Barak gets ten squadrons to charge my fighter carrier. I gaze in anticipation as I watch them approach.

I dial up my personal communicator. Ishtar comes on the screen. "Your turn."

"About time," she says with a determined smile.

Her vessels fire their drives and rush out from hiding behind a nearby asteroid. They break from formation, acting more like fighters than capital ships, making themselves a tough target. The two destroyers turn to engage in the impending battle, too. They outnumber us, but I hope our firepower and Ishtar's tactics will inflict more damage than Barak is prepared to take to get rid of my fighter carrier.

My ships weave in amongst the enemy's, firing maser blasts at will and destroying Barak's shielded ships with abandon. After ten minutes, Barak calls off his attack, and the remnant of his squadrons retreat, licking their wounds.

Within that time, my other ships have plowed through the main fleet and returned to our side of the battle zone again, causing a similar level of destruction to Barak.

Pride in what my people have achieved ripples through me, but I know we have barely dented Barak's armada.

A call comes through from Barak moments later. "I see you're not as weak as you look," he says. His face shows signs of frustration and irritation.

I shrug. "Did you expect me to be?"

"No. Regardless, you will succumb in the end." He breaks his communications.

"They're forming for another attack, sir," Conrad warns me.

I nod and contact Ishtar to start her next mission.

As I watch on the screen, her squadron highlighted in green, they return to the formation and join with the rest of my fleet as we make our next drive through Barak's armada. Just as we enter his phalanx, Ishtar's ships break off and pierce deep into the enemy, releasing a barrage of missiles before breaking off and returning to our base. Within seconds, the missiles explode, discharging a tsunami of destructive energy and destroying any ship within the vicinity.

After discussions with Mamagal, I have developed a means of using the crystal in the missiles without causing the spacetime rending destruction of my prior effort. These are the missiles Ishtar releases. Once the energy has dissipated, I gaze in awe at the result. We have decimated Barak's fleet beyond its ability to take part further in the battle in the immediate future. A few more of those strikes would even up the odds, but I suspect Barak will learn his lesson and not allow his ships to congregate into such tight formations again within range of my deadly squadron.

Barak's entire armada breaks off their attack after that and retreats.

The officers at my helm cheer at our success. I give a grim smile, knowing we are far from winning the war yet.

My personal comm blinks. I frown to see it's from Sentinel. Excusing myself from the helm, I retreat to my cabin before responding. Once I have privacy, I open the channel. Sentinel comes on the screen, the marks of battle smeared across his stern face.

I jump in shock. "What's happening?"

"We are at war, too."

"Klaus?"

"Klaus."

I nod. I should have seen it coming. "This is no coincidence."

"No, it can't be. But that isn't why I called."

I raise my eyebrows. "Why did you call then?"

"Korbinian has escaped." My gut clenches. Korbinian was Helmein's corrupt Grand Chancellor during the civil war. Adala's father had him imprisoned rather than executed as an act of mercy. Having him on the loose is the last thing we need right now.

"How did that happen?" I yell into the comm.

"I don't know how, but he had help from within our ranks. He's vanished and has friends attacking the palace while Klaus assaults the city. I fear we won't hold out much longer."

24

KIDNAP

My senses become numb with Sentinel's revelation. "Is Adala safe?"

Sentinel nods. "For now."

My mind races for a better haven. "I'd get you to take her to her yacht, but it's not secure up here at present either. We're amid battle too, and Barak is likely to do anything to achieve victory. What does Klaus want?"

"He wants to open channels with Barak to negotiate amicable terms of cooperation."

I shake my head. "He's naïve. Barak will not stop until he's subjugated the planet now. He murdered the refugee civilians just to warn of the consequences of disobedience."

As if the horror and evil of the news have flicked a switch, Sentinel's face transforms into rock, and the fierce determination I first experienced when I met him returns. "They will never get Queen Adala to surrender or capture her while I'm alive." He turns his head sideways before returning to me. "I must go."

"Be careful and keep Adala safe."

"I will."

The screen blanks, but I continue staring at it in disbelief. My heart wavers between continuing the battle here and rushing to Adala's aid. I fear for her safety but cannot afford to turn my back on Barak while he remains here, eager for my blood or to take me back to Shulgi in triumph. The skirmish on Helheim isn't a coincidence either. Barak has infiltrated the planet with his spies and agents before his arrival. They precipitated Klaus's uprising, tempting him with honor when he hands Helheim over to Shulgi. I know his reward. Slavery if he's lucky, death if not.

This news divides my concentration between the fighting up here and concern about what's happening down there on the planet. If Barak thinks I give in that easily, he's misjudged me. If he thinks he can distract me so easily, he's mistaken, too. My biggest consideration is not to let my anger fuel poor judgment and rash decisions, as Barak desires.

Taking a steady breath, I come back to the helm and the continuing battle, trying to keep my fear for Adala's safety out of my mind.

Barak's forces rally and maneuver into fighting formation again, a smaller contingent than his original armada. My fleet returns to their arrow attack positions. Neither wants to move first.

I consider my options and relay my decision to the fleet admirals. My fleet split into three and reorganize to create three arrowheads of smaller numbers. They race forward, taunting the enemy to join in the battle. Barak's forces hold back, whether in confusion or to set a trap. I can't decide. I contact Ishtar and instruct her to fly in on each flank, driving a wedge through the sides. It leaves my fighter carrier with little protection, but I get it to retreat to a safer location.

The ships engage in battle as before with similar results. Ishtar's guerrilla destroyers cut down the lighter, less protected ships as they plow through the phalanx from each side. Once through, they bank and fly further into enemy territory to attack another fighter carrier, destroying that before returning to our base rallying position to regroup with the others. As the dust settles, we take stock and reckon we have reduced Barak's force by a third while suffering the loss of twenty percent of our fleet. It's a pleasing result, but we still can't win on those numbers, even with the Helheim ships.

The statistics trouble me, and then I receive another communication signal from Barak. I get it placed on the screen.

"Impressive," Barak says. His mood has changed from before, puzzling me. It has gone from grim to jovial.

"You ready to go home and tell your master the sad news?" I taunt.

Barak chuckles. "I hear there's disquiet on your planet."

It shocks me that Barak has this intelligence, but it confirms he has spies there. "There's a slight disturbance," I acknowledge.

"A slight disturbance?" Barak smirks with victory. "You need to keep yourself up to date."

My discomfort deepens. What is he implying? As if to confirm his innuendo, my personal comm buzzes. I look at it. Sentinel is trying to reach me. My gut clenches with dread.

"You should get that," Barak says. "I'll leave you to it." He breaks the communication.

"What do you think he meant?" I ask Conrad.

"I don't know, sir. We've had no communications from the planet."

Barak's tone disturbs me. "I'll be in my cabin," I say as I hurry there. Once the hatch closes, I answer Sentinel. I know something is seriously wrong as soon as I set eyes on his face. Years of sorrow have poured onto it. "What is it?" I ask, my stomach clenching even tighter.

"I have failed," Sentinel says, averting his eyes from the screen as if confessing his shame. "They have seized Queen Adala, and the realm is in ruins."

"What do you mean, seized Adala?" Panic fills my mind, and I can't think coherently.

"Korbinian hatched a plot with Klaus to kidnap her, and they took her after slaughtering the royal guard."

"I will come and search for her without delay."

"We don't know where they've taken her, and we must still suppress Klaus's revolt."

I now understand Barak's gloating, and a suspicion germinates that he instigated the whole disturbance in Helheim. A fear beyond belief grips me. Adala is in Barak's hands. I look at Sentinel. "They arranged this beforehand."

My heart bleeds for Sentinel. Of every vow he has taken, the oath to protect Adala with his life is the one he has always held with absolute determination. And now he feels he has failed. His despair is plain on the screen. "Don't give up hope. You can't protect her against every evil."

"But I should have protected her, and I didn't."

"And you'd be dead with the other guards."

"At least I'd have died fulfilling my oath."

"And unable to help save her from Korbinian, Klaus, and whoever else is involved in this plot." I experience the same despair as him, but we must rally for any chance of finding her and rescuing her. A surge of rage sweeps up within me and soon develops into determination. Barak will not do this. He will not take my most precious possession from me. I realize he has discovered my relationship with Adala and is using it against me to force my surrender. But I will not run again.

"Sentinel, you must stamp out your rebellion. I suspect it will waver now they own Adala. Shulgi and Barak manipulated this and, if you condemn anyone, blame me for not foreseeing this possibility. They discovered what Adala means to me and are using that against me. But we must regain control of Helheim first. Take charge and place the planet under martial law. Klaus may have his followers, but he can't have the ear of the whole military. Once the waverers see you aren't surrendering, they will rally to you too and undermine Klaus's influence."

Sentinel nods. "I perceive the sense in your words. But I must concentrate my efforts on finding Queen Adala."

"If my suspicions are correct, you can achieve little to recover her. If Barak doesn't hold her yet, he soon will, and you can do nothing to prevent it. This is a battle I must fight."

"Very well. I shall do as you say. I shall quell this uprising and regain control."

"Open full communication channels with me now that they've ended this farce."

"I will keep you informed."

"And Sentinel ..." I stare into his sad eyes. "More is at play than you realize. I will explain everything in time. And I promise I will rescue Adala." With those words, I cut the link and close my eyes. Events are happening too fast for me.

I buzz Conrad. "Please get Zabada to come to my cabin."

"Sir."

"What is the status of the battle?"

"Barak is quiet at present. We rally for another offensive and will be in our positions in twenty minutes."

"Very well." I end the communication and wait.

A knock beckons me five minutes later, and Zabada enters at my invitation. He searches my eyes — I suspect to gauge my mood and gain an inkling of the reason for my summons.

"You wanted to see me?"

"Thanks for coming, Zabada." I stand and walk closer to him. "They have captured Adala, and the planet is in turmoil."

"I see."

"This is no coincidence. Barak orchestrated this to distract me from the battle."

"If what you say is true, he wants influence over you. For what other purpose does he interest himself in Helheim or Queen Adala's kidnapping but to leverage your weakness?"

I stare at the screen on the wall, watching the space outside and the blinking spots that show the positions of Barak's fleet and mine. After glancing at Zabada, my eyes return to the view, and I continue my deliberations. He waits patiently for my next words. I decide and blurt out, "It's time."

"No," Zabada replies. "You must not. Not yet. Not in your position of weakness when you are so distant from help."

"Of what value is support if Shulgi has Adala?"

"You do not know that. And besides, he doesn't have her yet."

"He has her. And you know his intent when he discovers her pedigree. This achieves his dream. A chance to claim divine providence in his rule."

"I do not agree. He may have her, and he may intend to exploit her for the very purpose you say, but he doesn't have you. His suspicions of a closer heir to the throne than he still restrains him."

"He will use her to lure me. He failed in his intentions last time, but he won't fail again."

"I implore you to wait until we take the battle back to Shulgi."

I gaze at Zabada and consider his words. "Then I must end this battle here. And with haste. You know what I must do. The one thing Mamagal forbids me to do."

"I fear you are right. But let's not get hasty. Those missiles worked well. I acknowledge more than their potency is now required. But let us meet with Mamagal and discuss our options."

After staring into Zabada's eyes while I consider his words, I perceive his wisdom and nod. "We will summon Mamagal."

25

CAPITULATION

Mamagal meets Zabada and me in my cabin ten minutes later. His eyes search ours, wary of the reason for the summons. Although he is integral to my cause, he has always been aloof and independent to the mainstream party Zabada inhabits.

I get to the point. "We're not sure, but we believe Barak has kidnapped Queen Adala to gain leverage over me and for other designs Shulgi will have in store when he finds out she descends from Alalgar. We must win this battle and move the war back to Eridu."

Mamagal nods. "I agree with you so far."

"One thing can end this in one stroke."

Mamagal's eyes flare in anger and disapproval. "No. I only agreed to use the downgraded crystals in the missile because they didn't interfere with spacetime. We must not use full-strength material. The risk is too great."

"Then what?" I ask.

We stand with eyes darting between each other, wondering if anyone can recommend a solution.

The mind's ability to think is amazing when it's searching for a resolution to a problem where an obvious solution is unavailable. With this dilemma focusing my attention, my mind sparks an idea. Its origin is unknown. It just inhabited my subconscious and needed a focused prod to germinate it into an inventive conception. As this thought takes hold, the other two stare at me, waiting for me to put words to my thoughts.

"Take a seat," I say.

We sit on the sofas facing each other.

"Have you ever wondered what the Alalgar emblem's star formation signifies?"

Zabada and Mamagal look at each other before turning their gaze back to me.

"It portrays the extent of the Rigel Empire," Zabada states.

"Is that true? The stars form the Orion constellation, showing the seven major stars, as seen from the legendary Earth millennia ago. Those stars sit far apart, and Rigel lies to one side. The empire stretches beyond the others."

"What are you implying?" Mamagal asks.

"They may have a hidden significance to us today in the location we now populate. A meaning that's not obvious."

Certain I'm right, I jump from the sofa and grab my tablet, bringing up the astrogation charts. Rewinding time and changing the stellar position, I display the seven stars of Orion making up the four limbs and the belt as viewed from an ancient record of where legendary Earth was. "Watch how these stars rearrange when seen from Helheim or, as you call it, Ur." I change the location coordinates, and the stars blur to a new arrangement with the seven stars highlighted. They don't have any pattern, and I see frowns of confusion on my guests' faces. To be honest, I'm unsure of my point, except it will be plain with the next integration. "Let's bring time forward to five hundred years ago." When I adjust the timeline, our eyes widen in amazement.

The seven stars change their locations so that six stars arrange equidistantly into a circle surrounding a central star — Rigel. That can't be a coincidence.

"That is interesting, but how does it help us?" Zabada asks.

"When I reconfigured the maser cannons on the *Queen Rosalind* to include the crystal into their circuitry, the extra power not over-loading the weapons amazed me. I now realize they aren't using more power. The maser beams are different: more potent and destructive. If we combine the beams, they should become more deadly still. What strength might we have if we focused seven beams onto a locus configured in this arrangement? I dare say it would have lethal force without the spacetime-destroying consequences of detonating a crystal."

Both Zabada and Mamagal nod, grasping my logic.

"What you suggest is that we arrange seven ships into this forma-tion, which should destroy any ship in Barak's fleet when we fire their masers at it at once."

I nod.

"That's fine in theory, but we must test such an idea to make sure it works," Mamagal says.

"We just try it," I say, shrugging. "At worst, they'll consider us raving lunatics clutching at straws. At best, we own a weapon able to slice through Barak's navy that he cannot stop."

"Which vessels do you suggest we use?"

"Ishtar's six ships and mine. I don't know why, but I believe it's important I'm at the center."

The door alarm buzzes.

"Enter," I say, puzzled by the intrusion.

Conrad stands before us when the door opens. "Sir, the enemy is stirring."

I nod and stride to the helm, assessing the image on the main screen. Barak has his navy split into three groups to match mine. Their strength is even, so I can't concentrate my firepower on any one squadron of ships. We have no choice but to use our arrowhead approach on all three, despite the tactic losing its effectiveness. Each enemy group can independently adjust their strategy to account for the circumstances with less chance of confusion and risk of striking each other amongst the enemy fleet. I relay my instructions and look on as we align ourselves with the adversary. Ishtar holds back, waiting for my further orders for her squadron.

With hands nervously folded behind my back, I wait for the battle to begin while I consider my choices with Ishtar and how to test my theory. Zabada and Mamagal stand next to me, observing with intense interest.

The engagement begins with similar results to the first attack. But as our vessels pierce through the enemy lines, Barak's ships concentrate their firepower on my empire-sourced ships instead of the Helheim ones. Since these ships have weaker shields and less firepower, Barak's weapons inflict damage on them at a greater rate than I can suffer. I gape in horror as Barak annihilates my navy before my eyes. When they complete their first pass, he has destroyed or disabled half of them. One contingent of Barak's flotilla continues to attack my fighter carrier, and I order Ishtar to protect it at any cost. I tell Conrad to join in to support Ishtar.

One of our arrowheads has lost its opponent to the attack on the fighter carrier, so it adjusts its vector and combines with another to tackle the remaining two enemy groups while the other arrowhead attacks the other.

I stare in despair as Barak again wreaks havoc on my fleet. We have inflicted heavy losses on his navy too — but at this attrition rate, only one outcome is possible.

As the major attack occurs, the other third of Barak's ships approach the fighter carrier. Ishtar and Conrad engage them in battle.

At one stage, our maser blast and one from Ishtar's ship accidentally cross paths, combining their strengths into one beam. The resulting ray slices through four enemy vessels as easily as paper. When I notice the effect, I nod in acknowledgment that my theory may be correct.

Despite the heavy bombardment by Ishtar and Conrad destroying many ships, the sheer numbers dictate my only fighter carrier's destruction, leaving my fighters without a home.

I lower my head in shock and shame. Volunteers losing their lives for my sake, unaware of the identity of their leader. I sense the urge to run and hide again, but I have nowhere to go this time where Barak won't find me, and I'm finished running. If I can't win, I'll die trying.

Once they destroy the fighter carrier, Barak's ships break off their attack and return to the safety of their main fleet of ships.

"Sir, a shuttle has just launched from the planet," Conrad says.

I glance at the screen and see it's the shuttle for the yacht. Assuming Sentinel has made use of it, I give it no further thought until it deviates from the vector it should be taking. Where is it going?

"It's headed for Barak's fleet!" Conrad yells.

Within an instant, I realize what has happened and who occupies the shuttle — Adala occupies it as a prisoner and victim of Barak's manipulations to force my capitulation. My head drops in despair, but I know Adala would want me to keep fighting for our cause.

"Shall we fire at it?" Conrad asks.

"No." I glance at him. "Queen Adala is on it. That's why they advance toward Barak's fleet."

"But we must rescue her then."

"How? We can't fire on it. And we are too distant to overtake it before Barak does." I stare at the screen as my stomach tightens, wondering what the next move is in this game of chess. I cannot save Adala yet, but I can inflict irreparable damage on the rest of Barak's fleet. "Ishtar, are you there?" I ask after connecting with her.

"Halwende?"

"Form your vessels into a circle surrounding me, equidistant from each other."

Ishtar raises her eyebrows and gives a bemused smile. "Why?"

"You'll find out."

"OK then." Ishtar breaks off, and her six ships maneuver around mine until they are in position. "Now what?"

"I need control of your navigation, and you are to fire your maser cannons when I order it."

Without asking why Ishtar sets in motion the commands to do as I ask. "You have control."

"Thank you." I pull up the remote navigation screen in my

command chair and adjust the alignment of Ishtar's ships until their orientation is right. "Fire your masers."

The six maser cannons of Ishtar's ships eject beams of maser particles, converging on a spot a third of the distance between our fleet and Barak's. Ishtar is still in view and looks confused. I don't blame her. I am unsure if this will work. Without further thought, I fire my maser cannon at the exact point of convergence. As the energy pulses into a crescendo of restrained fury, it overflows and jets into Barak's armada with a destructive force only outdone by the last show of my power at Uruk. As the beam smashes into Barak's ships, vaporizing them, I maneuver our ships to control the beam's direction, pulverizing ship after ship into elemental fragments.

This much power is addictive and corrupting. It makes me a god as my crew stares at me in disbelief. I know I must limit my ego for the sake of Adala. Reluctantly, I break off the attack.

While this display of my strength plays out, the shuttle completes its journey to the battlecruiser Barak commands. Within seconds of it docking, I receive a communication ping from him, which I put on the main screen. The same fear consumes his eyes that I saw the last time his ship and few others survived an attack against me.

"Your inventiveness never ceases to amaze me," Barak says.

"I enjoy surprising you," I say.

"Yet again, you have destroyed my fleet. The emperor won't be happy when I return." Barak's passive expression breaks into a grin. "But I will impress him with the present I bring him." Barak turns off-screen and nods.

Struggling defiantly, Adala comes into view. The crew on my ship gasp in horror, and my heart tears to see her helpless and in Barak's hands. It reminds me of her captivity with Egon and how that nearly ended in disaster. Knowing she can't escape, Adala stops resisting and stands erect with an air of dignity. They haven't assaulted her beyond that needed to restrain her movement. She looks at the screen, her eyes staring straight at me. They beg me for forgiveness.

My jaw clenches when I see the people in the background — Korbinian and General Klaus.

Barak gazes at me again in triumph. "We have a prize here, don't we, Halwende? Not only is she ruler of this backwater planet you love so much, but I understand you've taken a fancy to her. Emperor Shulgi's opinion of her will interest me. What delights she can offer to please him!"

"I'll kill you if you harm Queen Adala." I glare at Barak, enraged.

"Don't make threats you can't deliver." Barak eyes me with contempt. "It won't surprise me if you run away and hide like last time."

"I brought this on myself," Adala says, pleading with me. "Don't give in to his taunts."

"I'll come for you. It doesn't matter where Barak takes you, I'll rescue you."

"I'm counting on that," Barak says with glee. "I can watch you die like the scum you are."

"You don't know who I am."

"And neither do you."

Barak breaks the signal, leaving me glaring at a blank screen. Within minutes, the remnants of Barak's fleet retreat and enter hyperspace.

"Where have they gone?" Conrad asks, the horror of seeing his queen captive still plain on his face.

I break the trance I descended into and look at him. "To Eridu."

I must seek counsel. But first, I need to contact Sentinel.

26

PLANS ARE MADE

S entinel's face comes on the screen moments after I place a call through to him. His eyes show the failure I know he feels. He stands with shoulders slumped in defeat as he stares back at me.

"How did they overpower you so they could leave?" I ask.

"They had the shuttle pilot in their pay, from the word I received. While we fought, they headed for the craft and escaped. And now I've lost the reason to continue. With Queen Adala gone, the power base has descended into chaos."

The ease that Korbinian and Klaus could manipulate events on Helheim disturbs me. It seems Adala's hold on authority is more tenuous than anyone realized. My mind blurs with confusion as I consider my options. I must follow Adala to Eridu. But first, I need to stabilize the uprising on Helheim. And to do that, I sense I must confess my identity. I will seek advice from Zabada. My eyes lock on Sentinel's. "We are coming to the planet. Assemble Abelard, Frieda, and Sigmund. Bring Lilith too. She will be useful. We shall talk soon."

"As you wish. I look forward to your guidance."

I break contact with Sentinel and instruct Conrad to head for

Heimstadt. After confused protests, disputing my orders in prefer-ence to following Adala and rescuing her, I get him to see reason and he obeys. I relay the instructions through to Ishtar as well. My heart breaks when I realize Argandea, Lugal, Ninsar, and Yarla have all died. Barak slaughtered them in my fleet's destruction, and I must bear the guilt whenever I consider the foolishness of my actions.

We descend to the planet, and my destroyers hover over the city, awaiting my orders. I command them to wait while I travel to the palace in a shuttle. After another half an hour, I embrace Sentinel in the palace's main conference room. He looks weary and defeated. Lilith stands next to him. If the circumstances weren't so grim, I'd smirk at the sight. Sigmund and Frieda stand to the side, and Adala's father, Abelard, sits at the table, his eyes filled with sadness.

"Come and refresh yourself," Sentinel says, and he gestures me to a chair.

I do as he suggests, and a servant enters with water, coffee, and food. The others seat themselves and stay silent as if waiting for me to start the conversation.

After quenching my thirst with a glass of water, I gaze into their eyes, reflecting on their countenance. Despair and defeat saturate them. "Don't give up yet," I say.

"But what else can we do with Queen Adala taken away from us?" Sentinel responds.

"They may have captured her, but I will rescue her and return her to you. I promise you that."

"How?" both Sigmund and Frieda ask in unison.

"First, we must stabilize the position here. Have circumstances changed since we talked?" I ask Sentinel.

"Those monsters appearing above our city have panicked the populace."

"Good. That was their purpose. What of the fighting?"

"We gain ground in retaking the planet from the coup. With Klaus leaving, the others have no center of command to coordinate the takeover."

Happy that the rightful regime still controls Helheim, I give my attention to Abelard. "I must ask you to assume leadership until Adala's return."

"I am old and frail," Abelard protests.

"Yet your mind is sound and sharp. I need you in this interim role. Helheim needs you to do this."

Abelard glances at Sentinel, Sigmund, and Frieda. His resistance fails him, and he nods.

"We will help you, Papa," Frieda says.

He smiles and agrees again. "And what will you do?" Abelard asks me.

"I return to Eridu. That is where they took Adala."

"I'm coming with you," Sentinel asserts.

With a grin, I say, "I expected nothing else."

"And so shall I," Lilith volunteers.

My smile disappears, replaced by a frown. "You are safer here."

"My destiny takes me where you go." Lilith glances at Sentinel. "Where Ranulf goes."

Sentinel hides his embarrassment with a slight shuffle on his chair and then nods in acknowledgment.

"Besides," Lilith says. "I can be valuable to you by infiltrating the palace."

I can't dispute that. "It will be dangerous. If your father knows you go with me, he'll demand your return."

"Then you'll have to keep my presence secret."

I sigh. "It's settled, then."

With our plans made, Sentinel arranges for Abelard to be installed as Regent in Queen Adala's absentia by the cathedral bishop and for the ceremony to be broadcast throughout the realm, so no doubt exists about who is in charge. This has the desired effect. Filling the power vacuum rallies the royal troops, who overpower the coup without further conflict. They round up and imprison the ringleader generals and send them to await trial. The planet returns to normal everyday life for the citizens.

PREPARATIONS FOR OUR DEPARTURE INTENSIFY, and I'm eager to be on our way. But first, I must talk with Zabada, so I get him ferried to me, and we descend the palace corridors to the portal. I wish to show him its machines and technology. The presence acknowledges me as soon as I approach the door and we enter. Nostalgia overwhelms Zabada when he peruses the chamber and its contents.

"We have lost so much," he says once he completes a circuit of the room. He stares at me as he sits on the only chair in the place. "They had to hide this technology because of the conflict. In fact, it was redundant once the power source was unavailable."

"I still can't believe that Helheim possesses the only deposit of the crystal throughout the entire galaxy."

"The galaxy is a large place. There may be other deposits, but the Empire never located others to replace Ur."

"I must get used to naming this planet Ur. It'll be a shock to the inhabitants when they know."

Zabada chuckles. "Yes, it will." He sobers and returns his attention to me. "Now that I've seen this room, what do you wish to discuss?"

It's my turn to chuckle. I never could keep my intentions from Zabada. After glancing at him and the machines and the residual crystal, I broach the topic that presses me. "I sense the time is ripe for me to announce myself."

Zabada nods but remains silent for several seconds as he ruminates on his thoughts. When he is ready, he looks up at me. "I fear you are correct, but why do you think so?"

While I pace the room, I say, "They need hope here before I leave. With what has happened, they understand Shulgi's soldiers will return to subjugate the planet to his rule. There is now grave danger here. Once Shulgi understands the crystal's significance and the power it possesses, he could gain the knowledge to use it."

Zabada nods but replies, "You assume technology alone harnesses its potency."

I stop pacing and face him. "Well, doesn't it? What else could it need?"

"Didn't Mamagal or I tell you? The crystal has an affinity for those of Alalgar's blood." Zabada stares at me and through me with the same expression. "How do you explain your knowledge to tear space-time with its energy? Or to set up flerovium-powered masers in the correct configuration to unleash immeasurable destruction?"

His words confuse me. "I read it." Zabada's raised eyebrow unnerves me. "I must have."

"No written text exists for these applications. The knowledge is too dangerous. Imagine the power Shulgi would have with this technology. But to further counter your argument, how did you gain access to this chamber?"

I'm confused by the change of topic. "It allowed me to enter."

"Few know this room exists. How did you find it? Why did it allow you to view its doorway?"

"It was looking for someone from Eridu." Zabada's questioning unnerves me more.

"Anyone? I didn't see the entrance before you requested entry."

His revelation staggers me. That's impossible. Why couldn't he see it?

"It was seeking Alalgar's descendant from Eridu," Zabada continues. "It sought the rightful heir to the lineage."

"But Shulgi must have royal blood in him."

"No, he married into the bloodline."

The revelation both disturbs me and soothes my fears. "But we get off-topic. Shulgi will still destroy this planet when he returns, and I can't allow that while I'm alive. He will marry Adala when he learns of her heritage to legitimize his reign further and embed his dynasty. With my revealing my identity, people can rally to me."

"Why do you think they will risk upsetting the status quo by rallying behind a pretender?"

"They're sick of the tyranny. You see it in their eyes. They live in fear every second of their lives. You saw how the Resistance rallied to me once I proved my leadership. There's no point in continuing this charade with what's at stake."

Zabada nods. "The die is now cast then. Let the end game begin."

27

AN ANNOUNCEMENT

Zabada and I leave the portal chamber, and I race back to the shuttle and my ship. I must fetch the object, signifying my legitimacy to those who originate from Eridu and the Rigel Empire. With the casket in my possession, I return to the planet and the palace's conference room. Ishtar and Mamagal now join Sentinel, Abelard, Sigmund, Frieda, Lilith, and Zabada. They fall silent when I enter, focusing all their attention on me. I invite them to sit.

As I gaze into each of their eyes, butterflies play with my nerves at my impending announcement. Will they believe me? Will they acknowledge me? I won't find out by sitting here in silence, so I take a deep breath and begin.

"The Helheim citizens recognize me as the trader who crashed on their planet and helped return the governing body to the royal household. You have limited knowledge of my past — the death ... murder ... of my family, my cowardice. The people from Eridu perceive me as the Resistance general who fled and deserted them in their greatest need, leaving them to struggle without me in their battle with Shulgi to overthrow his tyranny. Two among you know my true identity."

The others mutter amongst themselves, wondering what I'm about to say.

"It is time to acknowledge myself to the rest of you," I continue. "I can no longer hide. The stakes are now too high. To be honest, I didn't learn my name until recent events unfolded, when I recovered historical records from the library on Eridu. But I keep you in suspense." I scan my eyes across them as I straighten my stance. "My true name is Sargon Halwende, direct descendent of Dumuzid, son of Alalgar and claimant to the Rigel throne."

Ishtar and Lilith both gasp. Abelard raises his eyebrows, as does Sentinel. Sigmund and Frieda, like two naughty children, suppress giggles.

"And to prove my legitimacy, I will place the signet ring of Rigel on my finger, the ring thought lost when Shulgi ascended the royal seat." I open the box sitting on the table and remove the jewel, the insignia of Alalgar sparkling on the bezel, and slip it on my right-hand ring finger. I don't expect what happens next. Power flows into me from the band. It doesn't make me grow ten feet tall or give me superhuman strength, but it distills a sense of destiny throughout me that I have never felt before. My presence bursts into a brilliance too bright to view.

As if to prove the transformation, Ishtar trembles as she rises and steps toward me, kneeling, almost collapsing, before me with head bowed. Lilith imitates her, as do Zabada and Mamagal. I'm embarrassed, but I don't belittle the size of this event with any comical quip to ease the tension within me. All I say is, "Rise. I have not changed. I want you to treat me as before today."

They do as I ask, but Ishtar says as she searches my eyes, "You may wish to be treated the same, but you won't be. I can never mock you again. To be honest, I was always suspicious of you. I could never fathom your presence. Now I know. And to think that–"

"That's enough," I interrupt before she embarrasses both me and herself.

"I sensed there was more to you than you admitted, too," Lilith says.

With the non-Helheim people considered, I glance at the others.

They sit, open-mouthed and uncertain of what to do until Abelard chuckles.

I raise my eyebrows.

"No wonder Adala took to you," Abelard says. "Even when we met in prison, you had an aura I couldn't grasp."

"We always knew there was something special about you from the first day we found you," Frieda says, and Sigmund nods.

Sentinel looks at Abelard and then at me. He has no words to utter, but his voice returns. "If I hadn't sworn my fealty to Queen Adala, I would commit myself to you now."

"There is no need to, my friend." I sigh. "But we have a mammoth task and insufficient time to act."

With the formality of my revelation dealt with, I wave the others to their seats and begin our deliberations. "Where do we start?"

"Announcing your lineage is the top priority," Abelard says. "That should rattle this Shulgi's bones."

"Won't it just make him even more desperate to get rid of me?" I had considered the same idea but thought it too risky. "He may be more determined to marry Adala at once when he finds out her heritage and the danger of her union with me."

"I don't know the politics of your empire, but I can't see him risking an uprising against him if he attempts such a homicide. The armed forces might even revolt."

"I'm counting on the military revolting. Without a significant navy, I don't see a means of defeating Barak now that he has destroyed what I had."

"We must send the announcement throughout the empire," Ishtar says. "When Shulgi finds out, the news will have spread to the extent he can't suppress it. It may give the forces in the outer systems an opportunity to consider changing sides."

"But why should they?" I ask. "Why put your money behind someone they've never heard of except in myth and legend?"

"Oh, they've heard of you," Lilith says. "Even I received whispers wondering if you had noble blood in you, and you appreciate how secluded my life's been."

I understand what they say, but I fear a royal tour would delay our rescue of Adala, and that must be our top priority. Without her removal from Shulgi's clutches, everything we do will be in vain. I shake my head. "We go to Eridu at once." By an unidentifiable invisible force, my head turns to Mamagal, who sits as if contemplating my every word, but he has an amused smile. "What?"

"I suggest you make a detour to Larsa first," Mamagal says. "There may be items of value there that prove useful in the coming battle."

Before my mind can consider his remarks, I nod in agreement, not knowing why I have but knowing the suggestion is sound and necessary.

"What are your plans for taking the palace?" Lilith asks.

"I hope you might help me with that, but we have time to prepare in transit."

No one has anything more to say, and the meeting descends into silence.

"Let's ready ourselves to leave, then." I rise.

"Wait," Sentinel leaves the room and returns five minutes later with Rickshaw and two others. "I'm sure Ishtar will station her own guards around you when you return to your ship, but for now, accept these as my contribution to your protection."

I haven't met the other two Sentinel brought along, except I recognize they belong to his personal spy network, but I know Rickshaw well and trust him. "My deepest gratitude to you, Sentinel. But do you trust Rickshaw?" I keep a serious face.

Rickshaw stares at me, offended.

I laugh at his expression as I slap him on the shoulder. "Come. We must prepare."

28

SHOPPING FOR WEAPONS

News spreads rapidly amongst the people making up the remnant of my navy when I return to my destroyer. A sense of awe envelops the helm when I step onto it, with the officers not knowing where they should look when they rise to salute me. Several Eriduans tremble as Ishtar did. I try to put them at ease but fear I cannot do so. Rickshaw and the two other bodyguards stand near me, primitive but effective Helheim weapons at the ready. Since leaving the planet, I discover the names of my other two guards to be Jacques and Lombard.

"Put them away," I instruct Rickshaw.

He shrugs, but they do as I say.

I intend to transfer to the *Queen Rosalind* and use that as my transportation. Conrad transfers with me as my second in command and we assemble a small crew from the other ships. I notice each person is proud to step onto the vessel, not only because they will serve me, but because of the prestige of the yacht's impeccable luxury and its modern fit-out.

After another two days of preparation, we leave Helheim, headed for Larsa and a return to the crypt. The reason we are returning to the crypt is known only to Mamagal.

I enter the Larsa system with my squadron of destroyers and we park within the asteroid belt, making use of the asteroid we occupied last time the rebels made their base there. Shulgi's forces have damaged it since then and the Resistance has deserted it, so we stay secluded there.

I prepare to descend to the planet using the shuttle on board. Sentinel, Mamagal, Ishtar, and my bodyguards go with me. My primary concern is reaching my destination without the planetary surveillance detecting my approach. I dare not return to the space-port. Security will be on alert for me. With no choice but to take our chances, we fly to the surface but receive no attention as we near our location. I direct the craft into the gorge where the crypt is located, and we disembark.

The cliff face fascinates Mamagal. "Where is the entrance?"

"Haven't you ever been here?" I ask, surprised.

"No."

"How did you know of its existence, then?"

"References and the map I gave you."

I shake my head and search for the secret passageway into the underground cavern. After a quick scan of the rock wall, I locate the spot and position my hand in the indentation, the doorway opening with a sigh. The Helheim people stare at the tunnel with skepticism but consent to stepping through, the stonework sliding shut behind us. We walk at a steady pace and reach the crypt within ten minutes, the unbroken expanse lighting up with a glorious yellow light. Sentinel and Ishtar gawk up at the Rigel insignia pattern on the ceiling, transfixed again by its splendor.

I go to the cabinets and retrieve several more flerovium crystals, placing them in a bag I brought with me. Afterward, I turn to Mamagal. "Why did you want me here?"

Mamagal doesn't answer me straight away. Instead, he studies the chamber walls with immense concentration, squinting at patches now and then, as if searching for a minute detail. He continues for several minutes before stepping back with an air of satisfaction. "Here."

I step closer to him. "What is it?"

"Recognize that?"

On casual inspection, all I see is a wall of rock, but when I peer at it more closely, I see the familiar hand indentation, the same as at the crypt entrance. I place my hand in it and hear a click before the rock swings open like a door. An arsenal sits inside a vast room.

"Did you know this was here?"

Mamagal shakes his head. "No. But I suspected from the writings I received describing the site."

I step into the chamber and inspect the weapons, picking up a rifle. It's a maser rifle, but unlike any I've seen. When I scrutinize it, I see a minute crystal of flerovium embedded in the power unit. I glance at Mamagal, raising my eyebrows. "This is not a normal maser rifle?"

Mamagal nods. "The armory of Alalgar. They don't make these firearms anymore."

I replace the rifle and grab a pistol. The same flerovium power supply sits inside it. I'd test it, but fear of its potential destructive energy in this cavern inflicting undesirable consequences prevents me. Instead, I treat it with a healthy respect. Still, I choose it and place it in a holster on my upper thigh. I grab another one for good measure before proceeding with my scrutiny. Muon grenades sit in a rack nearby — deadly and illegal to own. I put six in my bag, regardless. The room stores various other items of artillery, too. I leave them where they are. After a few more minutes of careful inspection, I retreat from the room but bring three rifles with me. I give a rifle to each of my bodyguards, instructing them on how to fire it with care. They take them, handling them as if they are holy relics imparted to them by a deity. I tell them to get over it. They're just rifles but particularly deadly ones.

Before I close the door, a sparkle attracts my attention, and I re-enter the room. A trinket sits on a shelf — a personal force field. I grab it and place it on my wrist. Another bracelet sits further along the shelf. It's not a force-field device. It has runes of the Emblem of Alalgar etched into the surface, but the bracelet's role escapes me.

Still, its presence in the room suggests it has a fundamental importance, so I keep it and go to thread it on my right wrist with the other wristlet, but it resists my efforts to thread it over my hand. Out of curiosity, I try my left hand, and the bracelet passes over it easily. I frown, as I've never heard before of a hand-specific bracelet.

Just before I'm finished, I grab two more pistols. I step over to Sentinel and Ishtar and give them a pistol each.

Once I close the armory, I say, "We must go."

Mamagal agrees, and we retrace our steps.

The sunlight blinds us momentarily before we return to the shuttle. I stand in its warmth and appreciate its rays soaking into me as I choose a moment to review my plight. With this side trip completed, we must head for Eridu and confront Shulgi and Barak, but I don't know how I'll convince them to release Adala at this stage. I'm hoping a bright notion will flash into existence before we arrive. Not an illustrious means of attacking an empire.

We parked the shuttle in an open field away from the crypt and now thread our way to it through the confines of the gorge. As we round the last bend to the shuttle's resting spot, and just before the craft comes into sight, Sentinel jerks up his fist, bringing us to an abrupt stop.

"We have company," he whispers.

We stop and step beside the gorge wall.

I inch to Sentinel's side. "Who are they?"

"You may have a better chance of answering that."

I nod and poke my head around the corner. "Imperial troops. Too many for us to fight, I fear."

"You won't walk up to them and ask them how their day's been?" Sentinel asks with a sardonic smile.

I roll my eyes at him.

They must have tracked us from space and allowed our landing, intending to arrest us by surprise. They've surprised us, but I don't intend to be captured. I move back from the bend and sit to think.

Rickshaw comes up to me. "Won't these give us an edge?" he asks, holding up the rifle I gave him.

I stare at him. To be honest, I had forgotten we carried the weapons, and he has a point. But too many of them confront us, and they can call for reinforcements. My nerve stimulator isn't of use either. They're too dispersed to incapacitate everyone at once. "They will, but they're not enough."

"We'd better think of something soon," Ishtar says. "They'll start sending out search parties. And we're trapped if we stay here."

I nod. We could retire to the crypt, but that would just delay the inevitable. They are aware of our presence, and we must return to the shuttle.

As if the troops are reading Ishtar's mind, Sentinel glances back at me. "A squad's coming our way."

"We'll fight here," I say. It's not my preference, but there's little we can do. With a grunt, I stand and prepare my pistol to fire.

Several boulders lie nearby, which will protect us, so we retreat behind them and wait. The first of the troopers round the corner, unconcerned and relaxed, rifles aimed at the ground. Once they come into view, we open fire with our newly gained weapons. The power of the beams rapidly slaughters the group. But it alerts the rest of the soldiers to the skirmish, and we hear them prepare to confront us. This worries me, but we have no other choice but to hold out, hoping they won't send for backup.

On seeing the slaughter of their compatriots scouting the bend, the troops retreat and take up protected spots from where to attack. The officer in charge yells for a mortar assault, and missiles rocket toward us moments later, earth and rock flying in every direction with the resulting explosions. We haven't given away our positions yet, but it won't be long till we do if they advance.

Our only chance is for one of us to climb the canyon wall and surprise them from behind, either by attacking them or firing up the shuttle. I scan the cliff for access to the top. A suitable spot is available further back along the gorge, but it means giving away my position, which would destroy any surprise. But it might just work. I motion to Sentinel and Ishtar my intentions. Both vehemently shake their heads, but I ignore them and prepare to dash to a climbing point out of sight of the besieging troops. Ishtar slaps her head and prepares to defend me from attack when she sees she can't deter me. After turning on my force field and psyching myself up, I rush to the wall, laser pulse puffing dust as it hits the ground near me. I dodge and turn, but one blast deflects from my shield as I disappear from sight.

Once I grab the projecting rock, I climb, my breath heaving with each step. Perspiration drips from me soon enough in the daytime heat. An exchange of fire starts as I continue my ascent. I reach the top after ten minutes and glance below, wondering how my friends are holding out as the sound of gunfire continues. The contents of my bag worry me, so I search for a place to hide it just in case, expecting I can return to retrieve it once things settle.

With no time to lose, I scramble toward the shuttle, hoping to avoid descending another cliff or facing any guards along the way. I'm in luck on both accounts as I run downhill to the shuttle. On reaching the hatch, I prepare to enter.

"Who have we here?" a voice says from inside. A soldier is sitting on a crate and pointing a laser rifle at me.

My force field might protect me, but I don't want to take any chances from such close range, so I say, "Saw the hatch open, so I thought I'd take a peek."

The soldier laughs and relaxes his grip, but he can shoot me before I can do likewise. "That's a first. Drop your weapons and raise your hands."

With no other choice, I do as he says.

He rises and trips me up, dropping me to the floor. I groan as my face scrapes the hard surface. He pins me with his foot while he places cuffs on my wrists, then raises me to a standing position.

"Now, you're going to tell your friends to drop their weapons and surrender."

"What friends?"

He smashes the butt of his rifle against my head. "Don't play games. I'm not in the mood."

I don't want my features rearranged, so I nod. "OK, lead the way."

He shoves me from the hatch, his weapon aimed at me the whole time.

I stagger to the gorge as the soldier keeps prodding me with his rifle.

The battle is still raging as we approach the enemy troops. The commander looks at me and then his trooper.

"He was sneaking into the shuttle," the soldier explains. "Thought he might help us stop this little skirmish."

The leader nods. "Tell them to cease firing and surrender," he tells me.

There's no point in refusing his command. The troops will wear my people out and kill them in the end. This way, we may have a chance. "Stop firing," I shout. "The game's over. Come out."

After several shots, the attack ends. Nothing happens for a minute. Then Sentinel and the others appear from behind the rocks with their hands raised. They don't have the new rifles but display their original ones instead. The imperial troops rush forward and secure my team with cuffs before they march them to me and the officer in charge.

He stares at each of us before he speaks. "I don't know what you were doing here, but we don't take too kindly to people landing on our planet beyond our spaceport. Goodness knows what diseases you might bring here."

I can't believe it. He's unaware of who we are, who I am. He thinks we're smugglers or other unsavory crew sneaking to their world to conduct suspect business. I glance at Ishtar and Sentinel to suggest we stay calm and search for a possible opening to overpower our captors.

They march us to their transport craft.

Just as we pile in through the hatch, shots fire at us — I should say them — as soldiers start falling dead around us. I fall to the ground, as do my friends, the troopers scrambling for cover and positions to fire back at the surprise attackers.

I squirm to get a better view of what's happening. While doing this, I spot Ishtar staring at me. "What?"

"Didn't I say you were trouble wherever you go?"

I shrug. "Know who our rescuers are?"

"Kalbum, I hope. I transmitted a message to him when you left on your foolhardy escapade over the cliff. I'm guessing someone's responded — unless they want both the troops and us."

Judging by the quantity and direction of the firing, a large contingent has arrived, overpowering the troopers' defenses.

Pings from kinetic missiles ricochet from the transporter's hull, making me cringe until the battle resolves itself with most of the soldiers dead. The others surrender and throw away their weapons.

With the danger over, I sit up, as does everyone but Mamagal. I glance over at him and stare in horror. His eyes stare back at me in a deathly mask as blood trickles from a wound in his chest. I close my eyes in sorrow as I absorb the tragedy. He so much desired to return to Eridu. I open my eyes to look at him. "Guess you won't be fishing in that stream again, my friend," I say as a tear escapes my eye. Ishtar looks on in sadness at our loss, too. The news of his demise will devastate Lilith.

A few minutes later, a familiar figure emerges from behind the transporter, beaming at us, proud of his success.

"You received my message," Ishtar says.

"Yes," Kalbum replies to her. He glares at me. "You're more trouble than you're worth sometimes."

I give him an indignant stare. "Hello to you, too."

Ishtar and Sentinel glance at each other. "There's something you should know," she says to Kalbum.

"What?" Kalbum stares at her, then me and back at her.

"Halwende here isn't who he says he is."

"I know. He's always changing names and acting the idiot."

Sentinel laughs, and Ishtar shakes her head. "Listen," she says. "Halwende is Sargon, direct heir to King Alalgar's throne."

Kalbum's eyes bulge. He gapes at me and at Ishtar to check she isn't playing a joke on him. His mouth wobbles open and closed several times before he produces a solitary word, "Bull!"

Ishtar nods.

Kalbum rolls his eyes. "No wonder he gets into so much trouble."

I chuckle out loud. "Can you please remove these cuffs?"

"Sure." He turns to move but then returns his attention to me. "Should I say your majesty or something?"

"Just get these restraints off before I clout you one."

"I'll leave them on if you don't behave."

Kalbum leaves and returns with a keypad to unlock them. He unlocks those of the others, too.

I jump up and hug him. "It's good to see you again."

"Yeah, well. Might teach you to come by the traditional route next time."

"I thought they'd recognize me."

"Humph. Let's get you going before reinforcements arrive, wondering what's happened."

I agree with him but scramble to the clifftop to retrieve my bag. The others collect their new weapons from behind the boulders. As I gaze at the aftermath, I see several soldiers still live. I don't know what Kalbum will do with them, but we can't allow them to report to their command. I tell him as much, and he says he'll fix it, whatever that means.

After discussing our position with him further, we agree that we'll return to the capital after securing the shuttle. I want to spend the night talking to Kalbum about the future.

29

A MEETING IN A TAVERN

The night is balmy when Ishtar, Sentinel, and I — along with my three bodyguards — meet Kalbum in a seedy tavern in an inner suburb of the capital. He directs us to a secluded part where we sit on lounges surrounding a large circular table — except for Rickshaw and the two other guards, who stand with their backs to the wall to keep a close watch on proceedings at the bar.

We drink a couple of beers before we start serious discussions. A quick glance at Sentinel tells me he is enjoying the diversion.

"You're full of surprises then," Kalbum says to me. "Crown Prince and whatnot."

"It surprised me too."

Kalbum rubs the lip of his glass as he considers his next words. "How does this change things?"

I stare at him for a few moments. "It gives legitimacy to the Resistance movement. That's where you get involved."

"Me?"

"Yes. I need you to spread the news, make people excited over an alternative to Shulgi's tyranny."

"It'll give me a quick trip to prison and death as well."

I sit back, unsure now of whether my judgment of Kalbum was

correct. He's right that spreading such rumors will prick the empire's ears, with the likelihood of execution for the perpetrators. But how dedicated is he? Is he willing to risk dying for it? Although why should he put his neck out for someone who ran away the last time we held similar hope?

Kalbum studies me, too. He says, "Security's tightened since the rumor of Barak returning from his mysterious expedition with a prize for his emperor."

My jaw clenches at such news. To think of Adala in Shulgi's hands is unbearable. As the story will leak, and I want Kalbum to know the facts for my own reasons, I tell him, "He kidnapped Queen Adala from the planet Helheim."

"Wow," he says, "I hear she's a goddess. Shulgi'll lust over her in quick measure."

Sentinel makes to attack Kalbum for insulting his monarch, but I reach out with my hand to calm him. "You are probably right. That's the reason I'm here. I intend rescuing her."

Kalbum has been gulping his beer, but when I mention freeing Adala, he gags and sprays the beer over the table. "You're what?"

"I'm saving her."

"Why?"

I stay silent.

Kalbum eyes me, confused, and then his brow clears. "That's where you crashed, isn't it?"

I confirm his suspicion with a nod.

He takes a sip to calm the residual tickle in his throat. "But why rescue her? What's she to you?"

"Remember last time I said I was Grand Chancellor?"

He nods.

"I am Grand Chancellor to her. She is in effect my Queen."

"But you're–"

"Yes, I am. That confuses things. Although Adala has royal blood, too."

Kalbum sits back, confused over all these revelations. He shakes his head to clear it.

"It's a long story. I'll retell it sometime when the atmosphere is more relaxed."

"Please do."

I take a sip. "Now that you know our history, maybe you'll tell me if you're still willing to help me."

"Security's tight." Kalbum rubs his chin. "It's much tighter on Eridu, from what I'm told." He sighs. "But my allegiance to you has been solid from the start. I have more incentive now." He nods. "You can count on me. I'll get the word out, and I'll even gather intelligence for you from Eridu while you're–"

Kalbum breaks off, staring at the entrance to the bar, his eyes squinting with suspicion.

"What?" I ask.

"We have company. Undesirable visitors at that."

Sentinel and the others become tense, ready for action.

Kalbum gestures to stay calm. "No need to panic. They're not security. They're spies, circulating between the bars to glean information worth buying for the empire. Although I consider them in Shulgi's employment. The selling is a cover."

I steal a glance at the newcomers but do as Kalbum suggests.

After watching the agents, Kalbum groans. "They're coming over here. Act natural. You're a merchant discussing business."

"With my merry group?" I ask, gesturing at my entourage.

"You're cautious."

I grin.

As Kalbum has predicted, two men stroll our way and approach our bench. I notice Sentinel and Ishtar reaching for their firearms. I give a slight shake of my head to them. They desist from completing their actions, but their hands hover over their weapons.

"How's it going, Kalbum?" The lead person positions himself at our table. He has a scar across his left cheek, partly concealed by an unkempt beard.

Kalbum acknowledges him with a smile and a nod. "Good, Tirig. Yourself?"

"Yeah. As good as we can expect. I could use more trade. Who're your friends?"

The other newcomer stands with Tirig, sipping his beer.

"Just merchants. We're discussing shipment possibilities to Santori."

"Good luck with that. New business is rare these days, what with all the extra security."

"Yeah, well, luck comes your way sometimes if you're in the right place. Any reason for this friendly visit?"

"Hey, just saying hello. Although I heard there was excitement out in the mountains today. A company of soldiers overpowered by strangers. Six of them, so I believe." Tirig scans me and my group to emphasize the coincidence.

I meet his gaze with a cool glare of my own. "I note your implication and won't be doing any business with you ... ever."

Tirig breaks his stare with me and turns his attention back to Kalbum. "Yeah, well, just thought you should know."

"Thanks for the tip." Kalbum shrugs.

Tirig and his friend leave us under Kalbum's watchful gaze. Once they vacate the premises, Kalbum says, "We should go. A patrol might come along soon if they report your presence."

Happy to agree with him, I finish my drink. The others do likewise, and we move to escape the way we entered, but Kalbum stops us and gestures for us to follow him through the backdoor. We weave a course past the toilets and the kitchen until we reach a door. Kalbum opens it, glances out both ways, and waves us through. We scurry along several back alleys before returning to a major thoroughfare and a scooter waiting to take us to a location only Kalbum knows.

We land and pile out.

"I wish you luck," Kalbum says.

"Thanks," I say as I hug him. "Just spread the news." I scan the spot. "But how do we return to our shuttle from here?"

Kalbum smiles. "Follow me." He leads us to a derelict shed and opens a door. Another scooter sits inside it. "With that. You know where you put it, I hope."

I nod. "I'll see you soon."

"Don't get yourself killed."

Kalbum leaves, and we stand in silence before Sentinel says, "Let's return to our ships. I'm feeling naked out here."

"With pleasure," Ishtar says.

We pile onto the scooter and fly from the city moments later. Two hours pass before our shuttle comes into view, with no imperial troops in sight this time. Once landed, we board the shuttle and take off before unwelcome visitors arrive.

The craft rockets into space and toward our ships. Five minutes later, several bleeps appear on my radar — fighters heading our way.

"We're getting an escort," I tell the others. They look troubled when I glance at them. I message Conrad and ask for defensive support with due haste, as the shuttle won't withstand the firepower coming toward us. To place distance between us and the fighters, I speed up with full power to reach my yacht and safety.

The enemy closes in as I watch the screen, beads of sweat developing on my forehead. Ishtar and Sentinel stand behind me. They say nothing, but I know they are as uncomfortable about our chances of survival as I am.

Maser fire rocks the shuttle as I weave to avoid their targeting. Where are Conrad and the destroyers? I can't see them on my scanners yet and, if they don't show up soon, we won't be here when they do.

A bolt of blue light shoots past us, aimed at the fighters, destroying them. I smile. They knew they couldn't reach us in time, so the destroyers formed the Orion formation and shot a volley. Whoever set the targeting must have a good eye. Heavy-handed but effective.

I relax again as we detect the yacht ten minutes later. We will land safely on it soon.

A violent jolt reverberates through the shuttle. My eyes widen as I search the screens, checking for damage. We have a hull breach in the ship's back, and it's beyond sealing. The rear bulkhead seals it from the front of the craft. Once I check for personnel, I find none occupied the section. We've accounted for everyone, and they're uninjured.

"What the hell was that?" Ishtar asks, her eyes wide, ready for action.

"I don't know. I can't see any enemy ships in the region," I tell her.

"Is it possible an asteroid hit us?"

"The automatic avoidance controls should have diverted us around any."

"Can they hide behind an asteroid?"

As if they heard Ishtar's question, another barrage hits the shuttle. On reviewing the status, I see our primary drives are offline. We're reduced to maneuvering thrusters only.

"You there, Conrad?" I say through our communication station.

"Yes, sir."

"We'd appreciate you getting here sooner instead of later. We're under attack and dead in the vacuum at present."

"Noted, sir. I'll maximize thrust. And our weapons officer will discourage whoever has you in their sights."

"Thanks, Conrad, we have little time." I break the link and watch our screen.

A destroyer emerges from behind an asteroid, its cannons locked onto us. "Surrender and prepare for boarding," a voice echoes throughout the helm from the speaker.

"What do they think we can do?" Ishtar says as she glances at me. "Jump into hyperspace with no drives?"

A bead of sweat sits on my forehead, and I wipe it away impatiently. "I hope Conrad gets here before they do." After a couple of minutes, the yacht shows signs of closing the gap between us, giving me hope of rescue.

"Approaching ship, shut off your drives and prepare for boarding," the enemy destroyer officer says. "Make no hostile actions or you will force us to open fire."

Under other circumstances, I'd be interested in the outcome of the power struggle between the two ships. But our shuttle might be caught in the crossfire between them. The *Queen Rosalind* isn't slowing. I hope Conrad knows what he's doing.

"Turn off your drives, or I'll destroy the shuttle," the destroyer's voice warns.

My head jerks toward the speaker as I hear the threat. More sweat accumulates on my forehead as I watch the screen for any signs of what Conrad intends to do. The yacht's drives power off, and it slows as it continues coasting toward us. Its shields still show full strength. I'd move away from this struggle, but I'm stuck without powered drives.

"Do you have any maneuverability?" Conrad asks me over a secure channel.

"Yes, but not much."

"When I tell you, dart to your left."

"Will do." I prepare my thrusters to do as he says, licking my lips as I shoot Ishtar and Sentinel nervous glances.

The yacht comes closer with each second, but the destroyer makes no move to defend or attack. The captain must believe he's convinced us both to follow his orders. I have my hands ready to move the shuttle.

"Now!" Conrad yells.

I bring the port side thrusters to full power, vectoring myself left at a snail's pace.

"What are you doing?" the destroyer's captain shouts. "Desist at once."

The yacht's maser cannon powers up in an instant and fires at the destroyer, missing the shuttle by a small margin. As its ordnance was still coming up to full strength when it fired, the blast only dents the destroyer's shields.

"Stop firing," the destroyer yells, "or I'll–"

We never do hear what he would do because Conrad fires another volley at the ship, this one at full power. It slices right through the shielding and the ship's hull, directly hitting the reactor. The warship disintegrates into nothing moments later.

"Nice shooting," I say.

"Thank you, sir."

30

DEFECTION

"That was unfortunate," Sentinel tells me as we view the aftermath of the destroyed ship.

"We're still here," I say. I understand what he means. First, he, as do I, detests wasting human life. Second, the destruction would have alerted the imperial fleet of our presence. I was hoping to leave Larsa without fanfare. We'll have to handle whatever happens while I return to the *Queen Rosalind* and the rest of my navy arrives.

Our disabled shuttle sits in the yacht's bay twenty minutes later, and Ishtar, Sentinel, and I weave our way to the helm.

Conrad snaps to attention when I arrive. "Good to see you unharmed, sir."

"Nice to be in one piece." I aim for the captain's seat and make myself comfortable, bringing up my screen. "Where are our other ships at present?"

"Flying toward us. They should be nearby in ten minutes."

"Good."

The door opens and Lilith enters, rushing to Sentinel and wrapping her arms around him. I raise my brow as he stares at me, helpless and turning bright red. I want to laugh but restrain myself. After a discreet cough, I say, "Maybe we could resume our work?"

Sentinel's reaction to Lilith shocks me. It's the first time I've seen him embarrassed in that way.

After noticing the rest of us, Lilith blushes, too. It's too much for me and I whoop with laughter, regardless. Ishtar is more restrained, but she has a snigger, too.

Lilith frowns. "Stop that."

"You should learn to control yourself then," Ishtar retorts.

"They could have killed Ranulf." Lilith straightens and stamps her foot, then stomps out in a huff.

"Ranulf?" I ask, raising my eyebrow at Sentinel.

"I will instruct her to be more reserved next time."

I shake my head but stay silent.

"Enemy vessels approaching, sir," Conrad says.

Alarm constricts my chest. "How many?"

After a delay for Conrad to count, he says, "A battleship, five destroyers, and ten corvettes."

"Not playing games."

"Apparently not."

"ETA for our ships?"

"Five minutes, but they are within communications distance."

"Get Hadanish on the com," I say. Any skirmish with the imperial ships will be messy. I could leave and suffer the few shots inflicted before we enter hyperspace, but they might follow us. I'd prefer to keep them intact, though. Further destruction of the fleet only diminishes its strength for defenses against outside enemies until we can replace them.

"Hadanish here," comes through on the screen in visual.

"You need to prepare for more fighting." Hadanish has impressed me so far. He's an excellent ship's captain and a good deputy to Ishtar's leadership of the squadron.

"Will do. You don't want the squadron to form into the Orion arrangement?"

"No, not yet. It's too drastic at present. Let's examine how serious they are about detaining us first."

"As you wish." Hadanish breaks the contact, and I see his ships rearrange themselves to meet the oncoming vessels.

With my squadron prepared, I wonder what else I can do. I don't know the intentions of the approaching ships yet. They have given no sign of aggression, which I find strange since they will come within firing range soon. I frown. "Hail the battleship," I order as I turn to Conrad.

He nods and gets his communications officer to carry out the task.

Thirty seconds later, an Imperial Fleet officer comes on the viewer. She stands impeccably dressed but is nervous, not someone confident of overpowering a few ships.

"This is Sargon Halwende." I dispense with any charade over my identity. "To whom do I talk?"

The person on the screen opens her mouth and closes it again, then gulps. "I am Captain Anunit, commander of the battleship *Stardust*."

I nod. "You have not formed attack positions yet. What are your intentions?"

"We intend to surrender to you, sir. We want to join forces with you."

Anunit's unexpected words leave me nonplussed. "I don't know you, Captain. How can I trust you?"

Her eyes fall in disappointment. She has nothing to say.

The communications screen flashes. It's Hadanish. I connect with him and place his image on the viewer screen. "What can you contribute, Captain Hadanish?"

"Sir, I know Captain Anunit."

"But why should I trust her?"

Hadanish fidgets before answering. "You can't except on my say so, sir. May I suggest Captain Anunit and her officers transfer to one of our ships for a meeting? We can further interrogate their credibility, then."

Hadanish's suggestion has merit. I glance over at Ishtar. She shrugs. Big help she is, but I'd do the same. We have no precedent but Hadanish to guide us with this predicament. At least if the officers are on our ship, we can hold them hostage if they prove untrustworthy. I worry this surrender is a ruse for a surprise attack, though.

"OK. Captain Anunit, are you amenable to Captain Hadanish's suggestion?"

"Yes, we are, sir. This might shock you. Once you hear our story, you will understand we have no other choice in the matter. And now we see the authenticity of the rumors with the band you wear."

I glance at the ring on my finger. It's clearly visible to her. "Very well. My crew will guide you to our ship." I break contact and look at Conrad. "Escort them to the *Queen Rosalind*."

"Yes, sir."

"You attend too," I say to Hadanish when I return to the screen.

"As you order, sir."

≈

≈

≈

Two hours elapse before everyone congregates in the yacht's conference room. Many officers must stand. The defecting officers stare at me when I stride in and seat myself at the table. Captain Anunit, seated, springs to attention and bows in obeisance.

"Sit," I say, embarrassed by the protocol.

Ishtar and Hadanish have grilled the captain and her officers. I'm counting on them to advise me about the defection. I worry the rest of the defensive warships around Larsa will chase them and us at any moment since they must realize the ships are missing in action by now.

As I scan the room, I stare at each officer, searching for the essence of their nature. A few avoid my eyes, unable to withstand my gaze. Others square their shoulders, considering it an honor to be looked upon by someone so noble. I wonder whether they realize who I am, or if they care. They came because of the cause I represent, not because of my personality, my blemishes. How do they know I won't be as despotic and decadent as Shulgi?

I sigh and focus on Ishtar. "What is your assessment?"

"We detect no deception amongst the defectors. They have an immense fear of the consequences of their actions, but I find resolve in them."

I nod. "And their crews?" I scan the room again.

"They vouch for them. Anyone who disagreed could leave."

"So, the fleet at Larsa knows of the desertion? We must prepare for engagement."

Ishtar nods.

Hadanish speaks. "I have delivered those instructions."

"Good." Hadanish is a fine captain. "So, what is the remaining forces' strength? Do we stay and attack or leave?"

"We can defeat the remnant," Hadanish replies. "But is that what we want? We need to hasten to Eridu, don't we?"

"Yes, we do." My thoughts turn to Adala. "But we don't want to be caught in a rear assault."

Anunit coughs to gain attention. "If I may, sir."

I nod.

"You will find little resistance in the fleet's remnant if you attack. They have no hunger for battle."

I glance at Ishtar and raise my eyebrows before returning my regard to Anunit. "Why do you say that?"

"Do you understand why we patrol Larsa? It's the quietest deployment in the whole empire." She bows her head but continues. "Only people wishing a quiet service while they whittle away the days to their retirement or discharge ask for a consignment here."

"Are you one of them?"

She nods and a tinge of red colors her cheeks. "Why play with death?" Her honesty impresses me.

Anunit raises her head, squares her shoulders, and straightens her stance, looking directly into my eyes with her jaw set. "Because we now recognize a fight worth fighting, I will wear this uniform with pride again."

Her declaration frightens and humbles me, but I see the same resolve in each officer. This satisfies me to trust them, but I will act swiftly if there is any deception. "OK. You can take orders from Hadanish. He knows your capabilities, I presume." I glance at him.

Hadanish nods.

Claxons sound battle stations. We tense in anticipation.

"Your services may be required sooner than you thought," I say.

31

KAMIKAZE SHIP

I contact Conrad via the conference room comm unit. "What's happening?"

"Incoming imperial vessels, sir." Conrad's voice stays calm despite the surprise.

"Battle formation?"

"Yes."

I gaze at the assembled officers. "To your ships." My stare lingers on Anunit and the other deserters. "You get to prove your loyalty."

"We won't disappoint you," Anunit replies.

They leave the room. I look at Rickshaw. "You want to fly again?"

"If I didn't have more important duties, I would, but your protection is my priority now."

I smile at him. "Very well." As I recall my first meeting with Rickshaw, I say, "We've come a long way from the labor camp on Helheim."

Rickshaw smiles. "Yes, we have."

"There's work to do." I stand and stride to the helm to join Conrad and receive an update.

Conrad sits in the captain's seat but rises when I approach him. I gesture for him to stay where he is, and we study the main screen in front of us. The ships are still distant. "When will they arrive?"

"Thirty minutes, sir."

"Any attempted communication?"

"Not yet. Do you wish me to try?"

"No, wait for them. Do you have numbers?"

"One battlecruiser, four battleships, ten destroyers, and fifty corvettes."

I contemplate the significance of the numbers. A large contingent of ships approaches us but far less than necessary for an intentional attack. No fighter carrier accompanies them, either. I frown. Unusual. "What do you make of it?" I ask Conrad.

"This is beyond my field of experience, sir. But given the number of vessels defected and our own ships, which they must know are potent, too few approach us to guarantee victory."

"They're my thoughts as well. So, what do they want?" I perch in the first officer's seat and stroke my chin as I consider our options. "Instruct our ships to maneuver to a defensive orientation until we know their intentions."

"Will do." Conrad relays the order to his communications officer.

I sit and wait. The other commanders board their vessels and move them into position. Ishtar's voice frequents the audio channel with instructions to her squadron. My confidence in her increases with each passing day. The psychological scars left by her interrogation still show, but her emotional strength has overcome them to produce a person of significant toughness.

The wait is agonizing, so I stand and pace the helm in the interim until we discover the reason for the advancing fleet's approach.

"Sir, a communication contact is incoming from the imperial battlecruiser." Conrad frowns. "It's a tight beam transmission."

"Accept it and put it on the front screen." I hasten to the first officer's seat again, eager to hear what they want.

An elderly man appears on the screen dressed in an admiral's uniform. His hair is black but gray at the sides, and jowls line his cheeks. His demeanor is one of nervous concern, not the arrogance I was expecting.

"How can I help you, Admiral?" I ask.

The person glances to the side as if checking he is online, then directs his gaze at me. "This is Admiral Jushur. To whom am I speaking?"

"Halwende."

"Sargon!" An expression of awe crosses Jushur's face.

I nod in acknowledgment but am astonished at the speed the word has spread. "What can I do for you?"

"It's what I can do for you. A ship that recently arrived houses an imperial agent with instructions to kidnap you and wipe out as much of your fleet as he can before you destroy him."

My eyebrows shoot up at the intelligence. "Why have you brought so many ships for one person?"

"Developments moved fast on Larsa. When news of the rightful heir to the throne was on the planet, the legislature absolved its link with the empire to join forces with you. Our navy is at your disposal."

"Isn't your allegiance to the imperial navy?"

"We foremost swear our loyalty to Larsa. It's in our constitution."

The knowledge leaves me breathless. I glance at Conrad and watch a smile spread across his face. "This is surprising, sir."

"It sure is." I take a moment to absorb the information I've received before glancing back at Jushur. "So, do you know this spy's identity?"

"Not precisely. He captains a ship. That's what we know at present."

So, he visited our vessel and might have planted a listening device or worse, a bomb. "Conrad, conduct a thorough search of the yacht and check for surveillance devices or bombs."

"But wouldn't that defeat the purpose of kidnapping you if he blew up the ship?" Conrad glances at me with a querying gesture.

"It could be a last resort. If he can't kidnap me, he'll kill me. They may be his instructions. Barak will have decided that would be the best outcome if it's impossible to capture and torture me again."

Conrad leaves to put together the search party.

I draw my attention back to Jushur. "Why shouldn't I consider this a ruse to maneuver within firing distance?"

"We lowered our shields and de-energized our armaments. A risky deception, considering our current location."

My weapons officer confirms Jushur's assertion. I can't fault that logic. So, if a dissident ship's captain occupies the first group, how do I force his move?

After pondering my choices, I decide on a plan of action. I contact Ishtar on a secondary channel.

"Yes, Halwende?"

"I want you to put together a party to board and inspect every ship that surrendered whose captain boarded the *Queen Rosalind.* You're searching for signs the captain could be a spy intent on kidnapping me and causing other damage to the fleet. I'll have Sentinel join you. He's good at sniffing out suspicious things."

Ishtar considers my words. A reserved frown crosses her face. "Will do. You sure this intel is reliable?"

I grin. "Admiral Jushur is listening. Yes, I'm sure."

With a sheepish smile, Ishtar says, "Okay. Send Sentinel across and we'll get started." She breaks contact.

I organize Sentinel and resume my discussion with Jushur. "Can you relay me to the Larsa President so I may confirm your information and understand her intentions?"

"I can. Give me a moment to set up the connection."

"We have time."

Jushur disconnects, and I sit back to await developments. The search will take hours, so I leave the helm and return to my quarters until I'm needed.

I receive news from Jushur confirming a conference call with the Larsa President an hour later. I open the link in the conference room, and the President comes on the screen moments afterward.

"Greetings, Madam President."

"Your Majesty." The President bows her head in obeisance. Her stance is formal.

"Just Halwende will do. Or Sargon."

"Sargon. It's an honor to talk with you, and I wait in anticipation to greet you in person soon."

"The pleasure will be mine on the proper occasion. But your rapid change of allegiance intrigues me."

The President sighs and slumps her shoulders into a more relaxed posture. "To be honest, it'll be a breath of fresh air to deal with an emperor without having to grovel for every leftover that Shulgi deigns to offer us."

I raise my eyebrows. "How do you know I won't be just as demanding?"

She smiles. "I have my sources."

"I'm wondering whether you've considered the implications of your actions. If I fail, Shulgi and Barak will retaliate with the full force of Shulgi's fury."

The President nods. "We are aware of that. We had an animated debate before deciding on this course of action."

"So, your resolution isn't unanimous?"

"It is unanimous. We convinced those wavering of the correctness of this choice. We will suffer the consequences of our decision if you fail to overthrow Shulgi."

"Before I do that, I must save Queen Adala from his clutches."

The President frowns. "Who is Queen Adala?"

"She's the Queen of Helheim, otherwise known as Ur, and someone of significance to me."

"Ur is a mythical place."

"I assure you it's real."

"Our entire fleet is at your disposal."

"So, I can trust Admiral Jushur?"

"Yes. I guarantee his dedication. He has no love for Emperor Shulgi or General Barak."

"Well, I thank you for your support. Next time, I hope it will be under less formal–"

I break off as the ship's claxons blare and the lights redden to general alert.

My eyes shoot up, attentive and confused. "I must go," I shout over the noise.

The President nods. "Until we meet again. Use Admiral Jushur as you need."

I break contact and rush to the conference room door in search of Conrad. When I find him, I ask, "What's happening?"

"A destroyer has powered up its drives and is headed our way at maximal thrust, sir. It intends to ram us."

"Can't we fire on it?"

Conrad blushes. "Our cannons were on standby. They won't be ready in time."

I stare at him. "Yes, they will." With no further discussion, I rush to the captain's chair and bring up the weapons screen familiar to me, punching instructions into it for the main maser cannon. "Connect me with that ship," I order the communications officer.

A captain's face shows moments later. Hate flows from it as his eyes glare through the space between us. "Your time is up, Halwende. You will never achieve your desires, and you'll never see your queen again."

I glance at the weapons screen. A few more seconds. "Please break off this futile attack. You'll kill every man and woman on your ship for your fanatical beliefs."

He gives a manic laugh. "They volunteered. They detest what you represent as much as I do."

The destroyer will soon be upon my yacht. Since our drives are off, we have no maneuverability to avoid the collision. To make his point, our ship rocks from direct hits by his maser cannons. At least our shields are up, the blows inflicting only minor damage to the ship.

I glance at the weapons screen again and see my cannon is ready. With one last gaze at the deranged captain, I sigh. "As you wish." I press the fire button.

A flash of maser energy blasts from our cannon with the intensity of a solar eruption. The people at the helm turn and stare at me in disbelief since they thought we had no weapons available. The kamikaze ship's shields hold for a few seconds. Then we witness the ship disintegrate into constituent particles.

MY EYES GAZE into the vacuum of space where the suicidal ship once flew. Sadness overcomes me as I mourn the lives lost in one fraction of a second and feel for the families that they leave behind. Disengaging the flerovium-powered part of the maser cannon circuit, I pack the screen away and notice the other officers. "As you were."

As if waking from a trance, the officers at the helm continue their activities.

"That was impressive," Conrad says.

I gaze at him with still sorrowful eyes. "Too many people lost their lives." I sigh. "Continue communicating with Admiral Jushur and have Ishtar and Sentinel include them in their inspections before we consider how to arrange this bedraggled bunch of ships into a formation to travel to Eridu. I wish to be alone." I rise and retire to my cabin. It's too large for one person, but I want to lose myself in it for now.

The door chime sounds, disturbing my contemplation. I frown, not expecting interruptions. Despite wanting to ignore it, I say, "Enter."

The door opens and Lilith stands just outside, her expression pensive. "May I speak with you?"

I nod. "Sure."

She steps into my cabin and the door closes. I gesture for her to sit in the chair next to me. "What's on your mind?"

"That was a narrow escape," she says as she sits.

With a brief chuckle at her understatement, I lean back and

inspect the ceiling before I close them. "You could say that. Not my worst, though."

"My father won't give up, you know."

My eyes open and I again straighten and gaze at Lilith. "No, he won't. Nor will Barak." I search her eyes. "Why are you here?"

"To offer my help in whatever way I can. I know many of Father's secrets and the shortcomings of the Imperial Palace security. More than he thinks I do."

"Didn't stop us from getting caught."

Lilith smiles. "No, it didn't. That was foolish of me."

"Once we defeat Shulgi's forces, we should overthrow him with little effort."

With a shake of her head, Lilith says, "You're wrong. He won't surrender. He has Queen Adala, and he will use her against you. And he will kill her if it means keeping his emperorship. Or he might kill her anyway, out of spite. I suspect his original intentions are to marry her to annex the Helheim kingdom without battle. But if that isn't possible, he'll slay her. His lust for power is insatiable."

"I do not forget this." I frown but then clench my jaw in resolve as my eyes wander to the window on the ship's side. "Events will transpire fast when we reach Eridu." I again lock my attention on Lilith. "But first, tell me of these security shortcomings you have located."

"The passage we used is not the only secret passageway in the palace. There are many I have discovered during my lonely wanderings through its corridors."

"Wouldn't Shulgi have this knowledge also?"

"He doesn't need to sneak through the palace. Since he never grew up there, he's unaware of its secrets. I shall tell you of these tunnels, and you can decide how to use them in your favor."

Lilith discloses her secrets, each one more astounding than the next. I find it incomprehensible that the palace's defenses have such serious shortcomings. And yet, according to Lilith, they do. As she divulges her information, a plan takes form in my mind that fills in the gaps in the scheme I had already fashioned. Each fresh development creates a new shell of complexity for the outcome.

Larsa's defection and its military hardware will also improve my standing as we move forward. For the first time, I smell victory.

But first, we must organize the flotilla into a disciplined fleet for the upcoming battle.

32

LET THE SLAUGHTER BEGIN

Admiral Jushur sits opposite me with Ishtar and Sentinel in the conference room as we complete our formations for the flight to Eridu. Captain Anunit is present for the discussions, too. Rickshaw, Jacques, and Lombard stand to the side as my constant protectors. Their task is, to an extent, symbolic because of the personal force shield I now constantly wear, but knowing they regard it as a special honor is enough for me. Besides, I may need their services before I achieve my destiny.

"Are we in agreement?" I scan those at the table for any dissent. The odd fleeting moment of trepidation crosses their faces as they contemplate the tasks ahead, but they nod and mutter their assent to the proposal.

"I wish we had more current information on the strength of Barak's forces around Eridu," Ishtar says. "We'd know what to expect when we arrive."

"You still have lingering doubts, then?" I ask.

"No. The plan is sound. I'd just be more comfortable knowing what we will face when we get there."

I laugh at the thought. "Expect the worst. Barak will concentrate his resources for this moment. He knows he can't afford to lose this battle. He intends only one victor, and the way he guarantees that the winner will be him is to use his entire force. He always has the leverage of Adala if he sees events going against him."

"How will you prevent Queen Adala from being used by Shulgi as a pawn in this deadly game?" Sentinel asks, his frown highlighting his concern for his queen's safety.

"I can't. She has her role to play before this war ends. Whatever happens, my goal is to secure Adala's freedom."

"She will give up her security if the alternative is your death."

"Then we must make sure I live." I smile, the warmth of friendship flowing between us as I study Sentinel's eyes.

I glance around the room one last time, inviting anyone to comment before the meeting ends, but they stay silent. "Let's prepare for our transfer to Eridu."

I stand, and those assembled copy me. They move out, and those heading for other ships withdraw to their shuttles to transport them there.

Sentinel hangs back. I sense he wishes to talk to me in private, so I stay with him and raise my eyebrows in query once the others have left.

"You haven't told us your entire plan, have you." Sentinel's tone signifies the words are a statement, not a question.

With a smile, I say, "No, I haven't. You have enough responsibilities for now."

He nods. "Whatever schemes you weave, you will need my help before this rescue ends. Please seek it. Queen Adala is my responsibility to protect. The duty I neglected."

I pat his shoulder. "I will ask. Although you may regret your offer when the occasion comes."

Sentinel grunts and leaves. I watch him disappear through the doorway as my thoughts turn to the dangers before us.

Our fleet takes another day to complete their preparations. During that time, I make a quick trip to the planet and the ruling authorities there to confirm their loyalty to me and the uncertainties ahead. Confident of their allegiance, I return to the *Queen Rosalind* and wait to leave. Our arrangements made, we enter hyperspace headed for Eridu, and whatever fate awaits us there.

WHEN WE ARRIVE in Eridu space, warships fill it. I had not realized Shulgi and Barak had accumulated such a massive navy. The shock nearly breaks my resolve. The expressions of Admiral Jushur and the other Larsa commanders on the main screen mirror my trepidation. But there is no going back now.

"Battle formations," I announce to the others with a confidence I do not feel.

The Larsa ships form into their squadrons and attack positions. The fighters from our accompanying fighter carriers dart out and line up, ready for the order to go ahead.

A communications ping comes through, and I instruct the officer to place it on the main screen.

Barak's smiling face looms before me, his confidence and menace plain. "About time you came. I was thinking you were going to abandon your queen. I see you've brought a gang of deluded followers, too. We will attend to their leader when this fantasy ends."

"You sure you've got enough ships?" I stay calm as I stare back at him.

"You're not getting away from me this time."

"That's what you said last time. And yet, here I am."

A slight doubt flashes across Barak's expression before he masks it again. "I recognize your tricks now, Halwende. You're more formidable than I ever imagined. It's a pity we're on opposite sides."

I give a grim smile. Barak doesn't know my true identity yet. Not that it will matter. I'm sure Shulgi will want me executed even more when he finds out. "So, how do you propose we play this?"

Barak bursts out laughing. "I'm glad you see this as a game."

With a disdainful glare, I say, "I play no game. You've caused enough damage. It's time we disposed of you."

"Well then, let the slaughter begin." Barak breaks the communication.

I continue staring at the now blank screen. "Yes, let it begin," I whisper as I mourn in advance the people whose lives we commit to their deaths.

33

NEGOTIATION

I contact Ishtar once my focus returns to the upcoming battle. "Prepare to strike with the Orion formation."

"This is it then," Ishtar says, her tone pensive.

I sigh. "Yes, we fight. Barak won't negotiate. He believes he's more powerful, so why should he?"

"He outnumbers us four to one."

"We must engage him, regardless."

"What will you do while we attack?"

"Devise a way to rescue Adala."

A tinge of concern crosses Ishtar's face. "Do nothing rash. We can't afford to lose you."

"When have I ever done anything rash?"

Ishtar raises her eyebrows.

"You need to get to work. I'll watch how things develop."

She nods and cuts the link.

I contact Admiral Jushur to tell him to take control of his fleet and attack as best he can but stay segregated from Barak's armada. I don't want his people getting killed by friendly fire from Ishtar.

With my instructions delivered, I sit in the captain's chair to watch the battle unfold. Admiral Jushur lines up his fleet into battle groups facing the enemy while Ishtar's ships move into position. My forces appear paltry compared to the armada Barak assembles into its attack formations. Fighters from both sides zoom in every direction, mosquitoes buzzing, ready to assail each other.

Our ships advance, and Barak orders a third of his to do likewise. They engage in battle, pounding each other's hulls with maser fire, weakening the shields until, within firing distance, both fleets unleash their missiles at each other. The ships with shields of insufficient strength buckle and explode into myriad fragments. The losses look similar on both sides, but Barak's superior numbers never place the outcome in doubt. Our ships retreat to regroup.

Once Admiral Jushur's ships are out of the way, Ishtar discharges the firepower of the Orion maser array and gouges a swarth of destruction through Barak's fleet. She damages or destroys more ships than Admiral Jushur did in one fell swoop of the beam. The slaughter cuts through me as I sit and watch. Why must it come to this? Ishtar adjusts her aim and scours another line of carnage through the enemy fleet, starting to even up the odds.

"Sir, a communication is coming from the planet," my comm's officer says.

My attention redirects to the officer. A sense of portent engulfs me. "Put it on the screen."

The image changes from the battle to Shulgi's face. His visage still displays confidence, but I see beads of sweat on his forehead. I wait for him to start the conversation.

"What is this weapon you own?" Shulgi asks. "Where did you source such firepower? On Helheim?"

I stare at him but stay silent, as I have no time or wish to answer the question. Let him wonder where I sourced it or if I have similar weapons even more deadly than Orion. My thoughts go back to when I used the full destructive power of the flerovium crystal as a weapon. But I have vowed never to use it again, regardless of how dreadful things turn out for us. It is a weapon of such potency I can't let it proliferate beyond my knowledge.

When I don't respond, Shulgi's confidence wavers. He wipes his forehead despite knowing it shows weakness. "That isn't what I wish to discuss. You are to surrender at once."

I smirk. "Why would I do that?"

Shulgi grins back. Seconds later, two guards shove Adala into the frame. She looks distraught, and she's been crying. She looks like she hasn't slept in days.

My jaw clenches as I glare at Shulgi.

"Or you will force me to harm your precious queen."

My heart stops beating as scenes of my life being torn apart flash past me. "Release her," I demand.

"Oh, I doubt that. Now surrender, or I'll show you what I intend doing to her in front of you."

"Don't do it," Adala shouts at me, her eyes pleading, and yet her immense love flows through to me.

One guard back slaps her on her cheek and nose, a red mark developing where he connected. Adala's head drops, and a trickle of blood escapes from a nostril.

"It gave me such pleasure ordering your family's execution. I have other plans for her but don't think I won't inflict the same fate on Queen Adala if you continue with this charade."

I stare at Adala and know what I must do. There is no other choice. I can't allow both bloodlines to end. How will I get out of this? I don't know, but Adala must stay alive. "I will surrender myself to you if you release Queen Adala."

"No!" Adala struggles but remains clamped between her guards.

A smug smile of victory spreads across Shulgi's face. "Call off your attack now."

"We will both stop our fighting. When we make the exchange, my forces will leave."

"How will I know you won't start attacking again?"

I raise an eyebrow. I could ask Shulgi the same question. "You have my word. I'll instruct my people to obey my wishes. Give me an hour to organize matters here and transfer to the surface by shuttle. I expect you to have Adala ready to leave when I contact you."

"Agreed."

I break the communication and lean back in my chair, closing my eyes as I despair of my plans. But Shulgi will always hold the upper hand with Adala in his custody. I see the entire crew at the helm staring at me when I open my eyes again. Disbelief and shock pour through to me. I sigh. "This is the only way." The mass of the galaxy weighs heavily on my shoulders as I prepare for my departure. "Get Ishtar and Admiral Jushur on the screen," I order the comms officer.

She hesitates for a fraction of a second and then nods and turns to obey.

They both appear on the screen a few seconds later.

"Please disengage your fighting," I order.

"What?" they both blurt.

"I've negotiated with Shulgi for Queen Adala's release. One condition is we both stop fighting for the time being."

"And the other conditions?" Ishtar asks, suspicion dripping from her voice.

"I surrender myself to him."

"You can't do that," Ishtar says. "He'll kill you." She frowns. "Does he know who you are?"

"Not yet."

"How can you cede to him? Your bloodline will cease if he kills you."

"That is why Adala must live." I give an enigmatic grin. "Besides, I must descend to the planet to achieve my goal."

"Like what?"

"Don't worry. You'll find out."

Ishtar shakes her head. I can tell she's not happy, but there's nothing she can do to stop me.

I break contact and see them cease fighting minutes later. Barak's forces cease and retreat, too, to organize into new groupings to account for their losses.

"Take command," I tell Conrad as I rise from my chair.

Conrad nods and then says, "Sir, do you trust this Shulgi?"

"No, I don't. That's why you must restart the engagement if things go wrong. Look after Adala for me."

Conrad stands to attention. "I will, sir."

I make my way to my quarters and prepare to leave.

The door chimes. Zabada enters when I accept, and the door opens. He approaches me with a troubled face.

"What is it?" I ask.

"This is a dangerous course of action you take."

"It is the only one available. I must resolve this deadlock and save Adala."

"So, you intend to announce your rightful claim to the throne?"

"Yes. Shulgi will find out eventually. I may as well be the one to inform him."

Zabada stares at me. "I can't say I'm happy with your decision, but you have made it. We must rely on the vagaries of chance for the outcome."

I smile. "I don't propose placing my life in the vagaries of chance."

Zabada crosses to me and hugs me, slapping my shoulder. "God-speed then."

34

KING OF RIGEL

As I hurry to board my shuttle to ferry me to the planet, a thousand thoughts rush through my head. Uppermost is the high probability of treachery on Shulgi's part. There is no guarantee he will release Adala or refrain from continuing the battle once he has me in his clutches. Regardless, I must do what I believe is right.

A familiar figure stands in front of the hatch as I arrive at the shuttle. Sentinel rests against the hull with his arms crossed, an enigmatic smile on his face. "Where do you think you're going?" he asks as I near him.

"To get Adala released." I prefer to avoid conversation with Sentinel, knowing where it will lead, but he intervenes between me and where I wish to go.

"Without me?" Sentinel raises an eyebrow.

"It's too dangerous. You need to stop here and help Adala when she returns."

"And who's going to protect you?"

"We are," Rickshaw says from behind me. He stands with my other two bodyguards.

I turn to gaze at him. "You must stay too."

"Not happening," Rickshaw says.

"You're meant to obey me."

"Not today. Not when you decide to do foolish things to get yourself killed needlessly."

I stare at him in frustration and back at Sentinel. They stand resolute in their determination to protect me and risk their lives. I throw my hands in the air. "Very well then. Let's move."

Sentinel steps aside and allows me to enter the shuttle first. He falls in behind me, and my guards bring up the rear. We strap in and I power up the ship, exiting the yacht moments later to descend to the distant planet and my destiny.

An hour elapses before we approach Eridu's atmosphere. After permission to land, I direct the vessel to the landing pad near the palace. Barak's soldiers with heavy weapons surround the shuttle in case I decide to leave, I presume.

I place a call through to Shulgi and wait. His visage covers the screen a minute later. "You've arranged a reception party," I say, noting the triumph on his face.

"You're not eluding my clutches this time."

"If you fulfill your side of the bargain, I won't resist."

"There's been a change of plans. Now that you can't escape, Adala is to remain safe with me. She doesn't need to be released."

I grit my teeth. I half suspected and planned on this happening. But I had hoped Shulgi would surprise me and release her. "So, we do this the hard way. I will order resumption of hostilities until you fulfill your commitment."

Shulgi gives a sinister grin. "We've jammed your communications off-plant. You can't reach your fleet."

"That's why they'll start, regardless, if they don't hear from me within the agreed time."

"My navy is dispensable now that I have you. I'm sure your people will desist with a few well-placed threats."

I sigh. "Have it your own way, then." I break contact. And prepare to leave.

"You're not going out there?" Rickshaw asks with disbelief.

"Yes." I smile. "And you're staying here until I've left. Sentinel knows what he must do, and so do you. Now make yourselves scarce until I leave."

I sense I'm a lamb heading to the slaughter. With a new uniform and my ring of office on my finger, I stand before Sentinel one last time. "Farewell, my friend."

Uncharacteristic emotion crosses Sentinel's face as he stares into my eyes. "You are a dear friend. Until we meet again." He steps forward and hugs me. We both slap each other on the back before releasing our hold.

I take a deep breath and head for the airlock while the others hide. Once the hatch is open, I step out into glaring sunlight and soldiers with maser rifles pointed at me. I notice several hesitate in their duty when they spy the royal ring, but they steel themselves straight away. The design on the bezel is unmistakable to anyone on Eridu. I make it easy and walk forward.

The captain approaches and says, "Follow me."

I nod and step to his lead as he marches me into the palace grounds. I steal one last glance behind me before the shuttle disappears from sight, hoping they don't discover Sentinel and the others' presence before they can sneak away.

The soldiers show me to the throne room. It is empty. I walk up to the throne and stand before it, waiting for whatever happens next.

Five minutes later, Shulgi and Barak appear from behind the throne. Shulgi sits on the throne, and Barak stands to the side.

"You're finally in my clutches," Shulgi says, ogling me like a miser who's found a lost coin.

"You've brought your lap dog with you, I see." I glance at Barak, who glowers at me, before returning my attention to Shulgi.

Shulgi laughs. "Oh, you're good." He stops and glares. "But I have something much more enjoyable for our entertainment." He snaps his fingers. "Bring her forward."

Moments later, two guards shove Adala from the behind-throne entrance. My heart breaks as I glimpse her tormented face. Despite being the jewel she is to Shulgi, he's treated her with disrespect. She stands with disheveled dress and hair, and tears blotch her complexion. I need every ounce of strength to stop myself from rushing to her. The soldiers push her next to the throne. She keeps her head bowed as if unable to look me in the eye.

"I thought it my duty to have Queen Adala present to watch your humiliation and execution," Shulgi says. "I have this joyous occasion on planetary holo-vision."

"No!" Adala shouts. She raises her head and looks at me. "You shouldn't have come."

Her despair crushes me, but I must bring my destiny to its resolution. I have shown all but one of my cards, and now I announce my last. Squaring my shoulders and staring at Shulgi, I speak with an air of authority that only the empire's ring can give. "You dare execute the King of Rigel?"

Shulgi jumps in surprise, and Barak does too. Adala looks up again in shock.

"What nonsense is this?" Shulgi asks.

"The true King of Rigel possesses the ring of the Rigel Empire, and I don't see it on your finger."

"They lost that ring years ago."

"They didn't lose it. They hid it." I raise my hand, making sure Shulgi and the cameras relaying this scene capture the insignia. "And I now wear it. I, Sargon, direct descendent of Dumuzid, son of Alalgar, come to reclaim the throne that is mine."

Shulgi gapes at me in shock.

No one moves, although the guards look confused, as does Adala.

Shulgi recovers sufficiently to remember the cameras. He motions to cut the transmission of the proceedings.

"Oh, you're very good," he says with another laugh, although this one seems nervous. "I executed every royal child. None remained." He projects his words with confidence, but I see the doubt in his eyes.

"You are wrong. They hid one and raised him in secrecy. I know you always sensed danger whenever you encountered me. Why else go to such lengths to rid yourself of me?"

Blotches of red and purple appear on Shulgi's face as he realizes his miscalculation. He explodes in rage. "Take him to the cells," he yells. "Him and her both." The guards stay motionless. "Now!"

Released from the trance I wove on them, the soldiers move me away, but less roughly than usual. I lose sight of Adala as I leave the throne room but hope they incarcerate her near me. At least we will be together for whatever comes next.

The guards are definitely treating me with more respect than before my announcement. After my performance in the throne room, they are unsure who to follow. I don't intend to make their job difficult, though. I walk where they instruct me as we descend to the prison cells of the palace. After a time, they bring me to a cell with better facilities than I've enjoyed on earlier occasions. I enter and they activate the force field to imprison me, but I detect a hint of fear in their eyes when I glance at them.

They don't lead Adala to the same jail, so I must tolerate our separation for a while longer. It would have been undignified if Shulgi had sent her to these cells, unsuited for royalty.

While I wait, I sit, brushing my thumb across the bezel of my ring, wondering if its significance is worth its constituent materials. To my surprise, the rubbing highlights the Stars of Orion, their flerovium facets illuminating in the dim light. I wonder why they haven't tried removing the ring from my finger.

An hour later, a commotion makes its way toward me as Barak enters the prison. He gets the guard to lower the force field and strides into the cell. Before I can make any comment, he peppers me with punches. I have no means of self-defense apart from throwing my arm up to protect my face. He then concentrates on my body until I fall to the floor, and he completes his battering with kicks.

"Whether or not you're king, I don't know. But we'll execute you, regardless. I've had enough of your interference."

I try to smile, but the pain shapes it into a ghastly grimace. "You bet on the wrong side."

My insolence rewards me with several more blows before Barak leaves.

To my surprise, I have managed to protect my eyes from damage. As I gaze after Barak, the guard stares at me. He's afraid of me.

Once Barak vacates the prison, the guard comes over and helps me into a chair again. I cry out in pain from the effort, and he asks if I need the infirmary.

With a shake of my head, I say, "I doubt you'll get permission."

He stands before me, uncertain what to do.

"Go do your duty," I tell him. "I'll remember your kindness."

He nods and retreats, raising the force field afterward.

35

REVOLT

What feels like hours elapse as I contemplate what to do. No sound penetrates the cell from the world above me. The pain from my wounds subsides as I ease into an agonizing plod around the confined space. The guard passes my cell on his regular rounds. He glances into it, his nervousness increasing on each round.

The next time I see him, he stops and faces me.

I raise my eyebrows and wonder what's changed.

"The city is in an uproar," he says.

The news both frightens me and gives me hope. "Is there fighting?"

"Not yet. But it comes."

I nod, wondering if the rioting is a spontaneous response or whether the Resistance has orchestrated it. "Is anyone attacking the palace?"

He shakes his head and walks away.

I continue pacing my confined space. It is unlikely Sentinel has any part in organizing the disturbance, but he must move soon.

The noise of fighting enters the prison shortly afterward and gets closer. I sit and wait for whatever the outcome will be. As the reverberations of maser fire and shouts approach the cellblock doors, my confidence soars.

The guard comes again. "Please don't let them kill me. I'm brave and loyal." He's panicking.

"You're just doing your duty. You've treated me well. I'll tell the soldiers to spare you if they reach us."

Not long afterward, the prison entrance blasts open as Resistance fighters burst into the room. Sentinel spots me and rushes to my cell. He can't raise the force field without the combination, so he pulls the guard over to do the task. The guard shakes as he punches the code.

"Don't harm him," I tell Sentinel and those nearby when I step from it. "Much struggle?"

"Enough." Sentinel's face is grim. His eyes dart to the other cells. "Queen Adala?"

"Not here. She's probably being held in the palace proper. We can't move in and rescue her yet. We need to break Shulgi's hold on the military. What's happening off-planet?"

"The enemy started offensive maneuvers as soon as you were in their clutches. Ishtar is slicing through them. The latest news I have is mass defections. Although, if they're caught by the others, they attack them."

The noise of battle abates, and Rickshaw, Jaques, and Lombard barge into the room, maser rifles ready for action.

"Whoa, Rickshaw," I say, a smile plastered across my face. "Point that somewhere else."

Rickshaw returns the grin. "Just doing my job, sir. Now, if you don't mind following us, we'll go."

"We can't leave without Queen Adala," Sentinel reminds everyone.

"No, we can't," I say. "We'll make a strategic retreat and regroup. Lilith's information should give entry to where she's being held." I allow Rickshaw and my other guards to surround me while we escape through the corridor out of the prison. "I must rally our forces and the planet first. Let them know I'm alive and relying on them."

Sentinel nods. "This way then."

We retrace the steps my rescue team made releasing me and leave the confines of the palace soon afterward, the breeze of the open-air welcoming to my senses. Flashes of light sparkle above us from the raging battle in space. I only hope the casualty load is minimal for us.

We race to a scooter that whisks us away to field headquarters to rally and assemble our forces for an earnest assault on the palace.

"Over here," Lilith says, motioning me to her.

I comply but raise my eyebrows. "What are you doing here?"

Lilith grins and glances at Sentinel before returning her attention to me. "Making sure you get the correct coverage when you announce your rescue to the citizens of Eridu."

I shake my head, thinking she wants to stay near Sentinel despite the danger. He casts a sheepish but respectful grin toward Lilith when I glance his way. By a mammoth effort, she has assembled a field holo-broadcast studio nearby, and we go to it.

"You can make a speech whenever you want," Lilith says. "We can break into the public transmissions and publicize your return."

Her suggestion is an excellent idea, and I prepare for my holo-cast. She organizes the technicians and counts me in moments later.

When the on-air light shines, I straighten my stance and say, "Citizens of Eridu, you received a broadcast earlier that showed Emperor Shulgi gloating over my capture. I announce I am no longer a prisoner of his, thanks to the bravery of the forces resisting his tyranny. I declare my rightful claim to the Rigel throne as King Sargon of Rigel, direct descendent of Dumuzid, son of King Alalgar of Rigel, and I urge you to renounce your allegiance to Shulgi and support me in overthrowing the usurper from my throne, your throne, so you can exercise your constitutional rights again. Help me in any way you can."

"Long live the King," soldiers shout behind me, to my surprise. The responsibility for so many lives humbles me.

I pace from the studio and over to Sentinel. "Let's assemble our forces to go back."

"You're not coming," Sentinel says, waving me away.

I stop what I'm doing and stand straight with my fists on my hips.

"Try stopping me. I have a duty to rescue Adala as much as you do. Besides, you'll just make a mess of it like last time."

Sentinel raises his eyebrows. "Really? I recall you were the one getting poisoned."

"And they shot you."

"Gentlemen," Lilith intervenes, "if you've finished comparing scars, we have work to do."

She's right, and I could burst out laughing if our task wasn't pressing on us. Before we can continue, we hear a buzzing noise and a swarm of gunships speed over the horizon toward us. As we react, a dozen missiles fire at us.

Rickshaw grabs my arm in a vice-like grip and drags me to a portable bunker with the other guards behind me, protecting me from the blast and resulting shrapnel. His strength astounds me. Massive explosions rock the shelter as we enter it. Sentinel and Lilith run close behind us. Moments later, I hear return fire from our forces, causing reciprocal bombardments on the attackers. The attack and counterattack continue for ten minutes before the guns are silenced, allowing us to peek our heads out again to survey the damage.

I pause at the bunker entrance in silence and gaze at the landscape. I can't help but compare it with the one I gazed upon many years ago. Now it's fading from my memory. Most of our fortifications still stand, and smoking gunships lie broken in the distance. The contrast in my countenance is palpable. I sense a hope I haven't felt before today. It's time for us to finish this war.

36

STORMING THE PALACE

Sentinel brings in more recruits to help storm the palace and free Adala from Shulgi's clutches, ridding the kingdom of his rule for good. A powerful company of soldiers assembles in readiness for my command.

We receive several updates from Ishtar as we prepare our forces. Her grin projects from the screen. She is enjoying herself despite reporting significant losses. With the might of the Orion weapon, she has the edge, though. She reports her steady progress in overcoming Barak's navy. I leave the space-based fighting in Ishtar's capable hands while we concentrate on rescuing Adala.

After an hour, we approach another secret entry to the palace compound known to Lilith. We have cause to be grateful for the isolated childhood that allowed her to discover so many palace secrets.

Once the entrance opens, we rush into the concealed tunnel, leaving a large contingent of soldiers outside to protect our flank and means of escape if need be. Unlike the other subway I traversed, this one is huge, wide enough to fit six adults across without interference. They must have used it for transporting loads of materials into the palace in earlier times.

Our footsteps echo as we march along the shaft, maser rifles ready for attack. Twenty minutes pass before we reach the tunnel's exit inside the palace grounds. I don't know what to expect when we open the paneling, but we will fight to the death to achieve our goal.

I call a halt and rally the team just before the doorway. They stamp their feet, keen to begin their assault but listen as I give last-minute instructions and encouragement to them. They nod and grin with determination when I finish my speech by turning to Sentinel and saying, "Let's go rescue our Queen."

He gives a satisfied smile. "Let's."

I stride to the opening mechanism and slam my palm against the pad. It lights up and, after a slight hesitation, releases the lock, activating the opener motor. The noise reverberates through the shaft as the seldom-used hinges scream in protest. Once enough room is available, we stream into the palace grounds and the bright sunlight outside the tunnel. The troopers fan out, ready to fight as we move forward and approach the palace proper.

Maser beams bombard us moments later, forcing us to shelter behind a building. When I look through the window, I see gardening tools and other maintenance and landscaping implements. My soldiers locate the direction of the maser attack and fire back in retaliation. I do not know how successful they are, but the enemy pin us down until we can remove the imminent threat.

"This is unacceptable," Sentinel blurts out after several minutes. "They will cut off our rear and enjoy slaughtering us unless we do something."

I agree but have no alternative strategy to suggest.

"Sir," Rickshaw says to grab my attention. "May I suggest I unblock the path for us?" He displays a miniature missile launcher in his palm.

"Where'd you get that?" My eyes boggle to see the deadly weapon.

"One of the many gadgets I now carry."

I glance at Sentinel, and he shrugs. "Go for it, but don't sacrifice yourself. I've become attached to your company."

Rickshaw creeps around the corner of the building out of sight. I lean against the wall, dreading the familiar barrage of maser fire and the scream of death when they detect Rickshaw's presence. Too many brave people are risking their lives for my sake. It is not acceptable, but I know it's necessary.

My fellow soldiers hazard rapid glances around the corner, firing a maser burst to distract the palace guard from Rickshaw's movements. One is unfortunate and is hit, his arm dismembered at the shoulder and the limb falling to the ground. He tumbles back in agony as blood spills from him. Our medic jumps into action to staunch the bleeding. The soldier will live, but he has finished his military life. The metallic stench of blood lingers in the air, and the smell opens the floodgate to the rising anger within me. This fighting and the devastation playing out in space above us are so unnecessary. Am I doing the right thing? I do not know, but as my thoughts return to the slaughter Barak inflicted on the defenseless civilians above Helheim's skies, my resolve returns.

While these images pass through me, a massive explosion reverberates from the palace. When I chance a peek around the corner, smoke billows from a gaping hole in the wall. Moments later, more fire chases Rickshaw to the protective cover of the building, a wide grin splitting his face.

"That should stir things up," he says.

I shake my head. "We wanted to get inside without attracting too much notice."

Sentinel grabs my attention. "It'll help us. Follow me." He winks. "You're not the only one Lilith divulged the palace's secrets to."

We prepare to move out with Sentinel in the lead. At his suggestion, we move in groups of three to decrease the chance of maser fire striking us, as it could if we moved as a larger group. Sentinel leads the first party, which dashes across the enclosure to another walled defensive location. It abuts the palace compound wall but encircles a courtyard, too.

I watch as he examines the far barrier. He finds what he's looking for and turns to me, making hand signals for me to come over next. I nod and prepare to move with Rickshaw, Jacques, and Lombard. That makes four, but they refuse to be separated from me. We brace ourselves and dash from our shelter.

Maser fire surrounds us as we weave and dodge to avoid being hit. Our luck lasts, and our safety is in reaching distance when I hear, "Ouch!" behind me. None of us stops running until we are under cover again. I survey my contingent and find Lombard holding his arm, blood seeping from around his hand, covering a maser injury.

He glances at me. "Just a flesh wound, sir. I'm still fit to continue."

I am skeptical as I stare at him, but we can't leave him here.

The rest of our group rushes over without further injury. One soldier slaps a plastic explosive on the surface, and we shelter behind a narrow projection and cover our ears as he detonates the charge. Slabs of brickwork fly past, followed by grit and dust, as the blast does its job. I peek around the corner and see that a section of the wall has collapsed, giving us entry to the inner palace compound gardens. With guns ready, we charge through and find shelter against the palace building, although it offers no protection from our rear. Sentinel posts a rearguard to defend us from any surprise attack.

A doorway stands in front of us. I have no inkling of where it leads, but we must enter it to protect us from an outside assault. Sentinel motions two soldiers to advance and explore how safe it is inside. They creep forward. One tries to open the door, but it's locked. He uses his maser to blast the lock and pushes the barrier open with ease. After waiting several seconds, they both rush through and disappear.

A minute later, we hear, "It's safe," from behind the doorway. We dash in and secure the door with whatever furniture we can muster. It won't stop entry for long, but it will impede anyone following us.

"Where to now?" Sentinel asks.

I retrieve the tablet containing a map of the palace grounds from my pocket and locate our position. "Lilith thought they'd hold Adala in the imperial palace east wing instead of the prison. It's just as secure and more comfortable — more befitting a queen. Unlike where he held me in my tenure of imprisonment."

"We need to cross the internal patio or traverse the palace corridors."

"Should have broken in closer," Sentinel says as he glances up from the tablet.

I shrug but agree with him. We've made our task more onerous and dangerous by entering the palace where we did. "We can't change that now. Using the courtyard exposes us. It's too great a risk."

"We use the passageways then. Lead the way."

Once I gain my bearings, I point in the direction we must take and start creeping through the passages, keeping to the shadows where we can. We meet no one as we progress, giving me an odd premonition, but we continue. After ten minutes, we reach a junction. A door blocks our leftward path, but the corridor on our right is straightforward and allows us to pursue our quest around the palace building perimeter to the east wing.

I glance at Sentinel a few times. The lack of resistance unnerves me. Sentinel often scans our rear as if he is having the same thoughts. Regardless, we keep going through to our goal until the corridor leads to a large foyer. At significant risk, we must cross it to the far side to continue our journey. Apart from our exit, two other corridors lead from the open space. We signal to rush across on my count. I raise my hand with three fingers extended, bending each one a second until I complete the countdown, and we run.

"You took your time," Barak says as he steps out from a corridor. Guards stream from the other corridors and soon surround us.

WE BRAKE when we see the maser muzzles pointed at us, herding us into a tight group. I should have suspected a trap when I noted the lack of resistance, but hindsight is irrelevant now. The soldiers in my possie, particularly Rickshaw, move to take a stand, but they'll just get themselves killed. "Surrender," I say to them. I turn my attention to Barak. "I will arrest you once I rescue Queen Adala."

After containing his boisterous laughter, Barak says, "You are a comedian. How do you intend to achieve that feat?"

That's a good question. I can't give the answer, but I know it lies somewhere in my subconscious if only I can retrieve it. My naivety angers me, and that anger sprouts a surge of power I haven't felt before. When I glance at my ring, it glows a brilliant blue. Glancing up again, I notice Barak and his soldiers staring at it, and then me.

Fear blossoms in Barak's eyes. "Shoot them," he orders.

I stiffen to prepare for my imminent death, drawing the others near me in my thoughts, especially Sentinel and Rickshaw.

Recovering from my shock, I shout, "Move!"

Rickshaw, Jacques, and Lombard surround me as we rush toward the exit corridor. As we run, we fire shots at Barak's troops, who shoot back, hitting and killing several of my group. Half my team lie dead or moaning on the floor of the foyer before we reach the doorway. But there is no time to return and tend to their wounds.

With me in the center, Sentinel and the others rush through the corridor, firing shots as we go. Sentinel throws a grenade behind us as we round a bend, a deafening explosion collapsing the passageway, preventing Barak from following us from that direction.

As we push forward, I stare at my ring, wondering what the luminescence means since we can only attribute our luck to the ring's blue glow and the fear it inflicted in Barak.

One thing the ambush confirmed is that we are moving the right way to locate Adala. Barak knows that I seek her and will do what he must to prevent me from achieving my goal. As if Barak reads my thoughts, a huge explosion blasts the wall away just ahead. Debris flies toward us, but we avoid all but the smallest of fragments. Dust clogs our throats as we cough the particles out.

We come to a halt, confused about whether to continue forward or find another way. We will meet an attack as we navigate the opening. I consult my tablet for an alternative route. "What do you think?" I ask Sentinel.

"Barak could be leading us into a trap."

"My thoughts too. Should we risk traversing the gap?"

"It is the most direct path and one giving us the most resistance. But once we pass over the debris, we won't have any alternative but to continue." He rubs his chin. "We cross."

I go with Sentinel's decision and signal our intent to the others. To confuse our enemy, I get a soldier to toss a smoke canister at the opening. The corridor is full of smoke by the time we're ready to move. We leave, dashing across the pile of debris from the barrier. I risk losing my balance when I stub my boot against a chunk of the wall but recover.

Several wayward shots of maser fire burst through the cloud, starting before we try the crossing and continuing as we run through, but we dodge them without further injury this time. Once we regroup, we continue our march along the corridor to the east wing and, hopefully, Adala's prison. But they don't leave us in peace for long.

When we round a corner in the passageway, shots rain toward us from further ahead. The intensity is so severe we can't defend ourselves against such a barrage, so we retreat to the nearest doorway, dashing inside the room. We lock the door and barricade it with furniture to prevent the enemy from entering. It won't deter them for long.

"This is ridiculous," I mutter to myself, although Sentinel overhears me. "We're always on the defensive." I glance at him. "Any ideas?"

"It's a tough place to plan an offensive. Its layout is unknown to us, and we have inferior numbers and weapons."

I pace the floor, frantic for an idea. I won't come this far, only to die as a caged animal. Noises at the door distract my thoughts. We must move. The only other exit is a window leading to the palace's interior gardens. It offers a tortuous route to the east wing, but there's plenty of foliage for cover — trees, shrubs, and the occasional ornament. "Through here." I blast the casement into oblivion. Barak's guard does likewise to the doorway as we make our escape through the hole.

We dash to the cover of the woods, the guards' maser blasts whizzing past us as we hide behind them. Now that there's adequate shelter, we fire back, with greater success, the groans of injured and dying assailants filtering through to us. Everything doesn't go our way, though. Another two soldiers fall from maser hits, dead before they strike the ground. At this rate, we won't get halfway there before we're defeated.

I glance at Sentinel and gesture to go through the forests to our goal. He nods and relays the command. We run to our destination, firing blasts behind us to delay the attack. Once we move further into the dense woodland, I realize a shortcoming of the woods. We have plenty of cover, but so do they when they push into the trees themselves. So, our battle resorts to delivering a barrage of maser fire and falling back to the tree cover again. Still, we make a slow advance toward the east wing.

Rickshaw sets up booby-traps for our pursuers once we progress deep into the woods. Where he stows the weapons, I can't imagine. The first detonates a few minutes later, the boom roaring past us and the ground beneath our feet trembling. Another blast reverberates soon afterward. It will slow our hunters, but I have no misconceptions. Barak has more soldiers where the ones he lost originated. We must get to our destination, and fast. Everything is taking far too long.

We break from the woods near the east wing, and my heart stops. As I glance up at the upper-floor window, I see the profile of Adala staring into the distance, oblivious to what's going on below her. She looks so forlorn in her imprisonment. I want to shout up to her, but our own problems take precedence as a maser shot fires past me, taking out a chunk of timber. Just as I move to look away, her attention is drawn to the ground below, and her eyes lock onto mine. Her sadness turns to joy and then fear as she sees the danger surrounding me. I burst into a beaming grin and send her a kiss before returning to the battle and preparing for our next maneuver.

WITH MY GOAL IN SIGHT, I find renewed energy to move forward. I gesture to Sentinel.

He dashes to me. "What now?"

"We have to get to that window," I say, pointing to where Adala stands, her frustrations and fear obvious in her expression.

A grin spreads across Sentinel's face when he sees her. After gazing at her for several seconds, he turns back to me. "We must end this distraction. They'll pick us off like stranded ships if we try running to the palace with so many behind us."

I frown and grimace in frustration. I can't envisage a strategy to sway the fight in our favor. The few men I have left defend our position with growing desperation.

To make matters worse, the sound of gunships overhead breaks through the noise of battle. I gaze up to locate their positions, but the tree cover prevents me from seeing them. Moments later, foliage explodes as the blast of a maser cannon strikes it only meters away from our position. I duck by instinct.

Rickshaw becomes agitated and grabs the backpack he has on his shoulders. After rummaging through it, he extracts a micro-missile launcher and primes it. He glances up at the sky and frowns. Too much cover interferes with locating any of the gunships. With a burst of energy, he sprints to the nearest tree and climbs it. I watch as he ascends into the canopy and disappears from our sight. After a minute, the familiar sound of a rocket launching resounds through the woods, and moments later, a massive explosion shakes the trees. Burning debris litters the foliage and starts spot fires where the wreckage comes to rest. Rickshaw re-appears with a jaunty grin as he reaches the ground, proud of his accomplishment.

In reply, another maser cannon blast rips through the forest, this time killing several of my soldiers. Our numbers are dwindling, and I despair of our success. Only Sentinel, my bodyguards, and two others support me now. I lean against a tree trunk and bow my head. I can't abandon my cause. Not today. I won't let Shulgi win. I won't let my present circumstances defeat me. But what can I do?

My eyes lock onto my ring and its iridescent blue glow as if it beckons me. I stare at it for inspiration. And then the spark of a foolish idea forms in my brain. How can it work? I must try anyhow if we are to survive our current predicament. I open the power pack of my maser pistol and manipulate the wiring so that it diverts through a flerovium crystal in my band. It's a primitive setup but hopefully effective. To test my improvisation, I point the pistol at the woods behind me and pulse the maser. Several trees disintegrate before my eyes. The others see my accomplishment and gape in astonishment. I shrug. It works.

Another cannon blast from the remaining gunship tears into the trees nearby. Pieces of shrapnel from the explosion catapult past us, the wooden splinters as effective as deadly darts. When I scan the vicinity, I see Jacques and Lombard lying on the ground, dead. Just the three of us now.

My anger returns, and I point the pistol at the sky, trying to get a fix on the gunship so I can shoot at it, but the canopy still interferes with my view. After several failed attempts to see the ship, I crane my neck one last time and just glimpse the fuselage. I aim and fire before I lose sight of it again, and it disappears from existence. To complete our annihilation of the enemy, I direct my pistol in the direction of the ground-based attack and blast three more shots, wiping out the impediment to our advance.

Sentinel stares at the weapon and then at me. "I'm glad I'm on your side."

I smile. "Let's get moving. Barak will send more before long."

We can't do much for our fallen comrades, so we take their weapons and any other useful items. The east wing is one hundred meters from the tree line, with no cover between it and us. After discussing our options, we decide that a fast, direct approach is the best of the poor choices available.

To make our rescue effort easier, I blast a hole in the palace wall for a quick entry. We dash forward, conscious of maintaining a separation between us and weaving as we close the distance to the buildings. With meters to spare before we must take cover again, a barrage of maser fire blasts our way. Fortune smiles on us. It misses. We enter the palace interior before they can get a second shot at us.

But Barak has another squad inside when we arrive, ready for us, who open fire as soon as we reach the wall's protection. We dive for shelter behind furniture as maser beams dart past us.

I marvel at our luck until I spy Rickshaw. He lies on the ground with a massive wound in his leg. He's still alive, but his participation in Adala's rescue is over, and he realizes it as he waves to us to continue without him. To help us on our way, he fires at everything that moves from his concealed position. With no surprise, the targets fire back at him, whittling away at his protective barrier. I give Rickshaw a hand by removing most of his aggressors in one shot. He smiles at me despite the agony he must be enduring.

Sentinel and I prepare to move forward. We must locate a stairway to ascend to the second floor, where I saw Adala. I point out a possible direction to Sentinel, and he nods. A lull in the attack allows us to dash along the corridor. After twenty meters, I spot a staircase and ready myself to scale it, only to be fired at from above. I just dodge the shot and step aside out of our attacker's line of fire.

I now have a problem. My pistol is too powerful to use for general fighting, but I don't want to reconfigure it to its earlier setup in case I need the increased firepower again. It's my only weapon, though.

Sentinel sees my dilemma. He dashes back while I wait. A minute later, he returns with a maser rifle and throws it at me. I check it. It's three-quarters charged, so I prepare it for use.

I signal Sentinel to lead and flush out our attacker upstairs while I protect him. He nods and moves forward slowly and steadily, bracing himself to fire his weapon or rush for cover at any moment. He fires volleys up the stairs and creeps up several steps at a time before stopping and checking for concealed assailants. More exchanges of weapons occur before he rounds the first flight and disappears. I move to follow him, keeping a close watch on our rear. The occasional shot resounds through from Rickshaw, too.

Once we reach the top of the stairs, we traverse the corridor leading to the east wing. It's too easy. We don't meet the opposition I expected. Barak must protect Adala with deadly force, both to appease his emperor's wishes and to prevent her rescue. Sentinel glances back at me, a frown creasing his brow as if he is making the same observation. We both glance to our rear with increasing nervousness as we near Adala's room, doorways on either side potentially hiding enemy soldiers. Her doorway is in sight, from my reckoning of her location. Resistance is still absent.

Just as we approach Adala's door to open it, the doors behind us open, and troops rush out with guns raised and pointed at us. We both dive for cover. I pull my supercharged pistol from its holster point and fire, killing everyone in the corridor before they fire a shot, although I believe they wanted to capture us instead of executing us. It doesn't matter now.

Sentinel and I glance at each other as we now have free access to Adala's room.

"It could be a trap," Sentinel warns.

I nod. "They won't risk opening fire on us with Adala in the room behind us. A misfire through the wall could kill her."

Sentinel raises his eyebrows. "You think she's no longer there?"

"Most likely."

"Only one way to find out."

We approach the doorway, still nervous of further attacks, and stand to the side. After studying the opening mechanism, I swipe the panel and the lock clicks, the door sliding open. Nothing blasts at us, so I peek into the room. It's empty. I venture a protracted survey, checking for booby traps, but don't see any.

"Looks vacant," I say.

Sentinel takes his own look, scanning the room for longer before straightening and daring to enter it. I follow him, cautious that our access is too easy. When we reach the middle of the room, the light dims, natural sunlight becoming the only source of illumination, and a hologram shows Shulgi holding Adala under duress.

"Welcome, Halwende, or whoever you say you are. If you hear me, you have entered the residential room of Queen Adala — and found it empty. She remains with me for safekeeping. I presume you will persist in your futile effort to rescue her, and I will wait, along with the strength of my imperial forces, to arrest you for the last time. I look forward to meeting you again."

The hologram disappears.

"That answers that question," Sentinel says to no one in particular. "But where has he taken her?"

"He'll have her in the main palace. It's where he feels safest and has his guards to protect him."

"The two of us can't defeat them, can we?"

I give a wry smile. "Only one way to find out."

WITH THE KNOWLEDGE that Adala is with Shulgi, Sentinel and I continue our mission to rescue her. We are aware we're more likely to be captured ourselves than escape Shulgi's clutches, but we persist in our search even while knowing that death probably awaits us. The palace hallways resemble a maze to negotiate as we advance deeper into the palace proper. We meet no resistance yet, but I expect Barak has prepared a trap for us in the best place for an ambush.

"Should we ask for reinforcements?" Sentinel asks as we continue sneaking along the corridors, following the map in my tablet.

"No time," I say. "Barak will only strengthen any ruse he's preparing while we wait."

With a sigh, Sentinel agrees, working his surveillance routine as we move forward.

We reach Shulgi's residential wing after half an hour with no resistance. "I don't like this," I say, glancing at Sentinel, nervous over the lack of opposition.

Sentinel chuckles. "I didn't like it when we first entered the grounds. But I get your point. It's too easy."

"Should we create a distraction?"

"I'm sure they know where we are, so it won't hurt–" Sentinel jerks his arm around to stop me. "Wait." He peers at the walls and ceiling before us. After finding a decorative apple in a bowl sitting on a side table, he tosses it ahead of us. It bounces and rolls ten meters before it explodes and disintegrates. "Our first trap."

"Where are the controls?"

"On the wall, over there." Sentinel points at the spot with his pistol before firing a blast at it with no effect.

"It's protected," I say, stating the obvious. "Let's see what this does." I fire with my supercharged firearm. The panel and half the wall disappear. The damage causes the ceiling and superstructure above us to become unstable, making me fear it might collapse on top of us.

"Doesn't that thing have a power-level control?"

I smile. "I'll try to remember next time."

We continue along two more corridors until we reach the entertainment suite where Shulgi used me to entertain his party. As the chamber is central to his regime, second only to the throne room itself, I regard it a safe bet that he is holding Adala in there and an even safer one that we'll have a welcoming committee waiting for us.

"We need to look in there." I point to the massive twin doorway leading into the room.

"You want to oblige?" Sentinel nods toward the entrance.

As I consider his comment from before, I temper the power level on my pistol and aim it at the doors. They splinter into pieces when the maser beam strikes them, giving us access to the chamber. We look at each other. I'm unsure of our next step, and Sentinel has the same uncertainty. We can't just stand out here and wait, so I inch to the gap and peek inside it. The suite is empty. I may have got it wrong. With a shrug, I motion to Sentinel and tread over the threshold. My memories of the space give me the shudders and create illusions of monsters lurking in the shadows.

Our footsteps echo off the walls as we edge through the interior, searching for any inkling of the enemy. We reach the center without mishap. I scratch my head. Now what? Before we have time to react, a force field surrounds us, trapping us within the potent energy it projects from floor to ceiling. I curse myself. How could I fall for such an obvious trick? We have no choice but to wait for what happens next ... unless? My eyes drift to my maser pistol as I wonder if I can overload the force-field generator by firing at it.

Before I can test my resourcefulness, a familiar voice reverberates throughout the space. "We should stop meeting this way. Although you're too predictable. You should have known I'd trap you in such an obvious place."

"Why don't you come out and show your face, you coward?" I yell. I'm sick of this game.

"Why should I? You won't be alive much longer. This isn't just a force-field prison. I have a surprise for you."

With a frown, I glance at Sentinel. I don't understand Shulgi. What else could he have within the confines of our entrapment? Sentinel shrugs in confusion.

A slight tingling sensation encompasses my body, increasing in intensity. My eyes bulge with dread as I realize a nerve stimulator is being used on us, and I imagine the outcome it may produce if the effect continues to increase. Sentinel looks uncomfortable as he shudders and shakes to rid himself of the same sensitivity. Pain radiates through me, perspiration erupting into beads that trickle from my forehead. This isn't good. What is this device, and how can I destroy it before it incapacitates us, or worse? Sentinel collapses to the floor in agony. Pins and needles flow through me as I resist my body's urge to follow Sentinel's lead. It must be possible to counteract this. On revisiting my original idea, I settle on trying it, as it can't hurt.

With effort, I point my pistol at the force field and fire a shot. The beam strikes the invisible barrier and splays outwards, dissipating the energy with ease.

When I pull my eyes to the settings on the gun, I cuss, as I haven't increased the power to full strength. With strain, I resist the effects of the nerve stimulator. My free hand moves at a snail's pace to the power knob on the pistol, the movement taking an eternity with the pain I now endure. I complete the action and select full power.

When I glance at Sentinel, he is verging on unconsciousness.

With the setting maximized, I press the trigger again, aiming at the force field. No immediate effect on the barrier occurs but, as the maser beam continues to splay across the wall of energy, the boundary glows, increasing in intensity until the barrier collapses with a massive explosion as the generator overloads and disintegrates. Chunks of ceiling crack and fall to the floor, narrowly missing us.

Yells emanate from the level above as two people drop through and crash onto the floor next to us. One person has hold of the nerve simulator device, but it rolls across the surface when he loses his grip on it. It's still operating, and I have scant time to turn the machine off before I join Sentinel in unconsciousness. With agonizing movement, I redirect the pistol, pointing it in the right direction and pulling the trigger again, destroying the stimulator. The relief floods through me as the pain ceases, but the removal has almost as painful an effect as the original sensation until my body works out what's happening and adjusts.

Heaving air into my lungs, I rise to a kneeling position and glance at the two operators. They are either unconscious or dead. Sentinel lies motionless on the floor, but I hear his breathing as he rasps air past his lips. With a reserve of energy that I didn't know I had, I raise myself and bow with my hands gripping my knees to recover. I don't have the time for this, but I must regain my strength. After a minute, I stumble to Sentinel and kneel next to him. He's still senseless.

A maser beam fires from the floor above us. It deflects from my personal force field. I'm tired of playing, so I raise my pistol and fire another shot above me, killing whoever attacks me and creating another avalanche of rubble. We stay too exposed where Sentinel lies, so I stand, grab his arms, and pull him to the room's perimeter. His dead-weight mass exhausts me by the time I stop and release him. I hope he wakes soon as I can't drag him any further, and we need to continue our search for Adala.

Movement catches my eye from the doorway. Enemy soldiers congregate there. What else can stack up against us? A wave of yearning passes over me to return to Helheim as in times past, where it's just Adala and me in each other's arms drowning in bliss. I shake my head to bring my thoughts to the dangers of the present. This must end. Shulgi's and Barak's taunting has gone on for long enough. It's time for me to stop this fiasco. I raise my maser pistol and pull the trigger, threading a line of destruction along the wall housing the entrance. Surprised cries and pained moans ricochet back, and troopers panic and rush for cover.

I comm to Lilith, but a full minute passes before she connects. The noise of fighting distracts both her and me.

"Sorry for the delay. We're busy," she shouts above the commotion. I see a streak of blood on her cheek.

"Are things in hand?"

"Yeah, we're keeping them at bay for now, but what of you? Where's Sentinel?"

Despite the seriousness of our predicament, I give a wry smile. "He's taking a nap." I glance at him.

Panic crosses Lilith's face. "He's not injured?"

"No. Just suffering the effects of a nerve stimulator. But I need information. Shulgi retreats whenever I get near him. I'm in his entertainment room, whatever you call it, but he's given me the slip again with Adala. Where would he go to from there?"

Lilith takes a moment to think. "His last sanctuary is the fortress. It's in the center of the palace compound and impregnable. Not even a maser cannon can blast through the walls." Lilith gives me a sinister look. "But a back door exists."

I shake my head. "Is there any secluded passage unknown to you?"

"I don't know. I–" An explosion overpowers whatever Lilith says. She glances behind her, frightened, but returns to the screen and outlines the secret entrance and how to locate it. "I'd better go. It's getting busy here again."

"Thanks for the information. I hope this will be over soon."

"So do I." Lilith cuts the link.

Her bravery amazes me. My concentration drifts back to my circumstances and Sentinel. He stirs. I wonder if the sound of Lilith's voice contributed to his recovery but don't dwell on it as I scan the corridor — or what's left of it — for any sign of the enemy. Sentinel's eyes flutter open.

"Refreshed?" I say with a laconic smile.

"They've stabbed me with a million needles."

"A nerve stimulator does that. We must move. Lilith told me where Shulgi's most likely to be, and we still have unwelcome guests around us."

Sentinel nods and sits, grimacing as he stretches. "I'm sick of this fighting."

"You and me both. Let's get moving. We've got more ground to cover."

SENTINEL STANDS, grabbing the column next to him to support himself as his body recovers from the stimulator's effects. If I had another personal force field, I'd give him one so this, or something worse, doesn't happen again. I wait a further minute for his recovery before I rise and prepare to leave.

"Set?"

Sentinel nods. "I'll survive."

"Let's move."

We bridge the distance to the destroyed entry doors and check in both directions for assailants. I don't see any, but I know they're there. Our best choice is to locate the secret entrance and use that to protect us from the rear. Lilith's comments suggest it's as impregnable to attack as the fortress itself is. After checking our route, I motion to Sentinel, gesturing the path we must follow. He nods and prepares to run.

With a heave of breath, I dash from the room along the corridor. Sentinel runs right behind me, his maser ready for any sign of assault. When we near the end of the stretch of hallway, I spy the descending stairs leading to our goal and, without a change in pace, leap downwards, taking four steps at a time. We descend two levels and divert our direction to a passageway to our left. I allow Sentinel to pass me, raise my pistol and send a blast of maser energy into the walls and ceiling of the stairway, collapsing the stonework into an impregnable pile of rubble to prevent anyone following us.

"We're not returning this way, then?" Sentinel asks, raising an eyebrow.

"If we don't leave by the front entrance, we don't leave." I run again with Sentinel beside me.

I catch him looking at me.

"Good to know," he says.

I smile but keep to the rhythm of my pace. The maze of corridors loses us. I'm unsure we can return by this route even if we desired it. After ten minutes, we reach a dead-end side tunnel and halt.

"Now what?" Sentinel asks, in between deep breaths.

"There should be a doorway here. We just need to find it."

"Lilith?"

I smile and nod. "Lilith."

"She had a neglected childhood filled with too much time to herself."

"Be thankful for it. She told us of this entrance. If only I can pinpoint the latch." I search the walls for the mechanism Lilith described but find it difficult to locate. I'm completely absorbed in my task.

"You should hurry," Sentinel advises after a time. "We'll have company soon."

Diverting my attention to my surroundings, I hear the thud of approaching and running footsteps. The imminent danger forces me to escalate my searching speed. Where is it? She said it'd be easy to find. Has her memory mistaken the variety of device used for the lock? Are we even in the right place?

Sentinel has his pistol ready to defend our position. He holds my rifle too, as backup. Troopers brake to a halt as they appear in the tunnel entrance, unprepared for an attack. Sentinel fires and kills several before they come to their senses and take cover. "It'd be great to discover it now," Sentinel says as he prepares for a counterattack.

I nod and renew my frantic search. My hand passes over an indentation to the right, just above floor level in a spot darkened by the shadow of the overhead light. I heave a sigh of relief and press hard on the depression as several maser blasts chip the surface, one glancing off my shield. After a soft click, a section of wall opens, revealing a dark continuation of the tunnel.

I tap Sentinel on the shoulder. "Fall back."

He takes a quick glance behind and nods, letting off rapid shots toward the juncture to dissuade our assailants from poking their heads around the corner. I decide to help and fire a shot from my pistol, aiming at the roof before the intersection, and the rock collapses. Why didn't I consider that? We move past the doorway, and it slides shut again. We stand in darkness.

"What now?" Sentinel asks.

"They didn't install lighting."

"Or it's deteriorated." Sentinel turns on the rifle light and aims it in front of us. "Let's keep moving."

We continue at a less frantic stride as we traverse the subterranean gloom. It has no detours and bends a few times before another wall blocks our passage.

"This is it," I whisper. "The fortress is behind it." I grope for the doorway-opening mechanism.

"You don't intend to make a more impressive entrance?" Sentinel gives a wry smile.

I glance at him. "It might be a greater bonus to check what lies beyond first, don't you think?"

"I didn't want to dampen your style."

I chuckle.

"What's on the other side?"

"Lilith didn't say. She was young when she discovered it and didn't understand what functions the rooms had back then."

"Let's hope we don't stumble on the fortress's main barracks."

"Full of optimism today." I continue feeling for the unlocking device until I find a matching depression to the last one. I press it and hear the familiar click before the wall swishes open.

I groan as a wall of guards blocks our path. How can so much rotten luck beset us?

"Good of you to drop in," Barak says, wearing his signature menacing grin. "Did you think we didn't know of this entrance?"

Sentinel stands behind me, my force field protecting him from the direct line of fire from most of the soldiers.

"Now that you're here, let me introduce Sledgehammer," I say to Barak.

As Barak raises his eyebrows with a questioning look, I raise my pistol and shoot into the troopers before they can react. Several of them get off a shot and hit me despite the surprise move, but my shield protects me.

Seeing the destruction of his forces, Barak panics and runs from the room. Those soldiers that are still able to walk rush after him.

Sentinel walks around me and disarms the wounded, piling their weapons into a heap. "What do we do with them?" He points to the troopers.

I gaze at them with pity. "I don't want to kill them, but we can't let them creep up behind us, either." After retrieving a weapon, I switch the power level to stun and fire a shot at each of them, rendering them unconscious. "That should keep them out of our way for now. Let's get moving before Barak has time to set up another welcoming reception."

We race up the corridor Barak used for his escape, remaining vigilant for any ambushes along the way. Rounding a bend, we meet a barrage of maser fire, making us retreat for cover. I poke my pistol around the corner and shoot my supercharged maser. Screams and falling debris result. I chance a peep again and don't see any resistance. Once I consider our path unimpeded, I step forward, double-checking for any soldiers lurking in the shadows.

"Clear," I call to Sentinel.

"Hope that's the last of them." Sentinel checks his rifle and starts running.

Caught flat-footed, I must sprint to catch up to him, getting ahead to offer the protection of my force field.

We burst into an open space, the perfect place to trap us. There are two exits and no protection. Both exits have barricades installed and masers converge on us from both directions. We take shelter and I let off shots toward both tunnels. The barriers disintegrate, and the people behind them either retreat or die since we meet no further opposition when we break cover.

"Which shaft?" Sentinel asks.

"Good question. I wonder if it matters. Both may lead to the fortress core, but one might be more direct."

"Did Lilith give any clues?"

"No. She might not have knowledge of the interior layout."

"We'll just pick one then." Sentinel looks at one tunnel and then the other. He selects the left and starts moving. I follow and reinstall myself in the lead.

We engage further resistance four more times before we reach stairs leading up to the next level. As we have no other choice but to retrace our path, we scale the steps, which spiral as we ascend higher. Once again, I find it more disconcerting than pleasing that we meet no further opposition but am grateful nonetheless that we've got this far without one of us becoming injured or meeting our death.

On reaching the top, we end up on a landing and a platform providing access to several doorways. Which door we should choose is undetectable from the clues we have. I glance at Sentinel and raise my eyebrows, seeking his advice.

"There is no other way," Sentinel says, "than to try one door at a time."

I shrug but agree and point to one end of the balcony as the start. The doors are unsecured, so we only need to press the opening button to slide the doors open. Sentinel and I stand on either side of the entrance when we scan the inside space. Most are storage rooms with no other visible exit.

We check each door, returning to the stairs we ascended to inspect the last doorway. I press the button and the door slides open. Sentinel takes a quick peek and takes cover again.

"A large room," he whispers. "This might be it."

I nod and make ready my pistol to fire at any enemies we meet. With my body tense, I rush into the space and am greeted by maser fire yet again. The intensity of this engagement suggests Barak has his last defensive line here — I hope so. I'm getting sick of this cat-and-mouse charade he's playing. I shoot back, eliminating most of those attacking me with one prolonged blast waved across the line of resistance.

Sentinel cleans up the rest when he enters, but the path ahead still puzzles us, as the space is empty after we finish our battle. A closed door stands on the farthest wall. Since Barak placed the soldiers here to protect the doorway from us, we conclude it's worth investigating what's behind it. We stand on either side, and I open the door, ready to barge into it.

"About time you got here," Shulgi's voice projects from within the space.

I stare at Sentinel and he at me, shocked now that we've reached our destination.

"Enter, please. I have a surprise for you."

After taking a deep breath, I prepare to step into the doorway. Every part of me says I'm entering a trap, but I must go ahead. I must end this. Shulgi's reign must end and end today. I raise my pistol ready to fire if necessary, and I gesture to Sentinel to hold back while I confirm Shulgi's intent.

I step through the threshold and stand nailed to the floor in dismay.

37

THE RING OF ORION

At first, my mind can't interpret what I see. Adala sits restrained in a chair in the center of the room. She's battered and bleeding and only semi-conscious, her clothes half torn away. Her face is so bruised she's barely recognizable. I stare at her and then at Shulgi, who stands behind her with a maser pistol pointed at her and wearing a smug expression.

"What have you done?" My words are barely a whisper. I'd blast Shulgi to eternal damnation if I had a clean shot.

Adala's head rises when she hears my voice, but she's too weak to keep it elevated and lets it slump again.

Tears of grief and rage and self-loathing well as I gaze at her. How could I have allowed this to happen?

Sentinel lunges forward to assassinate Shulgi, but Barak fires his maser at him, using a semi-stun setting. Sentinel collapses on the floor, his shoulder bleeding and arm half-blasted away.

"Ranulf!" Adala cries out when the disturbance draws her awareness again.

I am alone in my opposition to Shulgi and Barak. This is as it should be. I glare at Shulgi with hatred and contempt but keep my emotions under control. I need to fathom why he is acting with such impunity.

"Now that I have your attention," Shulgi says in his soft, sibilant voice. "Call off your minion from destroying any more of my navy."

My eyes rise from Adala to Shulgi, trying to comprehend what he says. As the words sink in, I blink. "I can't communicate with her. Barak has made that impossible."

"You can communicate with my loving, treacherous daughter, though. Don't deny it. We intercepted your earlier discussion."

That's how they foresaw our plans to infiltrate the fortress and our route.

"No."

"Then your beloved queen dies. A shame as I was rather looking forward to having her as my bride." Shulgi's arm tenses as he moves to pull the trigger.

"Wait!"

A satisfied smile crosses Shulgi's face. "See what the right persuasion does, Barak."

"He's as much a coward now as he ever was," Barak replies.

I disregard the taunt and reach for my communication unit, sending a message to Lilith.

"Lilith here. Everything progressing?"

"It's Halwende. Can you send a directive to Ishtar to cease the attack?"

"What?"

"Your father has Adala and is threatening to kill her if we continue."

"We can't stop for one person," Lilith says, annoyed. "Even Queen Adala."

"Do it!" I snap back. "Tell Ishtar I command it." I glare at Shulgi. "But tell her to be prepared to protect herself if the empire's navy keeps attacking." I break contact. "Now what?"

"Now, you dispose of your weapon that has so much power that it destroys half my palace. And take off your personal shield."

Shulgi thinks this will leave me defenseless, but he doesn't know the power invested in the Ring of Orion.

Adala gathers energy to glance at me and shakes her head, the pain of her bruises causing her to grimace. "Don't. Please. I'm prepared to die."

Tears escape my eyes. "My sacrifice is enough for you and your people. I came with nothing to offer, and I leave with the same." With a sigh, I disconnect the maser pistol from my ring — careful to hide the connecting mechanism from Shulgi and Barak — and throw the gun to the floor. I do the same with the shield bracelet and stand erect, head held high and proud of who I am. "Today, you dare kill Sargon, the true King of Rigel. Your punishment will be swift, terrible, and ruthless when it occurs." I turn to Barak. "And yours too."

Barak stands with a smirk but underlying that is a tinge of fear.

I bring my attention back to Shulgi. "Now what?"

"Now you die," Shulgi says as he levels the maser at my chest and fires.

I brace myself for death.

"No!" Adala gathers her last strength to shout in despair.

The maser splashes across me in the harmless dissipation of its energy.

Shulgi's eyes bulge in disbelief.

Before he or Barak can react, I rush forward and wrestle Shulgi to the ground, grabbing the maser from his hand. He yelps in surprise.

I see Barak recovering and preparing to take aim at Adala. Without thinking, I rush to stand in front of her and instantly blast him with the maser. He slumps to the floor, unconscious, and I think I have killed him. But the maser was on the stun setting. Either way, he is out of our hair.

Adala sits unmoving when I glance back at her. I believe she may have fainted, but my attention is drawn to Shulgi, who is attempting to rise and make his escape. In an instant, I remove the two steps between us and push him to the ground again, placing my foot on his chest and aiming the gun at his head. "You're not going anywhere."

"How?" Shulgi blinks at me in dismay.

"You should have conducted your research better and rounded up my father's advisers. This ring of office isn't just a symbol. That's why they hid it until now. But we don't have time to commiserate on your misfortunes. Call off your people, or you will suffer a slow and painful death." I don't intend to kill him, but Shulgi need not know that.

Fear radiates from Shulgi's eyes as he stares at the muzzle of the maser pointed at him. He fumbles for his communicator, gulping as he keys into the general leading his troops. After a quick conversation, he disconnects and looks back at me.

"And your Admiral of the Fleet."

Shulgi does the same with him.

"Stand." I take my foot from his chest.

Shulgi rises awkwardly and stands hunched over himself. He's aged twenty years in the ten minutes we've been together. I shackle him with restraints.

"Now, you will issue a statement to the empire, announcing your abdication of the throne that you illegally usurped from the rightful rulers of the Rigel Empire, effective at once. And Sargon, of the ruling house of Alalgar, will stake his legitimate claim to the throne of Rigel."

"You can't make me."

I raise my brow and adjust my aim to Shulgi's arm. "I have painful means of getting what I want, too. Do not tempt me to show you."

Seeing my determination, Shulgi capitulates. "As you wish. I don't understand how you escaped my dragnet. My generals insisted they were thorough in their purge." A frown crosses Shulgi's face. "Do you know who I am?"

"What does it matter? You are a monster to me and most of your subjects."

"I'm your uncle. I was married to your aunt."

The news unnerves me but makes sense. It also occurs to me that this makes Lilith my cousin. Perhaps that explains the affinity I felt for her from the start.

"You were too young to realize," Shulgi adds.

"Those who knew the truth were probably too embarrassed to warn me."

The news sends great sorrow through me. To think a member of my family could cause so much suffering. "Now, make your announcement."

38

BANISHMENT

A dala's eyelids flutter open as I sit by her bedside, staring at her, my face etched with worry. Her bruises and lacerations are still obvious and mar her beauty. I reach out and clasp her hand, caressing it in mine as she recognizes her environment and me. A smile blossoms on her broken lips.

"Where am I?" she whispers.

"In a hospital on Eridu."

She grimaces at a painful memory and struggles to rise. "Ranulf?"

I touch her shoulder, pushing her with gentle persuasion to return to her rest. "Is fine," I say. "He's resting in another room. Apart from the flesh amputated from him, he's uninjured. The doctors are grafting new muscle. He'll recuperate in a couple of months. He has his own angel tending to his needs."

"Lilith?"

I nod.

Adala smiles. "Good." She settles and closes her eyes, the momentary effort seeming to have drained her of energy. After half a minute, her lips curl. "You are usually the one lying in a hospital."

I give a hearty laugh. "Yes." But lightheartedness soon drains away, and Adala senses it and opens her eyes again. "I'd swap places with you without a moment's protest or complaint."

"I'm sure you would. Can I sit?"

I search for the bed-positioning controls and use them to raise her torso into a half-sitting position. Adala's spirits improve with the change in posture.

"Come closer, please," Adala says.

I frown, confused, but do her bidding.

"Nearer."

My face is only inches from hers. Without notice, she leans forward and kisses me before slumping back on the bed again, gasping for breath.

I accept the warmth of her lips on mine with gladness but fret over her over-exertion. She recovers her strength but remains resting. Her head tilts to the side facing the window. It overlooks the capital parklands and low-density buildings of the more prominent district. Scooter yachts hover over the greenery, banners fluttering in the breeze with the words, 'Long Live King Sargon,' emblazoned on them, and the crowds below us are enjoying the festivities.

"What's happening?" Adala asks.

"The city is celebrating the overthrow of Shulgi. Most non-essential work has ceased."

Adala turns her head back to me. "So, what name do I use? Halwende or Sargon?"

I smile as I stroke her cheek tenderly. "You can call me whatever you want."

"Even love?"

My face clouds with emotion as the words sink into me. I nod, then grin. "Even love." I lean over and kiss her, caressing her with a gentle hug. "My love," I whisper in her ear.

Tears pool in Adala's eyes when I withdraw, but her smile eclipses her other emotions.

A light rap comes from the doorway. We both glance that way.

"Sorry to interrupt," Zabada says.

"I doubt that," I interject.

He grins. "I do not wish to, but matters need attention, I'm afraid. And the sooner you settle them, the better."

I sigh and give Zabada a frustrated frown. "Run along, then. I'll be with you soon."

"As you wish," Zabada bows with a mocking smile but disappears from the doorway.

"I'll return as soon as I can, I promise."

Adala frowns. "I'm unsure I like that. I have ill memories of last time. You came back months later with a war chasing you."

"I must handle a distasteful matter, and then I'll come back to you. I'm not leaving you again." With that, I lean over and give her a lingering kiss, brushing her bruised and tender lips as I gaze into her eyes. "Until I return."

I rise and, with reluctance, walk out, turning to catch a last sight of her.

∾

∾

∾

SEATED in the palace throne room with Zabada beside me, I wait for Ishtar to bring in the prisoners. The guards shove four handcuffed men into the room, pushing them toward me and stopping them meters from me. They are all handcuffed and wearing restraining collars. Korbinian and General Klaus look frightened, but Shulgi and Barak wear insolent expressions. Ishtar parks herself to the side and stands at attention.

I'd sooner not cast my eyes on these four ever again, their presence sending vile emotions through me that I wish to forget. My mind wanders to Ishtar, but she keeps her passions covered by her mask of military etiquette. My soul smiles. I perceive the punishment she'd inflict if she had her way.

"What do I do with you?" I say to the prisoners, returning my attention to them. "I know what you would do if our roles were reversed. Give me a reason not to instill the same retribution on you."

The men stand in silence, apart from some sniveling from Korbinian and Klaus.

"Korbinian, you have proved twice that you cannot be trusted, and as for you, Klaus, you backed the wrong horse." The sniveling increases. I ignore them and turn to the others.

"Shulgi, you executed my family — indeed, your own family — without remorse and usurped the throne for your own glory and gain."

Shulgi answers proudly. "Your father, my brother-in-law, was weak. His grip was withering. It needed me to bring the treasonous generals back in line. Without me, the realm would have fallen apart."

"And yet you kill my father and family and take the empire for yourself instead of helping my father rule better."

"I have no regrets."

I raise an eyebrow, gauging his temperament. "Execution's too good for you."

"You have the power now."

"What should I do?" I glance at Ishtar.

"Execute him," Ishtar says with no emotion. "Execute them all."

My eyes lift to Zabada, but he remains silent.

I sigh and nod before my attention turns to Barak. "And my traitorous general, who defects to the winning side when it suits him. Do you wish to give your services to me now?"

Barak gives a stolid stare but has the grace to say, "We both know that's impossible."

"Yes. How I wish you had remained faithful to me. We were friends once, and I trusted you. That hurts me the most. I can forgive many shortcomings but not betrayal."

Barak remains expressionless.

As I chew my lip, I peer at Zabada, wondering if he has any advice for me. But he refrains from comment. My attention returns to the prisoners, staring at each one as I contemplate their fates. My choices are stark — execution, imprisonment, or banishment. I do not want to start my reign by executing people. How will that make me appear any different from them? Nor do I want to imprison them here where they could escape, as Korbinian did, and exert influence over weaker minds. I make my decision.

"I send you all to Hades to live your remaining days in exile. If you leave that planet, we will hunt you down and execute you."

"That is too lenient," Ishtar blurts out in disappointment.

I raise my hand, silencing her. "It is my command. And I doubt life on Hades is merciful." One look at the expressions on the prisoners' faces proves the truth of my words.

Ishtar bows her head in submission.

I turn to Zabada, who gives a barely perceptible nod of approval.

"Remove them from my presence."

39

RECOVERY

A month passes before Adala is fit enough to leave the hospital. Sentinel must stay another month, much to his irritation. I have a feeling he will find a way to circumvent the doctors' advice, as Rickshaw has already done. Despite his injuries, Rickshaw is already back at work.

I have too many duties to become bored with idleness. With Shulgi's defeat, I must reorganize the institutions he gutted or corrupted for his own purposes, including the military. After deliberations with Adala, Zabada, and Sentinel, I instate Ishtar as Head of Security and the Armed Forces, ignoring her objections. I can think of no one better suited for the job.

Many of the discussions between Adala and me focus on reuniting the two fractured arms of what was King Alalgar's empire before the cloaking of Helheim. After consultation, we both agree we'd realize the best outcome if the two realms amalgamated, recreating the original kingdom of Alalgar. My many visits to Helheim have resulted in city-wide celebrations at Heimstadt. Sigmund and Freida are ecstatic, and Abelard is filled with pride in his daughter and me. It has given him new energy to continue his role as monarch in Adala's absence.

My consultations with the bishop at Heimstadt Cathedral have unearthed the constitutional mechanisms for reuniting the two realms enacted when King Alalgar left it in Alulim's hands. With this knowledge, the bishop, Abelard, and I plan the empire's reunion, reinstating Helheim as the regal planet and changing its name back to Ur.

I return to Eridu content our intentions will help the entire empire in the long run. The prosperous families in the realm will need to adjust their political maneuverings to the new arrangements, but I have no reservations they will cope.

I ARRIVE JUST in time for Adala to be discharged. I stand outside her room, waiting to escort her.

After a delay, she walks into view, scanning the corridor for familiar faces. When she sees me, she bursts into the sun-eclipsing smile I love and rushes to me as fast as her injury-restrained gait allows. We hug and gaze into each other's eyes.

"About time you rose and did something useful," I say with a teasing smile.

Adala gives a feigned huff and slaps my shoulder. "I'll teach you to be insolent."

"I'm counting on it."

Her eyes twinkle in delight.

"Let's get you home and settled. We have much to discuss, and you still need rest."

"Stop mothering me."

"I'm just obeying the doctor's advice." I hold my hands up in self-defense.

"Lead the way, then. We have a kingdom to unite."

Rickshaw stands at a discrete distance from us. With Ishtar's aid, it took him little time to select new bodyguards. On the odd occasion when I've seen him and Ishtar together, I have wondered if their relationship is more than professional, but that is not my business. He smiles at me as we approach. "Ready, sir?"

"I'm ready. And don't call me sir."

"Well, you don't want me to say, 'Your Majesty' unless it's official duty."

I frown in frustrated thought. "Call me Sargon. I'll use my birth-given name."

"But Halwende has a distinctive ring to it," Adala protests.

"You can call me whatever you want."

"Be careful what you allow."

We both laugh.

"Let's get moving."

When we leave the hospital, we see that a crowd has congregated outside to welcome Adala, delighting her as she waves to them with practiced ease. The chatter and cheer within the group increase with the recognition. The imperial craft ferries us to the palace where my staff wait to shower Adala with enthusiastic greetings.

Sentinel stands there too. As I suspected would happen, the medical experts failed to detain him in hospital for the recuperation period advised. He'd have acted out of character if he had stayed. Lilith stands at his side.

"Welcome back," he says to Adala.

Adala gives him a hug. "I'm pleased to be rid of that place."

Lilith curtsies. "Welcome home, Your Majesty."

With a frown, Adala gazes at Lilith in discomfort. "I forbid you to curtsey to me. And 'Adala' will do unless you must greet me formally at an official function."

Lilith beams with delight. "As you wish, your– Adala."

"Especially since I suspect I'll be seeing much more of you." Adala gives them both a questioning, raised brow.

Sentinel blushes, making me laugh. He opens his mouth to reply but closes it again without a word spoken, bearing his embarrassment sheepishly.

We progress along the assembled welcoming line and stand before Ishtar. She stands at rigid attention in full military uniform and salutes.

"At ease, Ishtar," I say to her. I turn to Adala. "It's gone to her head."

Ishtar blushes, and I can tell she wants to rebuff my words, but her training prevents her from speaking unless I grant her permission. She changes to a relaxed stance.

"I believe Sargon has honored you with his most trusted military position," Adala says.

"He has, Queen Adala. And I intend to ensure that he doesn't regret his choice."

"I'm sure he won't. Here." Adala steps to her and hugs her, shocking Ishtar. "You don't need to be formal in private. You remind me of Ranulf too much."

"Heaven forbid," Ishtar blurts before she realizes it and reddens.

Both Adala and I burst out laughing. "I couldn't have put it better myself," I say.

And last in line, we step to Zabada, who supports himself with a walking stick. "I welcome your recovery," he says to Adala.

"It's great to be active again," she replies. "I understand you know Sargon's history. We must find time to chat." She gives first Zabada and then me a conniving grin.

"That's not fair," I say.

"I shall be happy to relate relevant details of his past," Zabada says in his diplomatic manner.

We laugh again.

"Come, let's mix and enjoy ourselves." I have organized for the palace to give a small reception party for Adala's return, and we mingle with the invited guests.

EPILOGUE

Many months have elapsed since we completed procedural matters, but both Adala and I now stand before the Bishop of Helheim and the head magistrate of Rigel in Ur Cathedral dressed in royal attire. We both wear flowing trains behind us and crowns on our heads. He conducts the formal rituals to merge the two kingdoms into one and announces the Kingdom of Orion formally, once again uniting the branches of Alalgar's empire. The ceremony is broadcast live throughout the realm, with the technicalities of performing such a task sorted beforehand.

We have no way of knowing, but rumor tells us the streets of the loyal worlds surge with celebrations, as does Ur's. We retire to the palace for our own reception.

During our festivities, I make several announcements. Yet again I stand to speak to those present. "I promise I won't disturb your enjoyment much longer. Adala and I wish to announce that Ranulf will undertake the position as Governor of Eridu, Eridu being the second most important planet in the kingdom." The assembled group cheer their congratulations to Sentinel. "My cousin Lilith will return to Eridu to act as Ranulf's adviser." A murmur circulates throughout the guests. "I trust any other relationship will not interfere with this role." Laughter fills the room, embarrassing both Sentinel and Lilith.

I glance at Adala and nod. She stands next to me, shuffling to get closer. "Lastly, Adala and I wish to announce a decision. After much soul-searching ..." Adala nudges me, and I give her a smile. "... Adala and I are pleased to declare our intention to marry." The audience bursts with cheers of congratulations. We can do nothing but bear the attention as one guest after the other approaches us with their good wishes. Sentinel adds an 'about time' comment with his.

Abelard approaches us last, eyes on his much-loved daughter, tears misting them. "I am so happy for you," he says. "If only your mother could see you now. She'd be proud of her gift to the world in you."

Adala bursts into tears as she hugs her father.

After they both regain their composure, Abelard turns his attention to me. "I can't think of anyone more suited to marry Adala, and I'm proud of you both." We shake hands and hug.

My time as Halwende ends. I've shed the cocoon I hid my true identity under, and now my time as Sargon, King of Orion, begins.

The End

You may be interested in reading more from John Wegener with Scorpius from his Zodiac series.

Type https://books2read.com/scorpius in your browser.

Thanks for reading this book. If you loved the book and have a moment to spare, I would appreciate a quick review on the site that you purchased the book from, as this helps new readers find my books.

Subscribe to my Newsletters and receive three free episodes of The Chronicles of Gatacus Todd.

Type http://subscribepage.io/g4r4f8 in your browser.

ALSO BY JOHN WEGENER

Books

Reach For The Stars Trilogy

FTL

Centauri

Ceti

Reach For The Stars Box Set (Books 1-3)

Loki's Fall

Zodiac Series

Scorpius

Libra

Halwende's Legacy Series

Halwende's Redemption

Halwende's Resurrection

Halwende's Reincarnation

Halwende's Legacy Box Set (Books 1-3)

Solar Dawn Series

Lunar Rift

Other Stories

The Dark Ages

SAGI

Short Stories

The Love Particle

ABOUT THE AUTHOR

John Wegener grew up in the Adelaide Hills of South Australia. He now expresses his imaginative dreams by engaging in writing after a 34-year career as a Chemical Engineer in the steel industry, which has taken him to many countries and allowed him to experience many cultures. John currently lives in Wollongong, Australia with his wife and children.

Click on johnwegener.com to find more of my books or read his blogs. Type subscribepage.io/g4r4f8 to subscribe to my emails for more stories and information.

f